'Deftly told . . . [illegible] study of the danger[ous] [power of] obsessive attraction'
Daily Mail

'Will have you turning pages long into the night'
Scots Magazine

'Compelling and compulsive. A perfectly crafted "just one more chapter" read. I loved it!'
Victoria Selman

'A suspenseful read right up to its shockingly unexpected conclusion'
Lisa Ballantyne

'Wonderfully constructed, this is at once a brilliant murder story, with enough spins of uncertainty to satisfy whilst remaining all-too-credible, and also a richly perceptive account of female needs for connection, affection, love and sex'
The Critic

'I struggled to put down this gripping tale of obsessive love and the dark shadow of the past'
Claire McGowan

'Compelling, engrossing . . . had me guessing right to the last page'
E. S. Thomson

'A stunning debut. Daring, exhilarating, and darkly thrilling. I could not put this book down'
J. A. Corrigan

'An addictive read: gripping from the first page'
Samantha Lee Howe

'Kept me guessing right until the end with fast-paced twists and turns'
Zoe Lea

Liza North is an academic, writer and former journalist. She has a BA from Oxford University and a PhD in Philosophy from University College London, and has written for the *Financial Times* and *Guardian*. A keen cyclist, walker and lover of fancy gin, she lives in Edinburgh with her husband and two daughters.

Follow Liza on social media:

 @lizanorthwriter

 @lizanorthwriter

 @lizanorthwriter

OBSESSED

LIZA NORTH

CONSTABLE

CONSTABLE

First published in Great Britain in 2023 by Constable
This paperback edition published in 2024 by Constable

1 3 5 7 9 10 8 6 4 2

A CIP catalogue record for this book
is available from the British Library.

ISBN 978-1-4087-1623-6

Typeset in Sabon by SX Composing DTP, Rayleigh, Essex

Printed and bound in Great Britain by
Clays Ltd, Elcograf S.p.A.

Papers used by Constable are from well-managed forests
and other responsible sources.

Constable
An imprint of
Little, Brown Book Group
Carmelite House
50 Victoria Embankment
London EC4Y 0DZ

An Hachette UK Company
www.hachette.co.uk

www.littlebrown.co.uk

For my mum, Vivien,
always my first and loveliest reader

1

Laura

4 March 2019

When your world ends, sometimes you carry on spinning. When Heather told me, I did not scream. Perhaps I did not even speak. I know only that I got away from her. I went into the nursery and I picked up Benjy and Evie and heard about their lunches and their paintings and said the right things about the boy who had bitten Evie and how it could easily have been the other way round. I got Evie into the buggy and she cried because she wanted to sit back to front, and then Benjy cried because it was dark and he had to walk.

I negotiated this, all of it, as though I was the same woman I had been ten minutes before.

At home, I couldn't find my keys. I knelt on the doorstep hanging on to Evie with one hand, upturning my bag with the other. She jerked away and ran for the road, and I screeched at her like the kind of parent I want not to be. At last I found the keys in my coat pocket, where they should always have been. I got the kids inside. Evie was raging. Benjy was whingeing. I shoved them in front of the TV, coats and shoes and all. Then I shut myself in the kitchen and looked up the local news on my phone.

It was true. He was dead. Alexis was dead. Stabbed minutes, surely, after we had lain naked together. I was sticky with his sweat and he was nothing. Flesh and bone, bleeding only because it takes time for our bodies to know that we are gone.

Benjy came to me, still whining, demanding a snack. I howled at him and he went out white-faced and accusatory. I didn't care. I picked up a fork and dug it into my thumb until I was no longer shaking. I filled the sink with cold water and put my face in it. I went into the sitting room, apologised to my son. I pulled my daughter, warm and protesting, onto my lap and sat with my chin on her hair and her hot weight fixing me to what had been normality. Over her head I watched the cartoon and hated everyone in it.

I started to laugh. Then I started to cry. Benjy put out a hand, puzzled and afraid, and rubbed me on the shoulder, as though he were clearing up spilled juice.

2

Laura

1 November 2018

The past caught me tonight. One moment I was examining a lump of clay Benjy had fashioned into half a rabbit, the next I was gaping at the man I had failed for nearly twenty years to forget.

I was at the nursery parents' evening, too hot in my winter coat, being talked at by Liam's mum, Heather. Which was Benjy's sculpture? Oh. Very . . . *surreal*. Was he going on the trip next week? Oh great, so was Liam. Was I volunteering? (No. I would rather eat scorpions.) Most important, had I met the new hot single dad?

I hadn't and I wasn't much interested. Any single dad would be hot. That was the rule, just as any single mum would be desperate. I took a mouthful of wine, examined a montage of skeletons, thought about what I'd watch later on Netflix.

Heather jabbed at my arm. 'By the pumpkins. Yazzie can't take her eyes off him.'

That was unexpected. Yazzie is the new toddler room manager. Purple highlights and a marble face. Loves kids but takes absolutely no shit. All the parents are terrified of her.

I drained my glass, abandoned the skeletons.

Yazzie *was* staring, so I took a long look too. I saw a man in profile. Broad shoulders in a grey sweater, straight nose, hair like maple leaves. My chest contorted. For an instant I considered running away, faking a call from Ryan. Then the man turned as though he had no alternative, and looked directly at me.

'Jesus,' I said.

It only lasted a moment. Then someone handed him a drink and he had his back to me again. I touched my fingers to the wall, hauled in a steadying breath.

'I told you,' Heather said.

'It's not that. I know him.'

Immediately I wished it unsaid. I started to drink and remembered my glass was empty. 'Not well,' I said, 'but we were at school together. Decades ago, actually.' I laughed, fake as a hyena. 'He's aged well.'

'So have you, apparently.' Heather looked me up and down. My body gave me away, fingers shaking. 'Well,' she said, 'aren't you going to say hello?'

I forced myself together. 'Later maybe. There's no rush.'

That was true. I knew we would find each other.

He came to me in the corridor, fluorescent-lit. I was gazing at the wall between two picture displays, empty glass in my hand.

'Hello, Laura.'

I twisted like a marionette. The same eyes, between amber and green. The same cheekbones. Oh God, the same mouth.

'Alexis,' I said. And, to say something, 'How've you been?'

He smiled, dismissed two decades with half a shrug. 'You know. All right.'

'I didn't know you lived in Edinburgh,' I said.

Of course I didn't. I'd known nothing about him since he walked away from me when we were seventeen years old. When I lay on my face in the grass, in the English springtime, and wept until I thought I would die from it.

He said, 'Nor I you. You've got kids here?'

Here, at least, was reality. 'A boy and a girl,' I said.

Heather was approaching. She stopped a few metres from us, picked books off a display shelf. I knew she was trying for an introduction, and immediately I panicked, as though even so basic an exchange would be beyond me. Then one of the nursery teachers came out of a side room and started talking about Liam. Reprieve.

Alexis looked at my left hand. 'You're married?'

'Yes.' I wanted to add something – express some loyalty to Ryan – but I couldn't do it. Not because I didn't feel it, but because this meeting tore away everything else. I said instead, 'I have a stepson too. Simon. He's fourteen.'

Alexis nodded.

'What about you?' I asked.

'I'm not married.'

'But you have a child here.' *Well obviously.*

'Gracie. She's three. I'm separated from her mum.'

Two dads walked past us carrying glasses. Alexis propped his shoulder against the wall, curved towards me. My stomach crashed through half a lifetime. I looked at his mouth – a fast, guilty glance. I wanted to touch him. I wanted to hit him, too. He moved a hand, then stilled it. I had a sudden vision of kissing him against a peeling wall, our bodies so hard together that we could have imprinted them in the plaster.

I looked past him to the photo display beside us and realised that one of them was my daughter, mud-splashed and innocent, in a flash of Scottish sun. Her grin was absolute: toddler joy.

Alexis said, 'Is that your girl?'

I nodded. He glanced from the picture to me, then along at the array of photos, the Early Years charts, the picture books with their innocuous covers. I saw that he was holding a piece of crayoned paper in one hand. *To Daddy, love from Gracie.*

'Christ,' he said. 'I can't talk to you, Laura. Not here. Not like this.'

I tried to keep my eyes on Evie's photo, but they pulled back to his jawline, his neck, his lips held resolutely still. I heard voices close to us. Yazzie, Heather again, and someone I didn't know.

I whispered, 'When?'

'I don't know,' he said. He turned away. He held his fingers up to his chest, his daughter's drawing, a talisman, tight between them.

3

Hope

4 January 1999

There is the common room for the cool girls and there is the locker room for the uncool ones. Laura is in the latter with me and Claire and Jem. It is a momentous occasion, although none of us knows that yet, because it is the day she will meet Alexis.

We sit on thin wooden benches with stickered lockers above our heads and winter mould on the ceiling. I am telling them about Alexis, who is joining the school that day and whom I know and they do not. Jem and Laura are teasing me, pretending to think there's something going on. They're only being kind. Hope Mitchell is no object of desire. But it's a game they feel obliged to play: their way of being friends.

Laura and Jem resent their status as locker-room pariahs. They don't say this, but we read it in their short skirts and sheer tights, in Jem's made-up face and Laura's deep-conditioned hair. They pout at the peeling edges of Robbie

Williams and Leonardo DiCaprio, no substitute for actual boyfriends, however inadequate. They squirm on the stiff pine and sigh at the smeary windows.

Claire doesn't care. She has her own plans: three As, a leading university, fancy career. She studies, she hangs out with us, she works some more. She thinks she can afford to wait.

I don't care either, or I may as well not.

I tell them that Alexis is just a friend.

The bell rings. Five-minute warning. Jem gets out her mirror, pursing her mouth and rubbing the tip of her nose. She smacks it with a powder puff, pastes gloss on lips already glimmering pink. Laura fiddles with her necklace, looking for a compliment. It's new. A silver bird on a silver chain. I ask about it and she says it's a good-luck present for the start of term. She doesn't say that it's from her parents, but I can see that she regrets telling me even that much. She swings away from me, tucking the bird into her top, and pretends to examine a poster on the wall. They're holding auditions for the school show this week, but she already knows the details by heart. We both do.

I go to the bathroom. I check that I am alone, then examine my face. It is as I thought: better than it might be. The acne has my chin today, my forehead, and either side of my nose. The spots are mostly early stage, smooth red mounds. Sometimes my whole face is covered ear to ear in bursting creamy pustules. Laura is my best friend, but on those days she cannot look at me. Usually when it is like that I have an orgy of self-hate and squeezing, and the next day they are scabbed or bleeding, stinging with antiseptic.

If I see Alexis today, I will look no worse than last time, perhaps a little better. I have a plan to make that a lot better. If I dare.

We see him after English. I am with Laura and Jem. He is walking with Mark Myres, who is in the second rank of cool boys. Mark grimaces at Jem and Laura, who have both, at various times, snogged him. He pretends not to see me, which is better than what sometimes happens. I see Alexis noticing this and wonder if he will do the same. It's like I am waiting to be punched. But Alexis is better than that. He stops and Mark goes on. I introduce him, trying not to sound proprietorial.

Jem wriggles like a maggot on a stick when she sees him close up, and snaps on her best smile. She'll be glad she did her make-up. Laura just looks at him. When I tell him her name, he looks back at her. Then he runs after Mark, who's showing him to his next lesson.

When he's out of earshot, Jem says, 'Well, *he's* gorgeous. I thought you said you met him through church?' Then she giggles. 'Sorry, Hope. I didn't mean . . .'

Only she did, so she can't finish the sentence.

'His grandparents go to our church,' I say. 'I don't think he's religious.'

Jem asks, 'Does he live with them?'

'For the moment.' I smile, enjoying the fact that I am in his confidence. I know – because Alexis has told me – that he has been sent out of the way of his parents' anguished divorce. I know he misses them, but is almost relieved to be out of the shouting line.

9

Laura is repositioning her bag strap. While she's doing this, she looks back along the corridor. Alexis has gone now, vanished into the crowd. Jem and I are watching her, waiting for the verdict.

At last, she's done fiddling.

'He seems nice,' she says.

She and Jem hurry off, late for economics. I stand where we were, less smug at the introduction than I thought I would be. Two fifth-form girls pass by, pretending not to look at my face. I gaze down at the blue vinyl, already striped with mud, and see something small and gleaming, settling in the dirt.

It's the bird from Laura's necklace.

Later, we eat our lunches in the locker room. Jem tells Claire about Alexis. 'Honestly, he's well fit. Beautiful smile, beautiful arse.' She swallows a mouthful of fat-free yogurt, waving the plastic spoon at me. A smear gleams white on her lip.

'Why didn't you tell us that before?'

'I didn't really notice,' I say.

I'm unfolding the strip of thin paper from on top of my sandwich. Handwriting so careful it is like a printed font.

> The soul of the sluggard desireth, and hath nothing:
> but the soul of the diligent shall be made fat.
> (Proverbs 13:4)

I want to tear it into pieces but I know better. I try, as I must, to commit it to memory. Claire watches me, but she doesn't say anything. At first, they used to make out that these notes were a form of kindness. 'At least she cares,' they'd say. After a while, they stopped saying that.

Jem is still chuntering. 'You could have warned us. I'd have undone more buttons if I'd known.' She sighs, takes another mouthful. 'You got quite a look, Laura. You'll be making Hope jealous.'

Laura says nothing. I pretend not to notice.

I refold the note and put it into my pocket. I can learn it later. As I do, my fingers touch something small and solid. Laura's bird. I waver, then leave it there.

She doesn't realise it's missing until we're leaving school, drawing on coats and gloves and emerging into the jagged cold. Laura is arranging a grey scarf around her throat and she starts scrabbling around her neckline, uncoiling the scarf, unzipping her coat.

'What is it?' Jem asks, and Laura says it's her new necklace: the pendant has come off.

We help her to check her sweater, her bag, the scarf, the floor. Claire goes back to search the locker room. Alexis appears beside us in a ski jacket and a woolly hat.

'What's happened?' he asks.

When Laura tells him, he joins in too. He walks in a circle around her, lifting the collar of her coat to examine it. His hand touches her hair. I look at her face. She's still upset, but she's smirking too.

On the way home, she's quiet. It might be because of her silver bird. After I've left her – when she is well out of sight – I stoop and drop it through a grate in the road.

4

Laura

14 November 2018

I have thought of Alexis every hour since I saw him. That's not an exaggeration. I have lived my work days like a somnambulist, occasionally surfacing to register that I have a job, communications to supervise, colleagues to appease. I have jogged miles on remorseless pavements and chancy paths. I have had sex once with Ryan and refused him twice, and it was the first I felt guiltier about, for I was not thinking of him. I have done almost all the nursery runs and felt bad about that too, because the children have been delighted and Ryan – always overworked – has been grateful.

I have seen Gracie. I made Evie point her out to me, a thin child with a sharp nose and her father's smile. I have not, I think, seen her mother, although I have watched for her almost as keenly as for Alexis.

Today I saw him when I delivered Evie to the toddler room. There was less shock, more pain this time. We left at the same time, the girls standing side by side behind the stair gate to bid us farewell. Gracie was crying. Evie and I went through our usual routine. She put out her hands with fingers wide apart and I held out mine to touch them, finger-tips to fingertips, thumb to thumb. Gracie stopped crying when she saw us and reached out for Alexis to do the same.

We stood quietly, joined to our daughters. Then we moved away down the stairs, through the double doors, onto the leaf-thick street.

The day was claggy, promising nothing. I told myself to go straight to the bus stop, then to the office.

I said, 'When do you have to be at work?'

He looked at me, really looked, as though he had been afraid to do it before. 'I can be late,' he said.

I couldn't. Not really. Not with two weeks of wasted ground to make up, a pivotal meeting, my new assistant to train.

But I would be.

We paced the wide, beautiful streets without speaking. Rose-gold walls, bay windows, regulated shrubs. At the gates to Blackford Pond, I scanned the path widening and parting ahead. Dog walkers, runners, a mother with a buggy and a toddler and a face like chalked stone. No one I knew. Sometimes nursery takes the kids here. But not this early.

Alexis said, 'We're not doing anything wrong.'

I walked through the gates, beside him. *No*, I thought. *Not yet.*

I watched him as we followed the curve of the path. It wasn't so much that he had aged well as that he had hardly aged at all.

'What is it?' he said.

'I was thinking of Dorian Gray.'

He smiled, glanced at me. 'I could say the same of you,' he said.

'Two kids,' I said, 'and nineteen years. I've changed enough.'

It was true in its way, but not in the only way that mattered.

We turned, without conferring, and went through another gate. The pond lay big and placid and tree-lined before us, familiar as my kitchen floor. I watched a duck dipping and shaking, then tugged my scarf tighter. It wasn't a day to be out.

'How long have you lived here?' I asked.

'Nearly four years.'

Dear God. And they say Edinburgh is a village.

We evaded the squabbling waterfowl, swarming a toddler with a loaf of sliced bread. Her grandmother hovered behind her, hands out. The swans were as big as the child.

I have been there with my two, time without count. Benjy is afraid of the swans.

I said, 'I thought you were in France. I thought you'd stay there.'

'I was,' he said. 'Mostly. I moved here when Diana, my ex, was pregnant with Gracie.'

I didn't want to think about Diana. Or Gracie. I said, 'You liked Paris, then?' My voice contorted. 'You were glad you went.'

He gave me a look. 'Hardly,' he said. 'For a long time, I hated it.'

I missed a step, caught myself. 'Tell me,' I whispered. 'Tell me what it was like.'

'Like what it was,' he said. 'Being in exile. My mother's boyfriend was kind. My mother tried to be. The school was . . . fine, I suppose. Afterwards, I went travelling. Asia. Australia. I worked in hostels, bars.'

I stared out across the flat, dark water to the trees, trying to stabilise myself. The leaves hung defiantly bright, waiting to fall.

'And after that?' I said.

'I came back to Europe. I went to university in Graz, got a job in Vienna, then in Paris. I was there until I moved here.'

With Diana, I thought. I longed to ask whether he had forgotten me then. With her or with her predecessors. There must have been predecessors.

A pair of greyhounds dashed along the path towards us. We moved aside, arms touching, then went on again.

'What was it like for you?' he said. 'It must have been hard, being still there.'

Being there, I thought, *and without you.*

'It was lonely,' I said. 'People knew there was something to set me apart. After a while, when I wouldn't talk, even my friends left me alone. I worked. I had nothing else to do. I stayed in and read.' *And cried. Mostly cried.* I smiled, so he wouldn't read the thought. 'My marks improved,' I said. 'I applied to the universities my parents suggested. I got into UCL.'

I could not lie to him. Not even by omission. I said, 'I thought I would lose myself in a big city. I was wrong, of course, but I tried my best.'

I had tried my best with drink and drugs and man after man. Emotionless sex, desperate each time to delete his face, his voice. The taste of his skin and the way loving him was like flying. To delete what we had done together.

It had never worked.

'Perhaps I was closer to losing myself than I knew,' I said. 'Only because I wasn't enjoying it, I didn't understand.'

'And then?'

'I started running again. After a few years, I moved up here. I loved Edinburgh on sight. I love it now. I met Ryan.'

I thought of my husband, of the parody of love we had made the weekend before, and felt ashamed.

Alexis said, 'Are you happy?'

I stopped.

We had gone beyond the pond now and were alone on the shaded path that twists round the side of the hill. 'Until two weeks ago,' I said, 'I thought I was.'

'Oh God. Laura . . .' He stepped sideways, off the path. He grimaced into the mass of vegetation, then back at me. 'If I'd known,' he said, 'I would have sent Gracie to a different nursery, moved across town.'

I should have said that was what I would have done too. I should have walked away and hoped to hell we never ran into each other again. Instead, I moved nearer to him, step by deliberate step.

He took my hands, both of them in both of his, pulled them down so we stood pressed hips to chest together. My throat was tight, my breath sharp. I could feel my body reacting, and his.

A dog ran, panting, almost into us. A child shouted. Our hands parted and we stepped back, so fast I nearly fell onto the piled leaves. Alexis caught my arm again, kept me upright, then let it go. The dog, an overfed Labrador, was leaping around us, tail wagging, nosing pockets for snacks. A middle-aged woman called him back, faux-apologetic. We smiled, exchanged niceties, stood there until she had gone. The dog pounded ahead of her, heading for the water.

I said, 'I have to go to work.'

Alexis nodded. We started back together, silent until we were back round the pond where the child had been and the swans still clustered.

'Tomorrow?' he said, then.

'Tomorrow night,' I said.

I didn't think about the lies I would have to tell. I thought only of how I could breathe through the hours to get there.

5

Laura

5 March 2019

The police were here today. I don't know who put them on to me. No one was supposed to know. They found me in my dressing gown, probably looking like I'd been crying all morning, because I had. I'd texted work and said I was ill. I'd told Simon the same and begged him to drop the kids at nursery on his way to school.

'You look like shit,' he'd said, and I didn't say a word, either to reassure him or about his language.

I could hear Evie testing out the phrase all the way to the door.

The detectives were women: one tall and faintly glamorous, one a squat prize fighter. I felt I'd encountered them before, but didn't know where. There was a woman last time too, but she was young and sympathetic, her bad-cop colleague taciturn in the background.

They showed me their warrant cards. I panicked and said I was ill. 'I think it's flu.'

The tall one said they wouldn't be long.

Next door, Mhairi was letting herself in, back from the school run. I saw her look at them, then at me. Perhaps she was wondering if Ryan had had an accident. That's what you usually think, isn't it, when the police show up at someone's door?

I took them into the sitting room, which was – and is – a tip. The kids had had tea in front of the TV last night. Half-eaten fish fingers accused me from the coffee table.

'Sorry,' I said. 'Like I said, I'm sick.'

I stopped, realising I should have begun with questions. *What's happened? My husband, is he OK? Oh God, just tell me.*

'I've seen worse,' the squat one said, of the room, but she gave that up at a look from her superior. The tall one *was* her superior, too, though she looked decades younger. Inspector something. They introduced themselves when we sat down, but I immediately forgot their names.

The short one got out a notebook. Funnily enough, the first thing they asked about *was* Ryan. Was he here? Was he at work? I told them he'd been away for a few days. They looked animated at that. I decided to take it as a cue.

'Is this about him?' My voice squeaked, a vent for real nerves. 'Is he OK?'

'He's fine, as far as we know,' the tall one said.

The squat one said. 'Do you know an Alexis Chiltern?'

Wrong tense. I wanted to shake her, to scream that no one could know him now. But of course they were trying for my reaction. I attempted to look puzzled, the right level of upset. I used to be able to act, but I seemed to have forgotten how.

'Very slightly,' I said. 'I heard he was killed. It's horrible.' I stopped, wishing I knew what to do with my hands.

The tall one said, 'He died very close to this house. On the footpath in the Hermitage of Braid.'

'I heard,' I said. 'It's awful. But I don't understand . . .' Was it the time to say this? 'I don't mean to be rude, but why are you talking to me?'

She ignored that. 'As though,' she said, 'he was walking home from somewhere near here.'

I shook my head. 'I don't . . . What are you *saying*?'

The short one said, 'We've heard you were a fair bit better acquainted with him than you're suggesting.'

I looked up, making my mouth an 'O' of surprise. 'What do you mean?' I said. 'I hardly knew him.'

Immediately I regretted that. We could have been seen out together. Not compromisingly, but out. I'd have done better to admit a few friendly drinks. And then there was the day in the Meadows.

'I knew him as a nursery parent,' I said. 'To chat to at kids' things, say hi if we ran into each other. That was it.'

I should have quit there. But they weren't responding. I shook my head, twisted my fingers together. 'You're making a mistake,' I said.

The tall one sighed. 'What were you doing the night before last?'

'Are you serious?'

'Just answer the question, please.'

'I was here.'

'Alone?'

'With the kids.'

The short one said, 'How old are the bairns?'

Christ. They weren't going to interview Benjy and Evie, were they? *Have you heard strange noises while Daddy's been away? Has Mummy been unhappy recently?*

'The little ones are four and two,' I said. 'My stepson is fourteen. Look, will you please tell me what it is you're imagining?'

'And he was home too?'

I considered asking Simon to lie for me, but I couldn't do it. Anyway, how would I explain why?

'He was out with his girlfriend,' I said.

'Until when?'

'I don't know. Late. I was asleep.'

'When did you put your younger children to bed?'

I grinned. It felt like putting on a mask. 'Do you have kids, Inspector?'

She shook her head. The short one, somewhat surprisingly, told me that she had two sons and a grandchild on the way.

'Well,' I said, 'as you know, it's less putting them to bed, more threatening and begging, and there's no knowing how long it will take.'

The prizefighter almost smiled. The tall one snapped, 'What time were you done that night?'

'I don't know exactly. I think Evie – my daughter – was asleep by about seven thirty. My son took longer.'

Benjy had dropped off at 8.15 and Alexis had been in the house, undressing me, by 8.25. The memory flayed me.

'What did you do then?'

That was the short one, curt again, regretting her lapse towards humanity.

I looked at the carpet, rosy with blackcurrant squash. I was about to say I'd watched Netflix, but I wasn't sure how much they could check. So I said I'd done the washing-up, then read a book.

'Which book?'

'*Anna Karenina*,' I said. Immediately I could have bitten my tongue out. They could read, these women, and they were gaping at me as though I was even stupider than they had thought.

The short one wrote something in her notebook. The tall one said, 'Interesting choice,' and got to her feet. 'Well, we'll leave you for now. If anything occurs to you, here's my card.'

The squat one shoved open the front door, dislodging strands of clematis, pink buds against her bulldog face.

'Where exactly is your husband?' she said.

'Frankfurt,' I said. 'It's a conference.' I gave a high laugh. 'Don't ask me what on.'

Neither of them returned my death's-head grin. The tall one said, 'When is he back?'

'Tomorrow night,' I said. 'But this can't have anything to do with him.'

The squat one thanked me perfunctorily for my time. I shut the door and watched through the glass for the car doors slamming. Then I ran to the loo and dry-heaved for what seemed like hours. Afterwards, I lay there keening, with my head on the bathmat and my knees on the bitter tiles.

Later, while I dressed to collect the children, I realised two things. It must have been Diana who'd tipped the police off about me. I'd always thought she knew. She'd be tormented at what had happened. If not for herself, then for Gracie.

Well, she probably would be. Unless she'd done it.

The second thing I realised was that I should have offered the police a cup of tea.

23 August 2018

From: Admin@Friends&Lovers.com

To: AlwaysHaveParis

Subject: SOMEONE'S INTERESTED!

Good news, AlwaysHaveParis. Khaleesi8690
has winked at you. Log in now to check
out her profile and send her a message.

From: Admin@Friends&Lovers.com

To: Khaleesi8690

Subject: IT'S MUTUAL!

Good news, Khaleesi8690. AlwaysHaveParis
has returned your wink. Log in now to send
him a message.

6

Hope

7 January 1999

My plan is to go to the clinic before school. I'm terrified, but I can't bear not to. I squeeze three spots first thing and the one beneath my eye spews a mass of red and yellow that slides down the mirror and drips to the tiled floor. Sometimes I look at my face and I want to scrape off the skin and start again.

I pat TCP on the holes, feeling sick at the pain but like I deserve it too. Then I dress and go downstairs. I can hear clattering in the kitchen and I want it to be Father, but it's not, it's Her, standing at the sink with Her back to me. Father is nowhere to be seen and that's worse again, because although he rarely stands up to Her, he might put a good word in if She's undecided.

She turns towards me, then back to the washing-up. 'Have you said your prayers?'

I nod, though I haven't. I gave up praying after I begged God for three years to take away my acne. I asked for other things to change, too, but they never did.

She says, 'Where's your brother?'

I realise I haven't seen Isaac, which means he slept through his alarm. I say, 'I think he's in the shower.'

I'll have to go back upstairs now, to wake him.

She can't object to cleanliness, so this is allowed to pass. I twiddle my fingers together. She snaps, 'You can dry the dishes. The devil finds work for idle hands.'

She always says that, as automatically as other parents say 'if you've got nothing better to do'. I've stopped thinking about it, but I saw Laura noticing it like mad, the first time she came round.

Laura hardly ever comes here now. She disapproves of Laura because Laura is pretty and not a churchgoer. I go to hers sometimes. Laura's parents are so lovely it makes me hate God.

I say, 'I would like to go in to school early.'

She doesn't turn, but Her shoulders stiffen. I go on because I've promised myself I will. 'We've got English first period. Claire and I were going to talk the chapter through.'

I've selected this alibi carefully. She doesn't hate Claire like She does the others, because although Claire isn't religious, she is studious and dresses like she doesn't want to attract boys. But I realise at once it isn't going to work.

'What book is it?' She says, not looking up from the sink.

I tell Her, then wish I'd lied. We're doing *The Mill on the Floss* and She doesn't approve of that any more than She does of Laura. Not so much because of Maggie's overnight boat ride with Stephen – she's punished for that, with biblical thoroughness – but because of the funny bits.

She stands still, holding a dish above the soapy water. I tense up, because although I know this isn't going well, I don't yet know what level of going badly it will be. But She just lowers the bowl again and turns to face me.

'It would be better if you went at the normal time.'

I don't argue.

The auditions are at lunchtime in the school hall. They've been running for three days, but Laura and I are going today. So is Alexis. I haven't told Laura this, but I have a feeling she knows. Jem and Claire aren't going, Claire because she isn't interested and Jem because it's *West Side Story* and she can't sing a note.

'What's wrong with a nice bit of Shakespeare?' she says, sounding like a disapproving granny.

I'm pleased by the choice because I *can* sing. I'm in the church choir and until I got my acne I did solos at Christmas and Easter. Now the vicar shoves me in with everyone else. He said he thought it was getting too much for me and that someone else deserved a turn, but I know better. So much for being equally beautiful in the sight of God.

Remembering this doesn't make me optimistic about today's audition. One of the music teachers, Miss Pendleton, ran into me last term and said I should try out. But it's not her who makes the final decision.

We put our names on a list by the door and sit on plastic chairs. I can just see Alexis at the end of the row in front. Mr Balmore and Mrs Henderson, heads of drama and music, are alone in the front row. Miss Pendleton is at the piano and a girl from the fifth year is climbing onto the stage.

'Do your parents know you're doing this?' Laura whispers, wriggling herself comfortable beside me. I shake my head. When I think about it, I alternate between fabricating lies so elaborate that even the thought petrifies me, and somehow hanging on in secret until it becomes impossible to extract me without a school-level fallout. And then doing my penance.

Laura tries to ask more, but I hush her.

Mr Balmore shouts, 'Go on.'

Miss Pendleton plonks away (it's not her fault: it's a crap piano) and the girl on stage jumps into 'I Feel Pretty', half a bar too soon. She doesn't catch herself up until just before they stop her, and she never quite gets the tune. Still, she *is* pretty, with lips like a jelly sweet and long, curved legs. I wouldn't be surprised if she gets a part.

The boy who goes next can't sing at all. Mrs Henderson rolls her biro, waiting for him to finish. Then there are two fourth-year girls, who bop about as though it's an audition for the Spice Girls. Mrs Henderson yawns; Mr Balmore stares. Alexis is shifting in his seat. He's never rude, so I guess he's near the front of the queue. The girls are followed by Mark Myres. He's been in the shows since he was fourteen. I think he does it for the sex ratios. He's not a great singer, but he's so confident that most people think he is.

It's hot in the hall, though it's freezing outside. The scar on my arm is itching. I push my sleeve up to rub it but see Laura looking and pull it down again.

'Oh Hope,' she murmurs, like it really hurts her, and she leans towards me as though she wants to give me a hug. I feel bad – for the first time since I did it – that I threw her pendant down the drain. Then Alexis gets up to sing, Laura moves away from me to gawp at him, and I don't feel bad any more.

He's good. Even better than I was expecting, and I knew he was musical because his grandparents keep nagging him to join the church choir. He sings 'Maria', and tears sting the half-scabbed spot below my eye. Laura grips her hands together. Mrs Henderson gives a jump in her seat and Mr Balmore lets him get almost all the way through before he remembers to stop him. Then he roars his thank you as Alexis walks down from the stage. We all clap. Mark, lingering by the door, says something. Alexis smiles and shakes his head.

The two of them are still there when we get through the queue to my turn. I've lost track of what the others are like because my heart is bumping so much. I feel as though the hall is full, even though it's nothing like.

'Hope Mitchell,' says Mrs Henderson.

Mr Balmore looks up, surprised and clearly not delighted.

'Good luck,' says Laura.

I climb the steps to the stage, into the light. Someone whispers. Someone else giggles. Mr Balmore scowls and Mrs Henderson looks at her feet. Only Miss Pendleton gives me an encouraging smile. I long to disappear into the black curtain behind me, fall away from them all like a bad dream. Then Alexis makes a thumbs-up sign and I straighten my shoulders and tilt my chin.

I've chosen 'A Boy Like That'. For the last month, I've nurtured a vision of myself as Anita. Red dress and black wig. Spots healed – or better enough to be covered in make-up – and Alexis, afterwards, telling me how amazing I was. Maria isn't an option for me, and not just because I'm a mezzo. I could sing soprano as well as anyone else here.

It's because of 'I Feel Pretty'.

The piano starts and so do I. When I sing, I feel undamaged, like the world stops and everything for a moment is as it should be. The applause afterwards is generous and surprised and gives me a feeling I thought I could never have. I gaze, blinking, to where Alexis is, and he's smiling and clapping like he's really pleased for me.

I want to pause time.

Then Mr Balmore says, 'Thank you.' There's no booming for me, no nudging Mrs Henderson. He says it as indifferently as if I'd collected his rubbish on a train. But he looks like what he is: a man with a dilemma.

Laura is next. She's picked a bit from 'America'. She can sing nicely and she looks right on stage, with her hair swinging and her eyes alight. She's wearing a short skirt, which will help with Balmore. But I know I was better.

I'm distracted all afternoon. Laura is too, but neither of us says anything. They're putting the cast list up at the end of the day, and I don't know whether I'm more scared of getting what I want, or not getting it.

I find out soon enough. I go to the hall as soon as the bell rings. The door is shut and Mr Balmore and Mrs Henderson are standing by it like bouncers. Neither Laura nor Alexis is there. I pass Miss Pendleton marching away down the corridor, her mouth thin. I think she's going to stop, but she looks away from me. When Mr Balmore sees me, he pretends he didn't.

I scan the list on the door, the names forming themselves slowly. Stacy Chambers is Maria. Last year, when they did *The Sound of Music*, she was Liesl. She's got a sweet voice, even if it is a bit poppy. She's popular. She's extremely pretty.

Alexis is Tony.

Mark Myres is Riff. Rick Nuccelli is Bernardo. He wears a leather jacket over his uniform and Jem has a crush on him. I've no idea if he can sing, but his dad is Italian, which is the closest this school gets to Puerto Rico.

Laura is Anita.

It takes me a long time to find my name, because it's among the extras at the bottom, half covered with Sellotape. I'm a Jet. I'm a boy.

I don't run. I stroll past the chatterers, trying to look like I don't care. I see Laura coming in the other direction.

'Well?' she says.

'See for yourself,' I say, not stopping. Then I make myself call after her. 'Congratulations.'

I pass Mark with his back to me and Stacy draped against a wall like a post-orgasmic Barbie doll.

'I didn't think I had a chance,' she's saying. 'I heard Hope Mitchell stunned you all today. The voice of an angel, Miss Pendleton said.'

'The voice maybe,' Mark says. 'But have you seen her face? We're not casting *Frankenstein*.'

Stacy sees me over his shoulder. To be fair, she looks

mortified. She grabs his arm and drags him away, whispering. I go to the girls' loos, shut myself in a cubicle and dig my nails into my face until my fingers are wet with blood and pus.

24 August 2018

From: Khaleesi8690

To: AlwaysHaveParis

Subject: Paris and Casablanca

Hi – thanks for the wink back.

Nice profile, and even better taste in films! Long-time Bogart fan here. Believe it or not, I've never actually been to France (or Morocco!), though I've heard wonderful things. I'm guessing leaving there would be a wrench, even to come here. What brought a Parisian to chilly Scotland?

Bye for now!

x

7

Laura

6 March 2019

Simon took the little ones in again. I didn't even have to ask. I called the office and said I was still under the weather. Kai sounded worried, but I have no head space for gratitude. I drank a cup of coffee, ate a stale bagel. Then I went for a run. Legitimate grievers are offered drugs, sleeping tablets, antidepressants. But I have only two tonics for my furtive grief: alcohol and exercise.

For now, I choose the latter.

I went by the road to Blackford Hill. Past iron gates and low stone walls, high hedges and houses I used to say I would give my soul to possess. By the gates to the pond, I turned my head away, guts twisting, and ran on through a rising scream. On, then up. I zigzagged on steep dog-leg roads, past terraces and bungalows. At the last bend, I left the road and followed rough paths on grass. I ran as though I could destroy myself, lungs and legs first, if I tried hard enough.

Obsessed

The Observatory, all tower and red brick. Salisbury Crags, looking close enough to touch. Curving slopes of grass, and false summit after false summit. I didn't stop. I saw the city with its slanting rooftops and white-rimmed windows; eyes in a thousand attic rooms. I saw the hills, stretching to the south. I remembered, with a stabbing pain, what I could *not* see but knew was there. A sharp-sided valley below me, with paths on high banks, and thick trees and a river. The spot where a man had died.

At the summit, students were taking selfies. I dipped past them and dropped down fast, finding paths through thickets. I didn't stop until there was no one in sight, and then I sank onto all fours amongst the gorse, hauling in lungfuls of damp air. The tears came hot and bitter, and the gasping sobs. I flopped back onto my knees, arms forward – child's pose – burying my face in spiky green. I stayed there for a long time.

When I got home, the tall inspector was waiting outside, being walked around by Mhairi's cat.

'I see you're feeling better,' she said.

I tried to lift the cat, but he slithered through my fingers, fatly, like a missed catch, and clawed his way over the fence. The sergeant emerged from their car, which was parked in a permit holder's space.

'You'll get a ticket,' I said. She smiled.

They followed me inside without asking. I kicked off my trainers and wrapped myself in Ryan's fleece.

The tall one said, 'Husband still away?'

'Yes.' *You know he is.*

I started into the sitting room before I remembered what I'd forgotten yesterday. I stopped in the doorway.

'Would you like a cup of tea?'

They exchanged looks. The short one said, 'Tell you what, why don't I get that? You go on in and have a wee chat.'

I flopped into the sofa. The inspector sat on the edge of an armchair, studying me with a curious expression.

'Laura,' she said. 'You know we have his phone?'

I didn't move. How could I not have expected this?

I tried to look blank. 'My husband's?'

She gave me a look. 'Alexis Chiltern's. We've read all your messages. We know he was here Sunday night.'

I said nothing. I could hear the kettle coming to the boil, the other officer clunking cups.

The inspector got something out of her pocket. A phone. She crossed the room, ramming her thin hips onto the sofa next to me. A touch of a button and there was Gracie, possum eyes, elfin face, filling the screen.

Not smiling. That smile would have skewered me.

'It was in his pocket,' the inspector said.

'There's no blood on it,' I said.

'No.'

The sergeant came in, carrying two cups pushed together in one hand, and a third in the other. We have trays. I could have told her that. She gave the single cup to me and her colleague took one of the others. I remembered to say thank you. She had given me milk, but I drank it anyway.

The inspector rested her cup on the coffee table and read aloud from the phone. Her eyes were the gleaming brown of coffee beans.

Outside xx

5 minutes. God, I can't wait x

I love you.

If there had been pity before, there was none now. 'These were sent between 20.17 and 20.22 on Sunday,' she said. 'Fairly unequivocal, wouldn't you say?'

I didn't. She sat on our sofa – the one I'd persuaded Ryan to buy, worn now, stained with baby sick – and made me listen to every message I had sent Alexis, every message from him to me. I swallowed my horrible tea and said nothing.

The short one said, 'You ken it's an offence, don't you? Obstructing the police in the course of their enquiries?'

Of course I bloody *kent*. I was shaking so hard I had to hold the mug with both hands. 'Please,' I said. 'Please go now.'

The inspector said, 'We'll need your fingerprints.'

I offered her my trembling cup and she shook her head, smiling like a disappointed teacher. 'This isn't a Dorothy L. Sayers novel, Laura. At the station.'

'Not today,' I said. My voice was Benjy's, pleading for a day off nursery. 'My head hurts. I'm not well.'

The sergeant looked up from her notepad. 'You're fit enough to be off running, though?'

I looked at the dregs of my tea. She said, 'We'll take you now. If you ask nicely, we'll even sort out a car to bring you back.'

I went.

8

Laura

15 November 2018

Until I got to the bar tonight, I felt guilty.

This morning, I said I had to take my new assistant for a drink after work. But Ryan said he had a late meeting, Simon his computer club. They turned away, apologetic but largely indifferent, to coffee and toast. I built anger out of shame, said why couldn't Ryan miss one bloody meeting. He said it was a bit late to mention it, and why couldn't I postpone my drink. I said why couldn't he take my work seriously, for once.

It was an old quarrel, resuscitated for convenience. Ryan, like me, works in a bank. But he is in senior management, earns several times my salary and puts in merciless hours. I do marketing, which means, in effect, rewriting endless emails so we can communicate with our customers without getting into trouble with the regulator.

If Ryan doesn't take my job seriously, it's because he knows it bores me stupid.

He didn't point this out. But when I said I'd have to ask Mhairi, if he wouldn't look after his own children for once, he tugged violently at the drawer he was opening. It slid from its runners, piling knives and forks onto his bare feet. Ryan swore. Evie cried. Simon carried her out of the kitchen, little arms hanging onto his neck, leaving his breakfast. Ryan and I picked up the cutlery in silence.

Later, he texted to apologise. That made me feel worst of all.

I asked Mhairi. Then, to make the lie credible, I went for a drink with Kai and a couple of other newbies, though I gulped it down with my eye on the clock. Kai was guilt-makingly grateful.

Alexis and I met in the Devil's Advocate, glowing warm and incongruous amid washed-out stone and grave-robber shadows. I walked from the New Town, trading vast Georgian houses and gated gardens for the blackened stairs and twisting corners of the Old Town; tranquil, austere Edinburgh for a city of secrets and dark violence. Against the velvet night, the castle glowed pale as a fantasy.

On the steps from Market Street, an old man in a sleeping bag shouted for change. I threw pound coins into his lap, four of them, as though the gold would buy me salvation. He was still muttering as I pushed open the glass door to the bar.

Alexis was standing by the counter in the dark grey coat and burgundy scarf he'd worn the previous day. He kissed my cheek as though he'd been meeting me for years, except his lips were burning hot. I didn't feel guilty then. I felt ter-rified, and frantically alive.

We stood close together, in the pack by the bar. I let the bodies push me against him, feeling him tense.

He said, 'I don't know what you drink any more.'

I asked for a gin and tonic, picked the gin at random. I could only think of how much I wanted to touch him. We sat in one of the booths that hid away, cave-like, beyond the main room, and talked as though this was the innocent old friends' catch-up we would pretend it was if anyone saw us. He told me about Gracie, conceived at the tail end of a fading relationship. I watched his mouth, nipped my lip with my teeth and shivered.

I bought time, sharing with him the things that should have stayed mine and Ryan's alone. I told him about Benjy, who was born four weeks early and spent ten days in ICU; about Evie, who had plummeted into the world with the confident abruptness with which she did everything. I told him about Simon: how he'd taken months to warm up to me and how I'd glowed when at last he'd come out of school and reached for my hand.

I didn't talk about Ryan.

I talked of Edinburgh, of London. I watched Alexis's jaw, his elbow hard on the table, his forearm. Would his mouth taste as I remembered; was his skin still sweet and salt and warm? I watched his fingers on the glass. I remembered how I had stretched over him, spent and shaking, hearing his heart beat.

I flicked my gaze up. He was watching me too.

I got up. I bought more drinks, pushing through chatterers at the bar – the friends, the first-daters, the work-night-outers. I asked for a glass of water and downed it at the counter.

'You OK, doll?'

The barman was watching me, mildly concerned. I thought, *I should go home.* Instead, I smiled and said I was fine. I took the glasses in hands that wouldn't stay steady.

Alexis was sitting completely still, staring down at the table. I saw his face as it had been more than nineteen years ago, when we parted. As though he was being taken out to be hanged.

I slammed the glasses down before I could drop them. He looked up, sharp and vulnerable and alive. I said, 'Do you think it's possible to forget the past?'

'No.'

I sat down, finished my gin and tonic in two gulps. My head wheeled, half settled, spun again. 'To move beyond it, then?'

I reached my hands across the table. He gripped them hard between his. I gave a little gasp, but not of pain.

'Alexis,' I said, as I had said decades before. 'It wasn't our fault.'

'Wasn't it?' he replied.

I looked at him, made him keep looking.

'Let's get out of here,' I said.

We took a taxi. We sat like strangers, not touching, but – not like strangers – exchanging no courtesies. His flat was in a Victorian tenement off Mayfield Road, top floor, up those worn stone steps that are so essentially Edinburgh. In the dim hallway, the street door clicked shut behind us, and we stood in shadows together.

He took my face in his hands, palms hard and warm along cheekbone and jaw, tilting up my chin. 'Laura,' he said. 'Laura.' The dark space of the stairs seemed to shift and settle and hold us there together.

I said, 'I can't not do this.'

We ran up the shallow steps, dragging each other. At the top, I gazed over the balustrade, edge of the abyss, one hand still gripping his, while he unlocked the flat. I thought of all those other doors, other secrets, in that one building. He spun me in through the half-open door, and I kicked it shut behind me.

We slammed into each other, mouth on mouth, pulled at clothes, fell against the wall. I tasted gin and memory and desperation. I felt his shoulders hard and bare beneath my fingers, his hands closing on my waist.

In the bedroom, where street light fed through the window, I saw his face. Shadow, pain and passion. I kissed him again, shutting out doubt. We fell together on the bed, bodies fast and frantic, more rough than tender. I cried out beneath him, as I had cried for years in the hidden parts of my mind.

Afterwards, coiled naked under a heavy blanket, I wept. I twisted his head towards me and kissed the tears I knew would be there. I found his mouth again and he groaned and uncurled and rolled onto his elbows. That second time it was tender, and afterwards I lay as I had remembered, naked against his chest, joined with sweat.

He fell asleep holding me, and I nestled against him in the murky night, feeling him breathe, until hours had passed and I had to go home.

It was after midnight when I got there. The house was locked and dark and silent. I showered downstairs and tiptoed up in my towel. Quiet darkness from Simon's room. I looked in on Benjy and found him asleep, stretched like a flung puppet with his toy panda in one hand and the covers clumped round him. Evie was in our bed, between Ryan and where I should be. I climbed in next to her and she half sat up, flung herself at me, then burrowed back into warm sleep. I hugged her to me until, much later, I fell asleep.

9

Hope

11 January 1999

First rehearsal today. It's not so much a rehearsal, actually, as a pep talk from Mr Balmore, who hands out schedules and spouts some drivel about how we're all key players. He doesn't look in my direction. Miss Pendleton hasn't shown up.

'Not everyone can be Tony or Maria,' Balmore says. Stacy Chambers jiggles in her chair. 'What matters is what you do with the part you've been given.'

No one believes him, though there's a lot of sniggering at his turn of phrase. There's already a caste system, with the principals clustered together nearest the stage. Among the extras, the girls who play girls whisper among themselves, thick-lashed and scornful. Everyone else is scattered across the hall. I sit alone. I'm not the only girl in the Jets, but I'm the only sixth-form girl.

Laura is next to Alexis. They waved when I came in, but I pretended not to see. Stacy is on his other side, stroking her pink nails. I change position and my notebook slips to the floor with a bang. Everyone looks at me. Mark Myres whispers something to Rick Nuccelli. Mr Balmore abandons his 'vision' for a lecture on paying attention.

'Nobody,' he says, 'is indispensable.'

After the talk, Stacy and Alexis join him on the stage. The rest of us get up and stand around, wondering if we're dismissed. Rick grouches half-heartedly. He auditioned for Tony and has evidently not taken Mr Balmore's words to heart.

'It's type casting,' he says, pulling a face. 'Just because I'm Latino.'

I look at Alexis. Chestnut hair and hazel eyes. I can't see them from where I am, but I know them all the same. All-American? Perhaps. And he *is* beautiful.

'I thought your mum was from Basingstoke,' Laura says, and everyone laughs. I watch the back of her head, shiny as wet paint. She wouldn't have said something like that before. 'Anyway,' she adds, 'what about us?'

She has a point. Anita and Maria are as Puerto Rican as Bernardo, but Laura is pale-skinned as the Abominable Snowman and Stacy could have been plucked straight from the Playboy Mansion.

Rick grins. Mark gestures at the stage. 'The point is,' he says, '*he* can sing. Do all the shite Ricky Martin impressions you like; you won't change that.'

A tussle follows, and Laura comes over to me. 'I've hardly seen you,' she says. 'Where've you been?'

'Nowhere,' I say.

In truth, I've been where I always am, but I've been quiet.

She's mostly chatted to Jem. I think she realises this, because she changes the subject. 'What did you tell your parents about staying late?'

'Study group,' I say.

This is true. I woke early and got my father as he was leaving. I told him the group was focused on prep for university admissions. He looked a bit nervous, but said it was OK.

'Well, I'm glad you're still in the show,' Laura says.

This isn't true. It's also tactless, since she's assuming (rightly) that I resent not getting Anita. I glare at her and she goes red.

'I mean, I . . .'

I wait for her to finish. When she doesn't, I say, 'Well, I'll see how it goes.'

We stand in silence until Mr Balmore summons her to join the favoured few onstage.

'Well, if it isn't Hopeless.' It's Mark, by my side.

'Very funny.' I don't look up. I've been called that so often, it doesn't even hurt any more.

'So you're going to be in my gang, are you?' he says.

I say nothing. It hadn't escaped my attention that Riff is the leader of the Jets.

He leans in. 'Don't worry, Hopeless. I'm delighted. I was just saying to Rick, you'd scare any Shark away. Or perhaps . . .' he steps back, leers at my scabbing cheeks, 'perhaps you've already been bitten by one.'

He's still laughing when he gets back to the others.

Up on the stage, Mr Balmore is nose to nose with Stacy (not for the last time, it turns out). Laura and Alexis are standing together, not talking. I would mind less if they were. Extras are drifting away. I was going to wait for Laura, but I trail after them instead.

I'm five minutes down the road when a bike steers onto the pavement, passing me so close I almost fall. It's Mark. I hear him whooping as he springs back into the traffic. A car hoots.

He's not wearing a helmet. I hope he'll get knocked over, but he doesn't.

I open the front door unwillingly, but the hall is empty. I soon realise why. Behind the kitchen door, I can hear Her voice, taut as a whip. My brother doesn't reply, but I know he's in there; I can feel him cowering against the cabinets. I wonder what he's done. Isaac – Her darling, Her youngest, above all Her son – usually gets an easier time than me. I shut the door and go upstairs. After a while, I hear him cry out. I feel bad for him, but mostly I'm glad it's not me.

10

Laura

16 November 2018

I faked a hangover. I decided in an instant, when Evie was wriggling into wakefulness and Ryan said, 'You were late back,' without lifting his eyes from his phone. I nestled my head into the pillow, muttered something about mojitos. In truth, my body ached, but not my head.

Ryan didn't comment, just lifted Evie off me and carried her downstairs for breakfast, still reading the *Herald* headlines over her shoulder. But later, when I was gulping coffee and he was pulling socks onto Benjy, he said, 'You weren't the only one out later than expected.'

I raised my eyebrows. He gestured upstairs.

'Simon? I thought he had some computer thing.'

'A "computer thing" at a pal's house. A *girl*.'

I laughed, but gently, at Ryan's expression. This was the first sign our introvert had shown of the slightest connection with the opposite sex. Three months back, Ryan had initiated a clunking 'if you're gay you know we couldn't care less, we just want you to be happy' talk. Simon had rolled his eyes and said he knew that.

'I'm not gay,' he'd said. 'I'm just not interested.'

'Which means,' Ryan had said, when Simon was out of the room, 'that *they* aren't interested.' Now, it seemed, one was.

Ryan went off with the kids, joking with Benjy, coaxing Evie out of a howling rage. I ate their leftovers and tried not to think about Alexis. I thought about Simon, instead, and how far he had come. Then he appeared, mangling his school tie with one hand, phone in the other. Like father, like son.

I got up to help him. 'I gather you've got a girlfriend.'

He looked simultaneously mortified, furious and slightly smug. 'Bloody Dad. She's just a friend.'

'Don't swear,' I said, tweaking his tie straight. 'If she was more than that, she'd be lucky to have you.'

Simon is taller than me now, so I had to reach up and bend his head before I could kiss the top of it. He let me, then wrenched away. 'Don't be embarrassing.'

I watched him as he buttered toast and thought about what it was like to fall in love at school. For all his denials, he was blushing. I felt the familiar, inevitable rush. Of relief, but also of protectiveness, for this boy who had lost his mother. For whom I must always be second best.

I hope it ends better for you, I thought, as I let myself out of the house.

At work, Kai greeted me with a flash of newly peroxided hair. 'You look good. Must be the early night.'

I smiled and said thank you. I stared into space through a group meeting, then texted Alexis.

I wish it was last night.

He replied immediately.

I'm working from home.

I said, 'I'm going to the gym at lunch.'

My boss, Danielle, glowered round her computer screen. She's head of marketing, very old-school, doesn't take kindly to the unexpected.

'I thought you went running every weekend,' she said. 'Isn't that enough for any normal person?'

'I'm not normal,' I said.

Kai laughed.

Four hours later, I lay twisted around Alexis, gripping him, still joined. I could hear our heartbeats, loud over the traffic below. He stroked my hair back from my forehead. I looked into his eyes, saw myself in them.

'I can't wish things had been otherwise,' I said, 'because I have my children and I love them.'

'I know,' he said. 'Or rather, I can regret the path that led to Gracie, but I can't regret *her*.'

'I never forgot you, though,' I said. 'Not once.'

God help me, I hadn't forgotten him even when Ryan and I first spent the night together. Not even on my wedding day. And I had remembered him, an impossible ideal, every time Ryan and I fought.

I shifted and lay with my hand on his chest, then ran it down over his stomach. In the daylight, I could see the scar on his chest that didn't show at night. I touched it, then knelt up and over, and kissed it. He pulled me back.

'We will have to talk about this,' I said. 'One day.'

'Not now,' he said.

11

Laura

6 March 2019

I didn't remember what day it was until I got back from the police station. Ryan and I usually work late on a Wednesday, so Anja, Benjy's key worker, brings the kids home and gets them tea. I showered and wandered round the house trying to make it less of a shithole for her.

The inspector's card was on my dressing table. *DI Fiona Capaldi*.

I ripped it into pieces, sent it swirling down the loo. In the kids' room, I realised why Capaldi and her sidekick had seemed so familiar. Evie's copper-haired plastic doll was propped up next to a faintly dissolute teddy that had once been Ryan's. The doll wore a black dress. To me, the bear had exactly the sergeant's seen-it-all stare.

I sat on the floor next to them and laughed until I cried.

Hours later, Simon came in while I was forcing crusty bowls into the dishwasher. His bags dropped onto the floor.

'What happened to computer club?' I said. Then I saw his expression.

'What's going on?' he said.

'What do you mean?'

'The police came to school today.'

I stepped back, thumped onto a chair. 'Why?'

'To see me,' he said. He was white, cautious-eyed. I thought of the seven-year-old who had grasped his father's hand, watching me with unfathomable distrust, and did not speak for an hour.

We had come so far since then.

'I got pulled out of class,' he said. 'Mr Armstrong was with me because I'm underage. I said why couldn't you be my accompanying adult. They wouldn't say.'

I tried to speak, failed, tried again. 'What did they want?' I said.

'To know when I got home on Sunday night.'

Oh God. I should have predicted that.

I whispered, 'When *did* you get home?'

'Five to eleven. I could tell them exactly because I checked my phone at the end of the road, and I remembered.'

Jesus. And Alexis had left at quarter to. A few minutes later, and they'd have passed on the street.

'I was asleep,' I said.

'I know. I heard you snoring.'

'I don't snore.'

He didn't laugh, didn't even smile. 'Well, doing that snorty breathing thing you say isn't snoring and Dad says is.'

I swallowed. 'Did you tell the police that?'

'Yes. Laura, what's going on?'

I put out a hand. He didn't take it.

'Darling,' I said. 'I can't explain. I'm sorry. Please trust me.'

'*Trust* you?' He stared into my face. Blue eyes so pale they were almost grey. Ryan's eyes are blue too, but close to navy. Simon has his mother's eyes: it took me years not to be disconcerted by them. They disconcerted me again, now.

'I have to talk to Dad,' I said. 'Please let me do that first.'

Simon walked out and slammed the door. I waited, shaking, for the outside door to bang too. Instead, I heard him running up the stairs. I took a breath of relief. Then I heard Anja's key in the lock and bolted to my own room. I hid there, shivering under the duvet, until Benjy and Evie came charging upstairs too and, delighted, squirmed under the covers with me.

28 August 2018

From: Khaleesi8690

To: AlwaysHaveParis

Subject: Kids & common interests

Hi A (so what does that stand for?!),

Thanks for the reply. Sounds like
we have even more in common than I
thought! Your little girl sounds totally
adorable.

Too busy being harassed for a drink to
say much more right now, but I can't
wait to grill you more later ;)

x

12

Hope

12 January 1999

Last year, when Laura got to know me well enough for it not to be rude, she asked if I had considered treatment for my spots. She said it delicately, *your skin*, as though it were a few blemishes, not a pus-ridden mass that makes strangers wince. I laughed. I told her it had occurred to me. Big-brand names with slick before-and-after pictures promising miracles; topical creams on prescription. I'd tried them all and none had worked. But when Laura passed on what her mother had told her – that there were hormonal pills, contraceptives, that would tackle the problem at its core – *then* I didn't laugh.

I knew that already too. I had been told two years before by a doctor. I had known for a few seconds the bliss of anticipated release. Then I had seen Her face, registered at the same time those words, *family planning*, and it had dropped the shutter on my joy.

She said, 'That wouldn't be appropriate.'

She meant that it would be ungodly, but even She wouldn't say so to the doctor.

On the way home, I had tried to argue, which I almost never did. She didn't say anything, but when we got in, She turned the gas hob on full, and that was how I got the scar on my wrist that makes Laura go pale and want to hug me.

Laura's mother is a nurse and a kind woman. My mother is not, and is not.

I think about this as I sit in the waiting room of the clinic when I should be at registration. I remind myself that this is not our local doctor. No one knows me here. No one knows Her. School thinks I am at the dentist.

Alexis is worth it.

But all the same, my scars burn. I pick up *Cosmopolitan* and feel sweat on the slick pages as I turn them without seeing them. A girl sits across from me with her boyfriend, hand in hand. I imagine being here, like that, with Alexis. Another is with an older woman. Mother? Aunt? I don't try to imagine that. A third is sitting alone, gripping her hands on the seat of her plastic chair. What is she waiting for? A test, surely, or a test result. Pregnancy or STD? Whoever her fellow risk-taker was, he's not with her now.

My name is called and I go in. The boyfriend whispers something. The girl sniggers. I wish they were the ones waiting terrified for bad results.

The woman I see is youngish and efficient. I explain what I want and she nods and peers at my face (bursting pustules today). She looks sympathetic.

She says, without apparent sarcasm, 'Are you also intending to use this for contraceptive purposes?'

I tell her that I am. Not necessarily right away, but there is someone. 'I . . . we . . . I would want to be prepared. When the time is right.'

She doesn't laugh. I suppose it's her job not to laugh, not to tell me that my face is the only contraceptive I could need and that in giving me this wonder drug she is also, perhaps, making it necessary. But all the same, I could hug her for it. She starts explaining the care needed to make sure it works. I nod, as though this is important to me.

When I am about to leave, she looks at me again. Not at my spots: at me. I wonder if she noticed the marks on my arm, when she took my blood pressure.

She says, 'Is there anything else you would like to talk to me about? We are in complete confidence here.'

I say thank you, but there is nothing else. She's been very kind, I say. She nods, unconvinced. On the way to the door, she gestures to my face again, and smiles.

'It will pass,' she says. 'It won't be immediate, but it will get better.'

I go with the packets in my hand to the clinic bathroom and I take the first pill there, without water. This is the beginning.

I'm still buzzing when I reach school. It's break time and Laura is sitting on a bench in the locker room, resting her head against the wall.

Jem says, 'Don't mind her. She's tired because she got up early to go *jogging*.' This is clearly the continuation of an earlier discussion, because Laura throws a Kit Kat wrapper at Jem and tells her to shut up.

'So what's new?' I say. Laura is always running. It's her thing.

'What's new is that she went with *Alexis*. I'm surprised you didn't know, Hopey.'

Jem is grinning. Claire picks up the wrapper and stuffs it into the bin. I glance at Laura. She looks as though she would like to throw something heavier at Jem.

'Didn't I mention it?' she says. Then she smiles too, unconvincingly. 'We'd have asked you, but I know none of you are into it.'

'No thanks,' Jem snorts. She twists her hair round, holding it up on the top of her head, looking sideways at her reflection in the window. 'We know when we're not wanted, don't we, girls?'

Claire has picked up *The Mill on the Floss* and is making pencil notes in the margins. 'You're insane,' she says to Laura. 'It must have been freezing.'

Laura smiles, tries to turn it into a shrug. 'Like I said, I know you don't get it.'

'Oh, we *get* it,' Jem says. 'We get it all right.' She lets her hair drop down again. It's henna red today and she seems pleased with it. 'He's all yours, Laura.'

I focus on taking the books out of my locker. I think of the hard-won cardboard packet, wrapped in my pencil case and stowed like a precious jewel at the bottom of my bag. But the dream has seeped out of it.

31 August 2018

From: Khaleesi8690

To: AlwaysHaveParis

Subject: Tired!

Thanks for your long message. It's
so nice to talk to someone else with
caring responsibilities. It can be so
completely exhausting, can't it? It's
only 9 p.m. and I just want to curl up
and sleep after the day I've had.

So I will! And I'll reply properly
tomorrow.

Have a good night.

x

13

Laura

6 March 2019

I must tell the police what they already know. My prints are all over Alexis's flat, as if the phone messages weren't evidence enough. Christ, we'd just had sex. For all I know, their grubby DNA investigations can prove that too, can turn our last intimacy into a piece of evidence to be smeared and showed off in court.

I will tell them. I was only putting it off so I could speak to Ryan first. I owe him that much. I owe him a lot more.

So that's what I did. Late tonight, when my husband was tired and plane-fogged and had just presented me with a box of chocolates from Frankfurt airport, I sat him down at the kitchen table. I poured him a whisky and I told him I had been sleeping with another man. I told him that that man had been stabbed to death five minutes from our door. He kept asking if I was joking. I showed him the news story on my phone, heart aching at the photo.

Ryan said, 'That's Gracie's da. I've met him. What kind of a sick game is this?'

I told him it *was* Gracie's dad. I told him the police had been twice. I told him they had messages from me to Alexis, and him to me. I told him they had interviewed Simon. Then he believed me. I watched his face as he understood and I realised, too late, what a monumental disservice I had just done him. I had spared him one ordeal, only to inflict another on him. For if the police had seen that shifting expression – incredulity to irritation, irritation to dismay – would they have bothered interrogating him, as they surely would now?

In all the injuries I had done my husband, I had forgotten that I had made him the prime suspect in a murder case.

I don't think he thought about that, at least not then. He was too caught up in the primary betrayal. He stared at me. His hands shook on the tabletop. I wondered, unforgivably, if this was how he had looked when they'd told him that Simon's mother was dead.

Naomi, his good wife.

He started to speak, but only a warped croak came out. He tried again, still watching me.

'Why?' he said.

I shook my head. I was remembering how we had viewed this house together, Simon quiet and eager beside Ryan, my stomach vast with Benjy. How we had talked of bedrooms and a pull-out bed so Simon could have friends to stay, and Simon had smiled as though, at last, he believed in the future. That had made Ryan grin too, and kiss me when the vendor wasn't watching.

Our first night here, we ate takeaway, sitting on boxes, and I made lists on the back of a magazine. Then the next morning I woke with what I thought was curry gut but turned out to be early labour. Ryan held my hand all night, and stayed all day by our baby in his glass cage.

Now he sat with his head in his hands, and told me, 'I can't process this.'

'It wasn't about us,' I said. 'There wasn't anything wrong with you and me. I need you to know that.'

He said nothing, didn't move. I said, 'It wasn't just an affair. I'm not . . . I wouldn't . . .' I stopped, finished lamely, 'This was different.'

My husband laughed. It made me want to weep. 'Is that supposed to make me feel better?'

I said, 'I knew him before.'

Ryan pushed his chair back. I jumped, but he didn't get up. He looked at me, and I knew he was staring into defeat.

'Was it him? The one from school.'

I nodded. Ryan knows a bit about that. Not all, but enough to know it matters.

He dropped his head again, fingertips so hard against his temples that I could see red semicircles under the nails. I moved towards him. He flinched away.

'Just go,' he said. His voice was resigned, heavy as lead.

I went upstairs. I got into our bed, curling into cold sheets. Hours later, I heard Ryan come up, hesitate, then creep in and lie down on his side, still as ice. Afraid of touching me. I fell asleep, woke in the early hours to a strange, stifled sound. It took me a long time to understand that he was crying.

14

Laura

1 December 2018

He's no Karenin, my husband, no Bovary. I wonder if it would be easier if he were. But he is attractive. He is clever and honest. He makes me laugh. At least, he used to. He loves our children and is good to them. He trusts me, who does not deserve it, as completely as I know I can trust him. He is marked by his first wife, dramatically and horribly dead. He is marked by the years going in and out of doctors' offices, building back his son's spirit. But he is made, for the most part, kinder by it.

If someone had asked me a month ago how our marriage was, I would have said it was good. I loved him well enough.

I still love him, only now it's not enough.

This morning, we watched our children rip the first chocolates from their advent calendars. We breakfasted together and I wrapped a birthday present for a girl in Evie's nursery class, and coerced Evie's hair into pigtails. We quarrelled about a broken door handle, and he stamped off to the shed, in search of tools.

I thought neither that he should apologise nor that I must.

I thought, *I do not care.*

I took Evie to her friend's party, sparing Ryan, because I knew Alexis would be there. It was in a church hall in Marchmont, with a bouncy castle and trestle tables full of sandwiches and carrot sticks, which the kids didn't eat, and crisps and cake, which they did. For the grown-ups, there was institution tea and coffee in plastic cups. Two energetic youths in purple T-shirts were rounding the children up next to a speaker system, a baby was screaming, and I was filled, as I often am on such occasions, with an overwhelming desire to be somewhere else.

Evie ran off almost before I'd got her out of her coat, insinuating herself into the centre of the group of kids, holding out her hand for the label with her name. I wish sometimes that Benjy had her confidence. I wish Simon did.

I wish I did.

I landed our present on a table piled with them, dodged a grandfather with a tea urn and saw Alexis as he came into the room carrying Gracie. I smiled and he smiled back, and I knew it had been a mistake to come. Better to have sent Ryan. Better to let Ryan meet him, talk, think they were friends.

Better that than to be here in the same room with him, separated, and sick with needing him.

He carried Gracie to the front, established her in the little group, helped her to collect her label and fix it on her dress. She wore a blue smock and her hair was in bunches with blue velvet bows. Had he chosen them, or was he just the agent of Diana's vision? It moved me to think of him sitting with Gracie as I do with Evie. Tying the bows, presenting his daughter to the world.

I shuffled from one foot to the other, thinking of Gracie. Half his, half Diana's, all her own. What will happen to her, and to my children? Will we tell Ryan the truth, get me a divorce, make stepbrother and sisters of them? When I think of this, I am stymied not by thoughts of my own little ones, who would retain two loving parents, nor even by what it would do to Ryan.

I am stopped short, in my castles in the air, by Simon. I have a claim on the other two, but he is mine only by love and implicit adoption. If Ryan – or Simon himself – decrees it, I could lose him forever. And Simon has been through far more, already, than any child should have to endure. He needs me. I love him too.

As to what Alexis thinks, I do not know. This is another thing we don't talk about. The future, like the past, is a foreign country.

He left Gracie with her hand in that of another little girl. One of the purple lads was booming at her in a way presumably intended to reassure. The other was switching the music on, cajoling the children into a circle. One of the dads appeared next to me, proffering a plastic coffee.

'Rather them than me,' he said, pointing at the front.

I tried to remember who he was, or even whose parent he was. I wished he would go away. I stood holding the coffee and mouthing nothings over the music, and watched as Alexis was buttonholed by a mum with a plate of brownies. Eventually I got away from the unknown dad under cover of going to the loo. I chucked my undrinkable coffee down the sink. When I came out into the corridor, Alexis was there.

He said, 'This is impossible.'

I nodded. I told him what I had told myself. 'I shouldn't have come.'

A woman came out of the hall, taking a child to the bathroom. A nursery mum; I should have been friendly. Instead, I waved my empty cup at her, grinned at Alexis like he'd made a joke. When they had disappeared into the loos, he caught my wrist, looked up and down the corridor, then kissed me fast on the mouth. I stepped back, my head bumping the wall, breath short and body gasping.

The door to the hall swung open again. A voice said, 'Oh, there she is. Laura, Evie wants you.'

I wanted to scream at her, at all of them, to leave us. To leave us together for one more kiss. Evie tore along the corridor and landed, tearful and imperious, at my side. 'Mummy, I called Jamie a poo, but I didn't pull his hair. I *didn't*.'

I giggled. Then I sighed, heavy with sudden guilt. I took her hand. 'Does Jamie say you did?'

She stuck out her lip and wouldn't answer. Alexis looked from her to me, smiling. She glared back at him.

'Evie,' I said. 'This is Gracie's daddy.'

'I know,' she said. She tugged at my hand. 'Mummy, come now.'

Later, Alexis found me by the door, waiting to leave. The children were milling round a mum holding party bags, like hyenas round a rotting buffalo. Other parents were picking up chairs, clearing the hall. We were briefly alone.

I passed him Gracie's scarf, felt fingers touch and nerves buzz. 'I want you,' I whispered, soft into his ear.

He looked at me, for an instant, as though he hated us both.

Gracie ran across the room, gripping her party bag, dark hair flying. He reached out his arms, lifted her into them. Over her head, he glanced into my eyes.

'Laura . . .' he said. But then he left without speaking.

15

Hope

18 January 1999

We're doing the Dance at the Gym today. Our first big rehearsal, when Sharks and Jets anticipate later battles with tense choreography (Mr Balmore's words) and Maria first sees Tony. Stacy is jumping around like a My Little Pony on heat, flapping her blonde mane, taking hold of Alexis and insisting that they practise their slow dance.

I don't care about her. I'm watching Alexis and Laura.

As far as I know, this is their first rehearsal together, but I'm sure they've met since last week's run. Laura has been away from the locker room a lot. If she's been jogging again, she's kept it quiet. Alexis was his usual self at church: kind, faintly humorous. He didn't mention her. Now, it seems they are always aware of each other, as I am always aware of them.

We plod about to the tinny drone of a ghetto blaster, with Mrs Henderson stopping and starting and sighing, and Mr Balmore yelling like a hooligan.

'It's like an aerobics class,' Stacy says, giggling.

I wouldn't know.

We're crap. I suppose we'll improve, but right now it's less dance, more rugby scrum, complicated by the fact that the Jets who are girls playing boys keep forgetting and following the girl instructions. Mr Balmore goes crimson with frustration. Mark is a terrible dancer. Rick, as Bernardo, is pretty good and Laura just follows his lead. Alexis can dance. So can Stacy, but she sexes it up too much for Maria. Mrs Henderson tells her off for that. Mr Balmore doesn't, for all his artistic integrity. I find that I can dance too, or at least follow instructions, but it does me no good. I'm still shoved to the back, with extra 'constructive criticism' from Mark.

We break after an hour and half the cast goes out for a fag. The main door to the hall is nowhere near an outside entrance, but from the backstage area (art classroom) you can get onto a high concrete walkway that joins this bit of the school with the science block. It crosses a road, cutting two storeys high over an alleyway then dropping down by a gate on the other side. The local residents hate it because of all the litter and cigarette ash that gets dropped. Not by me, of course. The bridge, like the common room, belongs to the popular kids. When I cross it – which is only when I have no choice – I go fast with my head bent.

Does this matter? It will.

But for now, the walkway is just where Mark and his mates smoke. Mr Balmore grumbles occasionally, then pretends not to notice. Mrs Henderson fingers her bag for her Marlboro Lights and looks like she wants to go too.

Everyone else goes to the loo or sits round eating snacks and drinking from cans. Laura glances at Alexis, but Stacy has already grabbed him, so she sits by me instead. We hardly talk.

Later, after more shouting and cavorting, I look for Laura to walk home. The hall empties, but I cannot find her. Then I do. Or rather, I hear her, as I am making a last check of the backstage classroom.

She's outside on the bridge, with Alexis.

I stop with my hand on the light switch and cross the room in near darkness. The outside door is ajar, and I stand behind it. Through the frosted glass I can see them as blurry outlines, half lit by the street lamps below. They're standing very close but not touching. They must be freezing. I listen.

They're talking about Stacy. Laura says something about 'your Maria', with a note in her voice that is pretending to be a laugh but isn't quite. Alexis replies, really laughing, 'Are you jealous or something?'

Laura says, 'What if I am?'

There's a long pause. Then she says, 'This is too important for faking.'

In the dim room, I can't see my breath as it cools on the glass, but I hear myself, gulp after gulp. Outside, the blurred figures move together, become one. I close my eyes, grip my hands together to stop myself from banging them against the door, screaming. This is not how it was meant to be.

I hear Laura murmur something, then she is muffled again. I open my eyes, and as I do, a hand grabs the back of my coat, jerking me backwards.

*

I don't shout. Even in this emergency, it matters that they don't know I'm here. Anyway, I realise almost immediately who it is.

Mark. He peers so close I can smell his breath. It stinks of cheese and onion crisps.

'Well, well,' he whispers. 'Thought you'd get a little action second-hand, did you? It's the closest you'll ever get.'

He lets me go, so quickly I nearly fall, and swings open the door with me still behind it. My chest constricts.

'Get a room, you two,' he says, and I hear their smug laughter and his footsteps fading along the bridge.

I'm breathing deeply, but I'm not relieved, or only fleetingly. If Mark hasn't used this ammunition against me, it's because he enjoys making me wait.

Outside, Laura says, 'I must go. I'm walking home with Hope.'

I load awkwardness into the pause that follows. Then Alexis says, 'Won't she have gone?'

'I'd better check, all the same.' I hear her smiling, see her lean in again. 'Just one second more.'

I take that long moment and use it. I slide into a store cupboard. Laura comes into the classroom, calling a soft goodbye, the smile still in her voice. She pulls the door shut behind her and I hear the lock click. She goes onto the stage and calls my name, over and over, with falling conviction. At last, she leaves.

The silence is complete. Alexis, like Mark, has ignored the rules and used the walkway as a shortcut to the street. I wonder what would happen if I stayed the whole night here, in this close, comforting space. I can't, though.

By the time I reach the main entrance to the building, the janitor is locking up. He isn't impressed.

16

Laura

14 December 2018

How many meetings has it been now? I have stopped counting. How many kisses and how many lies? Alexis has been away this week, in Paris with Gracie and his mother. He came back this morning and I have writhed all day with the knowledge. I went for lunch with Kai, so obsessed I almost confided. But I pulled myself back in time.

I do not have intimates; I will not change that now. The women I call my friends are the wives and girlfriends of Ryan's pals, or nursery mums like Heather. Play date and dinner party acquaintances, pushed back if they proffer more. In London, I had flatmates and course mates and colleagues. People to have around. To chat and drink and sometimes have pointless sex with. To stave off with shallow lies. Here, too, I have kept my colleagues at arm's length.

I risked love again, for Ryan. Sometimes I wonder how I did it. But not friendship. Not after her.

Instead, I asked for Kai's backstory. A gloomy one for a sunny Australian: caring for an ailing aunt. I wondered, briefly distracted, *Why an aunt?* It takes a peculiarly good person, or a very unlucky one, to get stuck in (I'm guessing) their late twenties with a broken dependent who's not even a parent.

I said, 'Did you come over from Australia to look after her?' and Kai said no, not exactly, but the aunt had been here, and it had become necessary. I changed the subject, chattered about Simon and his new girlfriend, whom we haven't been allowed to meet. But I thought how much this new information explained about Kai: that eager-to-please persona at odds with the surfer-bleached hair and beach-ready body, which gave a facade of confidence.

I thought, too, *That's a Christmas that will be even worse than mine.*

We did the tree after tea, weeks after Benjy started clamouring for it. Simon and I twisted tinsel and lights, Benjy shoved the least tasteful decorations onto the most prominent branches, Evie battered Mary with a sheep, and Ryan sent work emails from his phone. I watched my children until my heart stung, wondering if this was the last time we would do this. I studied Simon, pale face intent, attaching a star. The sting became a shot of fear.

I will not lose him, I told myself.

But afterwards, when the tree lights were on and the boxes stuffed into cupboards again and the children were climbing over Ryan, all of them laughing – and if anything should have made me stay, that should – my need for

Alexis became the greater pain. I went to the kitchen and messaged him.

I have to see you.

Five minutes later, I told Ryan I was going for a run. 'You can do bedtime,' I said. I didn't say 'for once', but he knew I meant it.

'It's dark,' he said.

'When else have I had a chance?' I snapped.

He said, 'I just want you to be safe.'

The thing is, I know he does. I looked at Simon, saw he was watching me too.

'I'll keep to the roads,' I said.

I did. In daylight, I'd have taken the paths: The Hermitage, dark and wooded; the edges of Blackford Hill. I know those ways like the fall of my running feet. I might have taken them now if I hadn't promised. But I had, and ridiculously, this minor loyalty seemed still to matter.

I took the wide, dim streets instead, past millionaires' houses set back and bright-windowed. Another world, in this city of infinite possibilities. Past villas to tenements, a thousand lives rising in stone above me. I dodged across roads, was hooted at by a cab. Perhaps I'd have been safer on the paths. In the next street to Alexis's, I almost collided with another runner. I staggered back, winded, and very nearly toppled into the gutter. They were gone before I could apologise, and I didn't stop to shout it.

Outside his building, I turned. I couldn't have said why, except that the image of that other jogger had stayed uneasy in my mind. Long leg and glossy jacket, vanishing round the corner. Hair flicking in the dark.

I fought back a flash of long-buried memory, pressed my finger hard down on the buzzer. Then I heard Alexis's voice, broken by the intercom, and forgot everything else.

'I'm all sweaty,' I said as he pulled me into the flat. It was half apology, half something else.

He was pale in the half-light. He undressed me, unzipping my fleece, peeling off Lycra. He paused with his hands on my hips, thumbs stroking the sticking-out bones, his face suddenly distant, his deft hands no longer a part of him.

'What?' I said.

'I wish we could run together again,' he said. But he said it like something that would never happen.

I had a flash vision of us, years hence, jogging along Edinburgh pavements and stopping to embrace, so that women in their twenties in shiny trainers would nudge their boyfriends and say, 'I hope we're like that when we're old.' I clung to it, but it was gone. He was kissing me, and now was now.

On the bed, he tied my wrists to the frame. The last time he had done this, we had used our school ties. I gasped, remembering how I had felt then, living how I felt now. 'Please,' I whispered, 'please,' and I twisted my legs around him, forced him to me, gripped my hands tight on the metal rail.

We lay panting afterwards. The street light I was coming to know, like a part of us, lay patterned on the bedroom boards. Alexis held my wrist, pulled it to his lips, kissed the mark from the ties.

Obsessed

'This is crazy,' he said.

'This is real,' I said. 'Everything else is crazy.'

17

Laura

7 March 2019

Today my marriage ended.

I lay feigning sleep while Ryan got the kids up, and didn't come down until it was time to say goodbye.

'Have a good day,' I said.

Ryan said nothing. Simon looked at me, puzzled-eyed, then he too left without speaking. What had he heard last night? I called work, said I was still ill. I got Danielle, who was not sympathetic. I ran round in a frenzy of tidying, emptying the dishwasher, mopping the floor, miming normality. On the table I found a brochure for Ryan's conference in Frankfurt. I don't know why I picked it up, but I did. Tucked inside, so it fell to the scuffed wood, was a printed piece of paper.

It was a refund confirmation for the pre-conference dinner on Sunday night.

For a while, it meant nothing. I folded and unfolded the slip, marooned in my weirdly pristine kitchen, staring at the last four digits of Ryan's debit card number as though

I would never see them again and had to learn them by heart. Then I reread the date of the dinner, and it meant everything.

Yesterday I had regretted not letting the police see my husband's unforced shock. Now, shaking, I wondered if he was a much better actor than I had ever guessed. I shook the brochure for more receipts. None came. I scrolled through emails on my phone for the details he always shared before these trips. I dialled the hotel, getting it wrong the first time by forgetting the international code. The woman who answered had perfect English. I told her I was a finance assistant at Ryan's work, said I was doing his expenses. I tried for the right level of executive-driven weariness.

I said, 'I don't seem to have all the documentation. Could you confirm his check-in date?'

'Of course, madam.' The sound of keys clicking. Then she said, 'Mr Reville checked in on Sunday the third of March and checked out yesterday. Would you like me to email a receipt?'

'The phone confirmation is enough, if I could make a note of exactly when he arrived on Sunday?'

If she was surprised at the request, she didn't show it. Another click, then that calm voice again. 'Nineteen thirty-three, madam. Can I help you further?'

'No thank you, that's great.'

I put the phone down. I tried to push the cancellation slip back into the brochure, but it crumpled concertina-like against the polished card.

I looked up. Ryan was standing by the door, staring at me.

He walked to the table, took the brochure from me, and the mangled receipt. I ceded them without protest.

'Ryan,' I said. 'I—'

He cut me off. 'Don't even bother lying, although I know you're a pro at it. You think *I* did it?'

I shook my head. 'No,' I said. 'You know I don't.' *I know you. But then I thought I knew myself.*

'So you were checking up on me for what, exactly? Fun?'

'It was just . . .' I gave up, tried again. 'You weren't at the dinner on Sunday.'

'Is that so?' He screwed up the paper, flung it across the room. 'And I can tell you where else I wasn't, Laura, I wasn't here. I wasn't in bloody Scotland. I wasn't stabbing that cheating fucker Alexis.'

'Ryan, please . . .'

He got out his phone, jabbed at it. 'I cancelled the dinner to eat with my colleagues, make a game plan. Look, if you don't believe me.'

I believed him, but I looked anyway. It was all in their WhatsApp group: the restaurant, the time they were meeting in the lobby, the thanks-for-a-productive-evening sign-offs, hours later.

I handed the phone back.

'They were on the same flight out,' he said. 'As you know, I checked into the hotel. Then I went to my room, unpacked, took a shite. They can't tell you about that, so you'll have to take my word for it. I sent you a message from the lounge, just before we went out. Perhaps you remember, though you didn't bother to respond.'

I nodded, groaning. I had been too preoccupied to reply, anticipating Alexis.

Ryan said, 'They can tell you I was there. Not being you, I didn't take anyone back to my room and shag them, but I can't help that.' He held out the phone again. 'You want to call them, do you? Give the office a bell? Humiliate me a bit more?'

'Of course not,' I said. I made myself look at him. My husband the stranger. 'But the police might.'

He walked to the kitchen door, turned with one foot in the hall. 'I'll take it from them,' he said. 'If I have to.'

I stood up, teetering, one hand on the wall. 'Where are you going?'

He looked at me, shook his head. I could see the anger fading, as though it had been painted on. A dim bleakness in its place.

'I'm going to pack,' he said.

I didn't argue. I sat back down, flicked my phone on, stared at the picture of Alexis in the news story.

Loving dad to three-year-old Gracie.

You could just see the back of her curly head.

I sat watching that picture, feeding the pain, until the front door slammed behind my husband.

8 September 2018

From: Khaleesi8690

To: AlwaysHaveParis

Subject: Saturday night

Hello Parisian,

I'm on the sofa with a large glass of white wine, deciding what film to watch. I'd say I was relishing some time to myself (I am, it's a welcome change!), but I've been enjoying our messages so much that I almost found myself pouring a glass for you! Does that sound too pushy? I hope not.

Maybe it's just because I've almost decided on Casablanca (for about the millionth time).

Anyway, Bogart and Bergman it is. I'll be thinking of you ;)

Speak soon!

xx

PS So, since I've almost said it anyway, I will. How about a drink IRL?

18

Hope

4 February 1999

In the locker room, Laura is learning lines and talking about Alexis. They went out last night and running this morning, she says. She is breathless at the recollection, gold-edged with joy.

I knew about the run already. I saw them. But I do not say so.

This openness is new. Or perhaps it is only new in front of me. This last fortnight, until today, Laura has been circumspect. Unsuccessfully, of course, because (unlike me) she's not used to hiding her emotions, but she's been trying.

This shift of gear makes me angry as well as afraid. I know she's been talking about me to Jem, and maybe Claire too: *It's not as if there was anything between her and Alexis. She said so herself. As for Anita, it's not my fault I got the part.*

Then one of the others: *Yes, just talk about him. It'll only get more awkward if you don't.*

Or perhaps it's her mum she confides in: *Oh darling, you mustn't be ashamed to be happy. Be honest and understanding. If she's your friend she'll be glad for you, but it might take time.*

Sometimes I envy Laura her mother more than anything else. Almost.

Jem is applying make-up. She never stops now that, thanks to Laura, she has an in with the boys on her hit list. Rick is back in the number one slot, but there are plenty of backups. Her mascara is tarmac-heavy, foundation thick as buttercream. Her face has barely a pimple, so it's unnecessary anyway. Perhaps I should ask to borrow some. Perhaps, one day soon, it might be enough.

'Have you shagged yet?' she asks Laura.

Claire glances up from her book, shakes her head, looks down again. Laura fakes being engrossed in her script.

'Not yet,' she says, when it's obvious Jem will wait for an answer. 'But I think it will be soon. He's . . .'

'Impatient?' says Jem.

'Male?' says Claire, not bothering to look up this time.

'Wonderful,' says Laura.

Claire laughs. Jem groans, not hiding her envy. I feel their gaze, combined, swivel towards me, then away. I say nothing. Claire gathers up her books and the four of us walk to class. As we pass into the daylight, Jem stops and stares at my face.

'You look different,' she says. 'What have you done?'

Laura looks too, and smiles. 'It's your skin,' she says. 'It's getting better.' She looks so happy for me, and I dislike her so much, I want to scream.

*

English. Another hour of *The Mill on the Floss*. Our teacher, Ms Barnard, is a George Eliot fan. Most of the class are not. They don't understand the bits she laughs at; they're baffled when Maggie is socially ostracised after her night with Stephen.

I'm not. But then my circumstances are unusual.

Ms Barnard spends a long time explaining the context, with digressions into the stagnation of women and Mary Ann Evans' own decision to write as a man. I'm not much interested, though Claire is. Then, suddenly, I am.

'Is Maggie to blame?' Ms Barnard says, in her determined-to-draw-us-out voice.

I look at Laura, and something strikes inside me. I don't often speak in lessons, but I do now. 'I think she is,' I say. 'They both are.'

They all stare at me. Ms Barnard looks delighted, and surprised.

I say, 'They betrayed Lucy and Philip.'

Laura says, 'Maggie didn't choose to do it.'

'Of course she had a choice.' My voice is high. Ms Barnard stops smiling and starts looking faintly anxious. Claire, next to me, moves as though she would stop me if she could. 'She knew what she was doing,' I say.

Laura says, 'Maybe, but not at the level that matters. Not when she was there, in the boat with him.'

Jem watches us, her black-rimmed eyes zipping from me to Laura and back again. Claire sighs. 'It's written as though she were sleepwalking,' she says.

Laura nods. 'Exactly. It's like that, or like she's drugged. She couldn't have done anything else.'

'She could,' I say. 'She didn't have to get into the boat.'

'She loves him,' Laura says. 'She can't resist.'

'She ruins herself afterwards,' Ms Barnard points out. 'She could have married Stephen then, but she won't do it to Lucy.'

Laura says nothing then.

'She felt guilty,' I say. 'She was right to.'

There's a silence. Then Jem says, 'Lucy took him back. She didn't have much pride. I'd have told him where to get off.'

Laura looks at me as though she's wondering whether I'll defend Lucy. But I've said all I'm going to say. Besides, it's not Lucy I identify with. Of course it's not. Pretty, popular Lucy in her happy home with her parents who adore her. It's not *Lucy* who is untouchable, pitied rather than loved.

It's Philip, the hunchback.

It's Philip who returns, always solitary, to Maggie's grave.

Afterwards, Ms Barnard keeps me back. 'It's great to see you getting into the discussion at last.'

I tell her thank you. We both know what's coming.

She smiles, plays with a ring binder on her desk, then fixes her eyes on me. 'But you know there is such a thing as *too* emotionally engaged.'

'Of course,' I say, as though I have no idea what she's talking about.

'Are you well, Hope?' she says. 'Is there anything you would like to talk about?'

I wonder if she's about to offer herself as confidante. I wonder what I would say.

'You know your form teacher is always available,' she says, stepping back and straightening a chair. 'We're here to help.'

This is not true. My form teacher is Mr Appleby, who teaches history and hates anyone born after 1900. I think about telling her this, just to see her face. But I don't. I say I'm fine. I stuff Maggie Tulliver into my bag, and get out of there.

I don't walk home with Laura. I hover in corners until she leaves with Claire, and then I trail them through the dull streets, past shops to suburban estates. If they see me, I can catch up, breathless, like that was what I wanted all along. But they don't see me, and then they say goodbye and Laura goes on alone. She steps faster now she's not chatting, moving briskly along Claire's street, where the lamps are bright, then into the alley that takes her to the cluster of pattern-made roads and houses and gardens where we both live.

I turn into it only a moment behind her, and a twig breaks under my foot. Laura jumps. I slide into the shadows at the side of the alley and stand motionless. She turns her head, looks about. Then she walks on. By the end of the passage, she is running. I'm getting good at this now.

Waiting there in the darkness, the germ of an idea takes shape. It is easy, it seems, to scare Laura. If she were frightened enough, often enough, what might she do? Lose her nerve? Give up on Anita? Or fall into distracted incompetence, lose the part? I let that thought linger, liking it the best. For if my skin continues to heal, who more appropriate, more obvious a substitute?

I let her pass out of sight. I tread the pavement jauntily, almost skipping, singing 'A Boy Like That', until I am at my own front door. Then I stop singing.

15 September 2018

From: Khaleesi8690

To: AlwaysHaveParis

Subject: Cocktails & taxis

Morning!

Last night was a lot of fun! My head isn't thanking me, though – and I'm more grateful than I probably was at the time that you said no to a last cocktail. It wouldn't have helped with brushing up the CV today. . . .

Seriously, it was so kind of you to get my cab. I didn't know you'd paid until I got out. Though feel free to be less of a gent another time. Speaking of which . . . but maybe I'd better not be presumptuous ;)

Until next time (oops, there I go again!).

xx

19

Laura

7 March 2019

This morning, after Ryan left, I went to the police. To get it over. I walked quickly, as though I could hasten time and time could heal me. I thought of my marriage, which I had thrown away.

I met my husband at a flat-warming party, somewhere near Haymarket, when I had been in Edinburgh two months. I had a new job as a marketing assistant in a corporate giant. I'd rented a tiny flat and I ran every morning, rain or sun, up the stony slopes and craggy summit of Arthur's Seat. Somewhere in my mind, still unacknowledged, was half an idea: here, perhaps, I might have a future.

The party was in an enormous flat with dark polished floors, thick-framed mirrors, and tartan prints shiny-new on the walls, all of which were being ruined by the numerous guests. I went with a man from my office: an American of whose personal attributes I can remember nothing now, except that he had a laugh like a barking dog. It was fancy dress, Scots-themed, and he was dressed as Burke (or Hare) and drinking bourbon out of a fake skull. It became unpleasantly clear to me, over the course of a long hour, that he considered this a date.

I escaped to the hall, not long after eight, and trawled for my coat in the heap below the hooks. Ryan was on the same errand.

'Not having fun?' he asked.

I told him about the skull and the misunderstanding. 'You?' I said. He said he had to get back for the babysitter.

I looked at his hand, saw the gold ring. 'You're married?' I said, just as – years later – Alexis would say it to me.

'Widowed,' Ryan said, and I said I was sorry, because what else can you say?

I noticed he wasn't wearing a costume, just an Aran sweater and jeans. 'What did you come as?' I asked.

'Sean Connery,' he said, straight-faced. I looked blank, then saw that he was grinning. I pulled my jacket from under a fake leopard skin and laughed. To be fair, he had the build for it.

When we'd got into our coats and onto the bracing street, he asked me if I wanted to go for a coffee. I said what about the babysitter. Ryan looked guilty.

'I exaggerated,' he said. 'She'll be fine another hour. I wasn't exactly having a belter either.'

We sat in a near-deserted Starbucks, me still in my Flora MacDonald dress. Ryan told me he was from Dundee, had been to university here, and never left. He talked to me about this city I was starting to love, and he spoke like a devotee, full of its glorious secrets, longing to show it off. He asked me about my work, my life. I gave him the version that had almost become truth; that was, on the surface, true.

He told me about Simon, how old he was (nearly eight), and how his mother had died in a car crash eighteen months before, with the child in the back of the car.

I looked at him across the plastic table. I felt pity, mixed with something more. He helped me into my coat, and asked, a little diffidently, if I would like to have dinner.

I thought, *I like this man.*

That was seven years ago, and now Ryan's ring finger wears the one I gave him. He keeps Naomi's on his other hand. I suppose he'll take mine off now.

The police station is modern. Clean beige and brown, blue lines and clear glass. Perhaps they think it's less intimidating that way.

I asked for Capaldi and waited interminably on a hard chair while the uniformed lad at the desk had a passive-aggressive and clearly non-work-related phone conversation. Eventually, the short sergeant came to collect me.

I said, 'I've come to make a statement.'

She took me to an interview room, grim and sterile, with a table in the middle and a recorder on the side. I thought how absurd it was, and how inevitable, that I should be there.

'The inspector won't be long,' she said. 'Tea? Coffee?'

What was this, the hairdresser's?

'I'd like water, please,' I said.

The sergeant fetched me a plastic cup and sat opposite me. 'What changed your mind, then?' she said. It was the second time in our acquaintance that she'd sounded human.

'My husband knows everything now,' I said. 'I've got nothing to lose.'

That wasn't the truth, but I hoped it was close enough to pass.

She said, 'You ken we'll have to see him?' I tried to place her accent. Not quite local. Fife, maybe.

I nodded. 'He knows that too. There's nothing he can tell you, but he can tell you that himself. Perhaps you'll believe it from him.'

She looked as though she'd do nothing of the sort. But Capaldi showed up before I could dig myself (or Ryan) any deeper. A sadist's vision in dark green today, with sharp heels and sheer tights.

'Before we proceed,' she said, 'do you understand that you could have a lawyer present?'

No Scottish accent here. *She* sounded like the product of every posh girls' school in the land. Which meant she probably grew up in Morningside. The mystery was why she was here, rather than stalking the corridors of Holyrood or Westminster. But it wasn't one I was likely to solve.

'A lawyer can't help me,' I said. 'I've done plenty wrong, but nothing that's against the law.'

As far as the recent past went, that was true. I had no intention of going further back.

The inspector nodded without speaking and the sergeant put the recorder on. 'Interview with Mrs Laura Reville,' she said, for its benefit. 'Interview commenced at 11.42 a.m., the seventh of March 2019. Present are Mrs Reville, Inspector Fiona Capaldi and Sergeant Esme Morse.'

So that was her name. It seemed inapt, on many levels.

'Mrs Reville,' she concluded, 'has declined legal representation.'

Mrs Reville indeed. Not for much longer.

After that, I forgot the recorder. I talked to those women, whom I dislike, as though they were my friends or my counsellors. I detailed my affair with Alexis from the first meeting to the last. I told them how I had tried to end it. I told them what I had told Heather, back in November: that I had known Alexis at school, slightly. They weren't noticeably interested. It was the last few months they asked about, with a curiosity that, if they *had* been my friends, would have bordered on the voyeuristic.

'Who knew about the affair?' That was Capaldi, when I thought we were done. I eyed the pristine suit, the lipstick, and thought about asking if she was on her way to a wedding. Or a funeral.

Christ, I hadn't even thought about Alexis's funeral. That brought a new, slamming pain.

'Laura?' she prompted.

I blinked back stinging tears. 'No one,' I said.

She leaned forward. 'Is that true? Please think very carefully. You must realise how important this is.'

I realised all too well. I waited, really thinking now rather than trying not to yell. Then I said, 'I wondered, sometimes, if Diana had guessed.'

'You mean Diana Mortimer? Alexis's ex-partner?'

I nodded. 'Did she tell you about us?'

The sergeant said, 'We cannae comment on that.'

I shrugged. 'Well, anyway. I wondered. But Alexis didn't think she knew.'

Capaldi said, 'Anyone else?'

'Not that I know of.' I picked up the cup, feeling the plastic buckle. The water was tepid. 'We didn't tell anyone, either of us.'

'That's not exactly the same, though, is it?'

I stared at her. What was she? A mind-reader. 'I thought . . .' I said. 'We thought . . .'

'Go on,' she said, fixing her witch's eyes on me.

'It sometimes seemed that there was someone watching us,' I said. 'I thought I saw someone, and then we kept seeing things.' I made myself smile, a ghastly and probably inappropriate effort. 'Jumping at shadows. But then . . . things happened.'

'Under the circumstances,' my interrogator said, 'we have to be interested in shadows.'

So I told them. They watched me like anthropologists, making notes on the monkey contorting in her cage. Occasionally, one would ask a question. At the end, the inspector did her fixed-gaze trick again. 'And do you have any idea, Laura – any idea at all, even the wildest guess – who this person could have been?'

'No,' I said.

They kept on asking. I kept on lying.

After that, they made me wait while a statement was produced. I signed it.

Outside again, I didn't go home. I went by side roads and

shallow steps into Holyrood Park. I wanted only to move and to forget, and here, at least, there was space. Barren wilderness and a dead volcano.

I crossed Queen's Drive, ran along the rocky paths and up the angular steps, straight up. I lurched on in my too-thick clothes, watching only each stone slab ahead of me, until my chest stung and vomit bit at my throat. I had to stop, twice, for walkers coming down, and both times they looked curiously at me, then passed with stilted greetings. I said nothing. I stopped, heaving, at the top of the steps, the city grey and green and distant below me. I scrambled across grass, feet sliding, away from the tourist paths, until I could sit with my chin on my knees, looking east to the sea. I watched the houses, the long slivers of sand, the silver-grey water stretching away. Portobello and Musselburgh and that beautiful coast that wound in and out and along, to the south. To England.

I sat there a long time, and let the pain spill out in salty tears.

At last I flicked on my phone, typed one name then another into Google, forcing my finger on the search icon as though I could stab through the screen into the past. Except I already knew I couldn't. *Hope Mitchell*. Nothing useful. *Isaac Mitchell*. The same. I tried combinations: their names with our school, our town. I got one local newspaper story, belatedly archived online. I read it word by word, my guts tangling, but it told me nothing new. I tried to remember what her parents were called, but I doubt I had ever been told. They weren't the type to be on first-name terms with their kids' friends.

I thought of how it had been, going into that house, and shivered. I stood up, put my phone in my pocket, extracted it again, cleared the search history, and stumbled back round the slope and down to the road.

20

Laura

20 December 2018

Our Christmas party was at a bar in the West End. Not my choice. Too busy and too loud and the only part of Edinburgh that always makes me think of London. Something about the competitive spending, the slither of posh clothes, the suited scrum at the bar, the fact – immediately evident – that I had not made enough effort.

A dash of lipstick and a pre-kids top do not a socialite make. Not when a glass of wine costs more than your average family's tea. Not when Kai glowed in tight green trousers, face and hair gold, and Danielle, highly out of character, wore a black satin dress designed for an adolescent, bursting at the seams.

I didn't care. I was preoccupied. *I must not let this consume me*, I told myself, then thought of Alexis all night. I longed with every tune to be dancing tight against him. I felt his hands, sparking nerves, whenever anyone brushed against me. Kai fetched me a cocktail and I drank it too quickly, then got two more. Danielle's boss, Graham, lectured me on the upcoming email campaign, breathing Prosecco and salmon. I watched his dull face and nodded and said I quite understood. I wanted to be alone with Alexis in a dark corridor, bodies clinging, twisting, thudding hard against the wall.

At nine, my throat was raw with shouting nothings, my ears buzzed with the music. Was it too early to leave? Kai was doing shots in a corner. Danielle was leaning against the bar, a thin man from HR falling into her boobs. Kai called me over, mimed drinking. I shook my head.

'Can't wait to get home to your lovely husband?'

'No,' I said, 'to see my secret lover.'

Kai's eyebrows went up. I laughed. 'All right then. Back to my husband snoring on the sofa. But a girl can dream.'

I hated myself then, for slandering Ryan. Ryan who'd asked me, this morning, if something was wrong.

Outside, it was cold and getting colder. Smokers thronged the doorway. With every step, I saw the puzzled smile on Kai's curved mouth. When I found a cab, I was shivering. I gave my own address. At the junction with Princes Street, resolve wavering, I picked up my phone to commit myself with a text to Ryan. Instead, I found one from Alexis.

Missing you. Have fun xx.

I will not let this consume me. But it already had.

I clasped the phone in my hand as we slid along Lothian Road and gazed through the glass at the city I had carved out a life in. The Usher Hall, a green-topped dome. The

Filmhouse, all bright arched windows and austere brick. The King's Theatre with its pantomime facade. I've been in them all. I've laughed and cried and forgotten reality. We took Benjy and Evie to *Cinderella* last Christmas. They hid their faces from the Wicked Stepmother, laughed at jokes they didn't understand.

We should be going this year, but I forgot to book.

The taxi came to Bruntsfield Links, dim and tree-lined, faintly sinister in the darkness. A woman in a red coat leaned against a bus stop, ignoring catcalls from the youths across the street. Her phone screen glowed like a blue and white beacon.

I leaned forward. 'I've changed my mind,' I said. 'Could you take me to Mayfield?'

'All right, darlin'.' The driver had seen it all already. He veered left, earning a hoot from a bus driver. I gave him the address, while my fingers messaged Alexis.

There was no space outside the tenement, so the cabbie pulled in a few buildings along. 'This do you?'

I nodded, handed him a note and coins. Too many. I dived out, started along the street. The air was chill and clammy, like hands in a dungeon.

Not a happy image.

I was only a street back from the main road, but the traffic sounded curiously distant. The doorways were black caves, fronted by silhouette gates and invisible gardens. Somewhere a window slammed, a gate creaked open. Along the road, a cyclist, dark-helmeted, face shadowed, was fiddling with his chain.

You're being ridiculous.

Something moved in the darkness. *A cat*, I told myself. *A cat, or a fox*. But I turned, sliding like a figure skater. I ran back to the taxi, leaned in at the still-open window.

'Will you stay until I'm inside?' I said.

Again the driver evinced no surprise. 'Aye, nae worries. Scared of a ghost, are you?'

'Something like that,' I said.

In the flat, leaning into Alexis's kiss, I was still breathing fast.

'Did you run here?' he asked, smiling. I shook my head, moved back.

I said, 'Do you believe in ghosts?' and his smile dropped.

'What do you mean?'

'I think we're being watched.'

I wrapped my arms round his waist, crushing myself against him. I felt his mouth on my hair, his hands on my ribs, excitement rising through fear. I waited for him to deny it, but he said nothing.

Again, I thought, and the word echoed back to me in his lips, his breath, his closing eyes. But we neither of us said it aloud.

21

Hope

12 February 1999

I hate Mark. I thought I could only hate Her, but now I hate him. Not because of the day-to-day bullying. That grazes me, nothing more. I hate him because he makes each rehearsal like torture, waiting to be given away.

Laura isn't here today; she's with Alexis. She didn't tell me, but I watched them leave together. We're doing the opening scenes, and you'd think Mark wouldn't have time for me, but being yelled at by Balmore just gives him extra spite. He says things when the teachers aren't listening but other kids are. Most of them laugh. Then he gets me alone when we stop for a break.

'Hey, Hopeless.'

He's on his way out for a fag and he rams a corner of the pack into my arm to get my attention. I almost laugh. If he thinks I'm going to mind a bit of cardboard, he has no idea. Then he leers in. 'Peeping Hopeless. That's my new name for you. Like it? Been doing any more perving lately?'

I turn away. This is standard stuff now. He seizes my arm. 'We both know where Alexis and Laura are now, don't we? Nice bit of fun away from prying eyes. Bet you wish you could be watching, don't you, Hopeless?'

Worried he'll get further than you did?

I'm remembering what Laura told me about the after-show party last year. But I don't say it. Last rehearsal, I tried something along those lines and he hit me, quickly, while the teachers weren't looking. Then, more worryingly, he looked immediately round for Alexis and Laura. He'd have told them, too, all about my pathetic watchings, except Laura wasn't there and Alexis was on stage.

So I swallow the line, and try to leave. Mark follows.

'You should be wondering,' he says, 'what you can do to stop me telling them.'

A flicker of hope (ha, ha). Then it fades. What could I give him? I have no money, nothing of value. Least of all myself. He's watching me like a rat deciding whether to bite. He puts his mouth against my ear, and I feel bits of spittle land inside it.

'Nothing,' he says. 'There's nothing you can do. You'll just have to wait.'

'You'll miss your smoke,' I say. He leaves me with a nasty look. I walk off in the opposite direction, to the girls' toilets.

In the corridor, there's a bike leaning against the wall, right in my way. I know it's Mark's. He's been moaning for ages about having to go to the bike shed and cycle the long way round the school, so last week Rick said why didn't he just leave it outside the hall? 'It's not like anyone would steal that piece of shit,' he added.

The corridor is empty. Just me and my opportunity. I go closer. I've never had a bike, but I've watched my father teach Isaac to look after his. Rick's right about this one. It's years old, with deep scratches and a layer of dirt all over. Even Mark didn't bother defending it, just boasted that he's getting a new one for his birthday.

The fantasy is not new; acting on it is. I pull tissues from my pocket and lay them over the brake calliper on the back wheel. Through the gossamer layers, I feel the attachment. It's loose anyway. Detaching it takes no effort at all.

I pull the tissues away, surveying my handiwork. It could easily have caught on something. If Mark checks, that's what he'll think. He should check, every ride. That's what Father told Isaac. But I doubt he will.

I hear voices down the corridor, and hurry to the loos. I shove the tissues into the toilet bowl, then pee on them. It seems symbolic. When I come out, I stare in the mirror, like I do every chance I have now. My face is noticeably better. I thought Mark might be easier on me when I was closer to normal, but that hasn't happened. As for Her, I live in fear that She will notice and ask why.

When we are finished, Mark and Rick emerge from the hall just after me. Mark wheels his bike along the long corridor and out of the front doors, yanking it when it gets stuck. Outside, he flings his leg over without stopping to check.

Careless, I think, and smile. He spots me in the doorway and I stop smiling. But with Rick there, he limits himself to generalities.

'See ya, Hopeless,' he calls in his Riff accent. 'Wouldn't want to be ya.'

Rick waves goodbye. He walks off in one direction and Mark cycles away in the other, slightly uphill. No need to brake. I follow, watching, until he is out of sight.

22

Laura

28 December 2018

Today was bright, breeze-touched. What they call a lovely day for the time of year. After lunch, we put Evie and Benjy in Christmas-present hats and hauled them out into the crisp freshness. Simon refused to leave his computer game. Ryan's dad evidently thought we shouldn't let that one pass, but we did.

The rest of us went along the Braid Burn, high on the bank where the path lies, with the trees climbing above us. I listened to Ryan's mum as she babbled about the kids, Ryan's overdue promotion, her own volunteering. Ryan and his dad jogged ahead, Ryan overseeing Benjy, who was learning to cycle, Malcolm lumbering like a dinosaur as Evie shot ahead on her balance bike. I watched them, unseeing. I watched the water, slithering in and out of view.

All was as it should be. Only it wasn't.

I longed, with an urgency I was afraid Jean would see, for Ryan's mum and dad to leave. Not because I do not like

108

them – I do, very much – but because they require something of me. I am glad Christmas is over. I'm glad the kids enjoyed it. I am even glad, disloyally, that this was Ryan's parents' turn, for I couldn't have hidden my distraction from my mum as I have from Jean. My mum, whom I make excuses to email now instead of call. Who has already watched once as I disappeared before her eyes; whose face grew a little older every time I refused to let her in.

She adores Ryan; the children have bound us back together. I want her to stay thinking I'm OK.

I thought all this through Ryan's sister's dog's operation and a crisis in Oxfam Dundee. Then I saw Alexis.

He was by a bench where the ground is lower, the burn wider, fixing Gracie's helmet and smiling into her anxious face.

'Laura?' Jean said. 'Are you all right?'

Alexis was bent over now, tying Gracie's shoe. Maybe if we walked quickly by, it would be OK.

'Sorry,' I said. 'I thought I saw someone I recognised.'

'And did you?'

'N—' But Evie had wheeled round, come trundling at top speed towards us, and spotted them too.

'Gracie,' she called. She hauled her bike towards her friend, across grass and mud. 'I got a cycle. It's orange.'

Alexis straightened and saw me. He smiled, as if by instinct. My mouth twitched. I followed Evie sedately, picking my way with Jean across the treacherous ground.

'Hi,' he said.

Gracie was lifting her own bike to show Evie, who immediately, loudly, listed the advantages of her own. Gracie's face contracted; she clung to Alexis's leg.

Jean said, 'They're *both* brilliant.' She went over and pretended to examine the bikes. 'Aye, both A-star. No' like your grandpa's, Evie. That has two punctures and he fell off it last week.'

Evie cackled. Gracie smiled and detached herself from Alexis sufficiently to put a proprietorial hand on the frame of her bike. Alexis and I looked at each other, then away. Malcolm appeared, jogging, in belated pursuit of his granddaughter.

'She'll gie me a heart attack,' he said.

Then Benjy was there, braking at the last moment. And Ryan, who put out a hand to Alexis.

'I'm Evie's da,' he said. 'I've seen you at nursery.'

Alexis shook my husband's hand, introduced himself. He'd never told me he'd seen Ryan. But then would I have wanted him to?

'Grandpa fell off his bike,' crowed Evie, letting her own fall and dancing across to Malcolm. 'Grandpa fell off his bike.'

Malcolm scooped her up, held her shrieking in the air.

Ryan said to Alexis, 'This is Laura.'

'We've met,' I said. I dared not take Alexis's hand; I might never let go. Ryan introduced his mum, who shook hands, and his dad, who waved Evie around by way of greeting and said it was a braw day.

Benjy was impatient, making little sorties along the track, returning disgruntled when we didn't follow. I would have gone, but Ryan was making conversation.

'Good Christmas?' he said.

'Very nice. Yours?' Alexis glanced at me, then back at Ryan.

'Lovely,' I said.

Malcolm had put Evie down, was loudly straightening his back. She pummelled his shins with her fists, shouting, 'Again, again.'

Gracie raised her hands to Alexis. He lifted her, held her on one forearm with her arms around his neck. I watched him, under cover of smiling at her, then could not look away.

'Were you here?' Ryan asked.

'I was in France,' Alexis said. Jean would clock the pronoun, even if Ryan didn't.

None of this was news to me. I knew Alexis was in Paris for Christmas, just as I knew he had asked friends from Vienna for Hogmanay.

Evie gave up on Malcolm and followed Benjy.

'Hang on,' Ryan called after them, and then, to Alexis, 'We'd best go.'

'Bye,' Alexis said, through Gracie's hair. 'Nice to see you.'

'Good to meet you,' Jean said. 'Happy new year, when it comes.'

If you only knew, I thought. Malcolm said nothing; he was already in unwieldy pursuit of the children.

As we turned the corner, Evie steered her bike into her grandmother's legs. 'Gracie's mummy and daddy,' she said, 'don't live with each other.'

'Well, that's sad,' Jean said, 'but sometimes it happens. Her da seems very kind.'

Evie shrugged, no longer interested.

'Oh God,' I said. 'Benjy's dropped his glove. I'll go back.'

I ran without waiting for contradiction. Gracie was perched on the bench now, back straight, a small potentate.

Alexis was gazing down at her, doling out chocolate buttons. He didn't look up until I was very close.

'Laura,' he said, and my heart buzzed.

'I've missed you,' I mouthed, over Gracie's absorbed head.

'Me too,' he whispered.

'When can I see you?'

'Very soon.'

'Numpty Mummy,' Benjy said, when I caught up with them. 'It was in my pocket.'

Among the reproofs, my confusion was allowed to pass.

Later, Mhairi brought her sons round for drinks and mince pies.

I like Mhairi. We have lived for years now on that curious divide between neighbours and friends. In the early days, when we first moved in, she made overtures, as if she would push us over the other side. I almost accepted them, secure in my new happiness. But something kept me back. And I had nothing to say to her today.

I wanted her children to entertain mine. I wanted her and Ryan and Jean and Malcolm to distract each other and I wanted to sprint like a wild thing to Alexis, pull open his clothes and peel off my own, slowly, while he watched. I wanted to lie luxuriant in his arms.

I left the others in the sitting room and stood alone by the kitchen window, chilling my face on the pane. Ryan came through, collecting bottles, and said, 'What's up?'

'Nothing,' I said. I found a smile, which felt like a blow. 'I'll be through in a second.'

112

He set the wine on the counter, came to me by the window. 'I mean it,' he said. 'You've not been yourself all Christmas. Longer.'

I said nothing. I thought, *He knows*, and wondered if I had the energy for a convincing lie. I thought of the truth unravelling while our neighbour and his parents made polite talk in the next room and the children chased each other up and down the stairs.

He took my hand, tried to make me look at him. 'Laura,' he said. 'Are you sick?'

I almost laughed. Then I remembered Naomi, dead without warning. I wanted to throw myself on the hard floor, push thorns under my nails, cauterise this love that would destroy everything.

'No,' I said. I hugged my husband, hating myself. 'I'm not ill. I swear I would tell you if I were.'

Ryan was so pleased, he didn't ask anything else.

Afterwards, he handed out mince pies and told jokes in a voice made bright by relief. I drank red wine, dark and plummy, and sat with Evie on my knee, remembering my husband's words. Thinking of Alexis, whom I couldn't let go.

Not yourself.

More myself than I am.

I could have laughed aloud. Catherine Earnshaw, hardly the heroine to emulate. Better or worse, I wondered, than poor Maggie Tulliver, with whom I was once compared? I had to shut that thought off, too, if I were to last the evening.

23

Laura

8 March 2019

Ryan is often away, but not like this. Today the future tightened on me like drying mud, lining the children's clothes, the plates on the kitchen table, the unemptied dishwasher. I squeezed too-small shoes onto Evie's feet, promised to get her fitted for new ones. I poured honey on thick toast, thinking, *This is how it will always be*.

The little ones clamoured for Ryan. I said, 'You'll see him soon.'

I thought of Gracie, who will never see her father again. I crooked my head into the cupboard so they would not see my face. When I straightened, Simon was looking up from his Weetabix, his mother's eyes on my untwisting neck.

'He only just came back,' he said.

Benjy exploded into tears. I said to Simon, 'We'll talk later. Don't worry,' and he gave me a bleak look. Evie wailed too, and I shouted at them to hush. Instead, they yelled louder. I burned my finger on the kettle and was pleased because it gave me an excuse to scream. Simon watched me, not speaking. Then he pulled Benjy onto his knee, fed Evie her toast.

We were late to nursery. Benjy whined all the way to Cluny Gardens and then, when we crossed at the lights, ran on down the hill as I was turning right. I swung the buggy after him, shouting like a harpy for him to come back *now*. Evie joined in, kicking her legs. 'Bad Benjy! Bad.'

He stood on tiptoes where the road crosses high over the railway, trying to see over.

'Help me, Mummy. I can hear a train.'

I grabbed him by the wrist, not looking over, and dragged him back wailing after me. I know that drop. Some twelve, fifteen meters, and then the hard earth and relentless metal below. I never stop there if I can help it.

'There's no train,' I said. 'And *never* go off like that. You know how dangerous it is.'

He doesn't know. He's four.

'Daddy lets me,' he said, through escalating sobs. 'Daddy lets me look for the trains.'

'Well, I'm not Daddy.'

I pushed on, listening to him cry, avoiding the glances of other pedestrians. It's true that Ryan takes him there. He lifts him so they can study the rusty tracks together, waits patiently for the freight trains that shudder intermittently through. Once they spotted the Flying Scotsman, taking on water, and it was the highlight of Benjy's life.

He yanked his hand from mine and stood on the pavement, rageful as a thwarted despot. 'I want Daddy!' he screamed, so loud that a cyclist, overtaking, shouted a reproof.

I stopped the buggy, kicking on the brake. I bent down to Benjy, gripping both his hands. 'I'm sorry, darling,' I said. I bit on anger. *This isn't his fault.* 'I'm not Daddy. I'm me, and we're very late.' I brought him back to the buggy. 'He'll take you,' I said, cutting across his whingeing. 'He'll take you another time.'

Yazzie met us at the toddler room door, guarding it like a troll. Evie ran to her, was lifted and held tight.

'You're better, then,' Yazzie said to me, hard-lipped, accusatory.

'I'm on the mend.' I met her gaze. 'Thanks.'

I looked over her shoulder, skimmed heads. Gracie wasn't there. Benjy pushed past us, climbed the pile of boxes at the back of the room.

Yazzie said, 'I thought it would be Ryan this morning. I thought he was back.'

'Well, it's me.'

She hugged Evie, turned my child from me. 'You're here now, hen,' she said.

I walked round her. I kissed my daughter, called my son back with a sharpness he did not deserve. I looked back from the stairs and saw Yazzie still cradling Evie.

Downstairs, I asked about Gracie. 'She's not been in since,' Anja said. 'I expect Diana thinks she's better at home.'

We stood in silence, watching children who were not Gracie as they charged about or built castles out of sand. Benjy was making a pile of it, tall as a tower for a fairy princess. Anja shook her head. 'That poor kid,' she said. 'I don't know how you get over something like that.'

No, I thought, as I walked through the garden to the street. *I don't know how either.*

The path was lined with flowers. *Lilacs out of the dead land.* Only it's March, not April, and these were daffodils, bright and thrusting, an insult to my unsleeping grief.

I thought of Gracie. She and I are linked by the loss of Alexis. We two alone, in this pensive city, are daily scourged by our memories of him. For all I have done wrong, I am not entirely selfish. I do not equate my loss, tarnished by my immorality, with hers. If I could spare her her suffering by making mine worse, I would do it. But I cannot.

I cannot even comfort her openly, or myself by proximity to her. I cannot talk to her of her father, of his smile that was like her smile, of his voice, which once made me cry for love, of his integrity and his pain at the loss of it. I cannot tell her how much he loved her.

When I got home, Simon was sitting on the bottom step of the stairs, kicking the floor.

I said, 'Why aren't you at school?'

He said, 'Dad's moved out, hasn't he?'

I dropped my keys, caught them, raised my head to face him. He was in his school uniform, his bag on his knees. He looked tired; at once much younger and much older than he really was. Above the rising stairs, seven framed years of family holidays lined the wall.

'Yes,' I said.

Simon started to cry, his head dipping onto his rucksack. 'Why?' he said. 'Why would he do that? Why didn't you stop him?'

I sat down next to him, put my arm round his shoulders. 'I'm so sorry,' I said. And then, because I could not turn this boy against his father, 'It wasn't his fault. It was mine.'

He turned a moment in my grip, stared at me with Naomi's pale eyes. Candid, tear-stained, dragging the truth from me. 'What do you mean?'

'I had an affair,' I said.

He let his bag, book-heavy, thud to the floor. I thought he might yell, but he just sat with his arms around his knees, staring into space. That was much worse.

I stroked his back. 'I'm so sorry,' I said. He gulped. I said, 'It's not . . . I'm not . . . It's over.' And then, because anything else was an implied lie, I went on, 'He died.'

Simon made the same movement his father had, putting his head in his hands. He looked so like Ryan that I was unable to speak. 'The cops . . .' he said quietly when he lifted his head again. 'The man who was killed in the Hermitage.' I stared at the wall. He said, louder, 'Was that him?'

I nodded. *Please don't ask more.* But he did.

'He was here with you that night?'

I said nothing. The tears were hot on my eyelids.

'*Was* he?'

'Yes,' I said.

He looked blank. Then he looked angry. But his tone was almost forensic. 'You were cheating on Dad, with Benjy and Evie in the house.'

As I watched, his face twisted, his voice cracked. 'With them in the next *room*?'

'Simon, please don't . . .' I stopped, swallowed. 'I'm so sorry, darling.'

'Don't call me that.' He banged his fist on the wall, not violently, but repeatedly, once for every obscenity. 'Shit. Shit. Shit.'

I didn't reprimand him. I let the pause last, taking deep breaths. Then I said, 'We both still love you, whatever has happened.'

Simon stared, as if I were an idiot. 'It's not about *me*,' he said. 'It's about Dad. Don't you think he's had enough crap to deal with?'

That wrenched my heart, or the nervy pulp that had replaced it. Simon, too, had had enough crap to deal with.

'I didn't plan any of it,' I said. 'Alexis and I . . . I can't explain.'

'It's still your fault,' he said.

Of course she had a choice. She knew what she was doing.

I fought memory. Simon said nothing. I put out a hand, rested it on his knee. I didn't expect him to take it, and he didn't.

I said, 'I won't try to defend myself. This is where we are now. I'm truly sorry.'

Still silence. I hadn't wanted to do this now, either, but it was too important not to.

'I love you, Simon,' I said. 'I hope you will stay here with me, and then be part of whatever arrangement Dad and I reach for Benjy and Evie. I know it's different for you because you're older, you have a choice. But I hope – I hope so much – there'll be no other difference.'

He jerked his knee, and my hand flopped to the ground. I said, 'I know you're angry. But I love you.' I swallowed. 'I'm still—'

He cut across me. 'Dad will forgive you. He'll come back. This is temporary.'

I'm still your mum.

'I don't think it is,' I said. 'I'm sorry.'

'He loves you.'

'It's not that simple.'

'And it's over, your affair. That man is dead.'

I told myself that Simon wasn't even fifteen yet. He didn't mean to be brutal – or if he did, he had provocation.

He said, 'You wouldn't do it again. Would you?'

'No,' I said. 'But some things change a relationship, so it can't be mended.'

'Does Dad think that?'

'Please,' I reached out to him again. 'This is something we have to determine for ourselves.'

Simon shoved my hand away, bouncing it against the banister like an unwanted toy. It hurt and I yelped, then bit down on my lip.

He said, 'You're deciding for me too, and Benjy and Evie. This isn't what we want.'

I said, 'I know it's unfair. I know it's hard for you.'

He ignored this. 'You have to mend it.' He stared past me, as though he was reading a law. 'We're a family,' he said.

19 September 2018

From: Khaleesi8690

To: AlwaysHaveParis

Subject: Past mistakes

Afternoon!

Having quizzed you about your relationship history last night (or tried to!), I suppose I should come clean on mine. I didn't mean to avoid the subject. It's just there's nothing interesting to say. The usual run of bad choices.

I'd say things look different now, except I don't want to jinx anything.

Xx

24

Hope

15 February 1999

Our classroom stinks. It always does. The two main suspects are Mr Appleby's trainers, which he kicks under his desk thinking we won't notice, and his lunch, which he keeps in a drawer. Either way, it's cheesy and repulsive. But this morning, no one seems to notice. There's no nose-wriggling or fake gagging, just rippling disquiet. Mr Appleby is unusually upright, eyes open, his gaze creeping across the rows of students. Rumours glide from line to line, though never to me. I am always the last to know.

Laura slithers into her seat next to me, only just not late. Her face is tense with suppressed information. I'm about to ask what's going on when one of the cool girls leans in from her other side and whispers something.

I curl back into my place. Laura nods. 'It's awful,' she says.

I will not ask her now, but I do not have long to wait. Mr Appleby coughs, gets to his feet. He still has his shoes on.

He takes the register like he's the vicar welcoming us to a funeral. Then he stays standing.

'I'm afraid,' he says, 'that I have some very sad news. Your friend and colleague, Mark Myres . . .'

I understand then, with a quiver of fear and elation. I should have guessed before.

'. . . had an accident cycling home on Friday night.'

He pauses. The room is still as a taxidermist's gallery.

'I'm very sorry to tell you that he was killed.'

There is more, of course. Not the details I want, but about how we must be there for each other and the teachers are there for us, and there is counselling available for Mark's friends. I don't listen. Some of the girls are crying. I'm sure half of them never spoke to Mark. Laura is tugging at a strand of her hair, staring at the desk.

The rest of the story drizzles out over the morning, reaching me at lunchtime in the locker room. Jem says, 'His brakes failed,' and I need suddenly to go to the toilet.

I sit down, instead, and my gut shudders still.

Claire says, 'Are you OK, Hope? I didn't think you were such good mates with him.'

'I'm not,' I say. 'I didn't even like him much, but we were in the show together. It's horrible.'

Jem nods, plonks her bottom beside me.

'I can't believe I snogged him,' she says. 'There he was, making me feel a bit icky and embarrassed whenever I saw him, and now he's . . . nothing.'

'I don't understand it,' I say. 'Brakes go wrong all the time. People don't usually die.'

I just wanted to give him a shock.

But it turns out that the first real descent on Mark's way home is the steep downhill, beyond the shops, on the main road out of town. And I already knew that he cycles (cycled) like a maniac. I can see him now, showing off at full pelt, then yanking on the brakes at the last moment.

'He went over the handlebars,' Jem says. 'A lorry hit him.'

Hit him? Went over him, she must mean. Crushed him. I don't ask. Jem is looking queasy and Claire as though she thinks we're talking about it too much. I untwist the quote from my sandwiches (*Honour thy father and thy mother*, a favourite with Her) and chuck it into the bin.

Perhaps there are some real tears for Mark, but I see only passing hysterics. By the afternoon, cast members are starting to say, 'I wonder what will happen' and 'Perhaps they won't want to replace him', and by the time we gather for rehearsal, there's open speculation about who will be playing Riff.

We don't find out. Mr Balmore and Mrs Henderson show up drab-faced, only to send us away again.

'Rehearsal is cancelled, my dears,' Mr Balmore says, and the endearment sounds wrong. Too stagy even for him. 'There will be a time and a place, in the next weeks to decide how to proceed with our show. Speaking for myself, I believe Mark would have wanted it to continue.'

Mrs Henderson gives him a sidelong glance. He reddens.

'But that time is not now. Please, go home and remember him in your own ways.'

Laura hurries away with Alexis and Stacy, who has red blotches around her eyes but has found time, I notice, to redo her mascara. I rearrange my bag, put on lip balm, so it doesn't look like I'm following them. Then I do.

Rick stops me in the doorway. 'I think we should talk to the police,' he says.

Real fear hits me then. A cramping slowness, as though my world is about to end, and all I can do is watch.

'What do you mean?' I say.

He sounds impatient. 'We saw him, didn't we? We saw him leave. His bike caught on the door. That was probably when the brake got damaged.'

My life comes back into focus. Of course that would be what he meant. I say nothing.

Rick says, 'From what I've heard, it must have been the back one; maybe the calliper was undone.'

Rick is a cyclist too. I'd forgotten that. A proper one. Mountain bikes and jumps and tyre changes by the trackside.

'You know what I mean?' he says. 'You saw it too.'

'Yes,' I say. 'I saw him pulling the bike to get it through the doorway. I think it jammed on something.'

Rick kicks at the wall. 'I should have told him to stop and check. I'm so angry with myself.'

'I hadn't thought,' I say.

'That's because you're not a bike person. I am. I've thought about it all day.' He takes a breath. 'There'll be an investigation, I suppose. They'll want to know what caused it.'

'Of course,' I say. I fight to keep my voice sombre. 'You're completely right. I'll go with you. Tomorrow?'

'Tomorrow,' Rick says.

Perhaps fate is giving me a break at last.

I walk home imagining how Mark felt when that rear brake failed him and his bike upturned and hurled him into emptiness. I wonder whether he saw the truck coming. I wonder if he had time to be afraid.

23 September 2018

From: Khaleesi8690

To: AlwaysHaveParis

Subject: Last night . . .

. . . was amazing.

I know I shouldn't say it. I know I
should play it cool, but I'm not that
kind of girl and I figure you know that
by now. It was amazing. You are amazing.

That's all.

xx

25

Laura

8 March 2019

Bedtime broke me. It was my own fault. I gave the children chocolate and too much TV and sat tracing the scratches on the kitchen table, as though each one recorded Alexis's fingers on my skin. Then I wrenched the kids too abruptly from their screen fix. Benjy cried and Evie shouted and slammed hard fists into my thighs. When I got her upstairs, she had a poo accident. I shoved her into the shower and crawled around the bathroom floor splashing detergent and rubbing at shit with an old towel with a hole in it, and all the time Benjy was in a quaking heap by the radiator, pleading, 'TV, TV,' over and over like a junkie forced to go cold turkey.

By the time I had them in their PJs, teeth cleaned, I was shaking too, and hating myself. The way I was shouting, a neighbour less understanding than Mhairi would have called social services.

Perhaps she should have. Perhaps I should call them myself.

Ryan came in when the worst was over, though Benjy was still shuddering with intermittent sobs and telling me he hated me. I was reading Julia Donaldson and wondering whether I should hand them both over to their father and walk out of this life altogether.

He took over without a word, though he looked plenty. As I left the bedroom, I heard Evie shrieking, 'Daddy, Daddy,' and Benjy asking, 'Have you come home properly?'

I winced at that; I expect Ryan did too.

'Na, Benjy-boy,' he said. 'No' to stay. But I'll come and take you out tomorrow.'

He said it loudly, defying me to contradict him. I didn't. I drifted into the bathroom and stood there a full minute, staring at the detritus around me, at the black growth on the grouting. Eventually I gathered up Evie's clothes and the bathmat for the wash, but I swayed on my feet, dropped them in a fetid bundle by the bathroom door, and went to our bedroom instead.

My bedroom now, I suppose, but for how long?

Evie had left a doll there – a flimsy wool-haired object – and I lay on top of the duvet, under the blanket, and hugged it to me like a live thing until I fell asleep.

Ryan woke me. It was less than an hour later, but I felt as though I was being pulled from hibernation. He didn't come in, just stood in the doorway and said my name until I sat up trembling and blinking and wondering, for a long moment, what had changed.

'Are they asleep?' I said.

'I've seen the police,' he said. 'I thought you'd want to know.'

'Oh God.'

I pushed the blanket off me, swung my legs over the edge of the bed. Ryan didn't move. He hadn't shaved and looked older. His beard has been grey for years, though his hair is only just going that way.

I asked what he had told them.

'What I told you,' he said. His expression didn't change.

'Will they check with your colleagues?'

'Aye,' he said, 'if they haven't already.'

'But they believed you?'

He looked at me as though I was crazy. 'Laura, it's not me they suspect.'

'What do you mean?'

'It's you,' he said, as if it was obvious.

I gripped Evie's doll, held on to reality. I shook my head at him. He said nothing. I said, 'But Simon came back, just after . . .' I stopped. *Just after Alexis had left.* 'They spoke to him,' I said, quietly.

'Do you never read crime fiction?' (Ryan does, pile after pile of Ian Rankin.) 'They can't time it that exactly. There was time for you to nip out and stick a knife in your boyfriend's back.'

I recoiled, huddling the toy against me, shaking my head like a wobble doll myself. 'Did they say?' I said, at last. 'Did they tell you they think it was me?'

'They didn't need to. They only have your word for when he left this house, or what he did here. It's a shame for you Simon didn't walk in and find you shagging the fucker. Then you'd be in the clear.'

'Christ,' I said. 'Don't say that.'

'I'll say what I like.'

We stared at each other across the battleground that had been our marriage. Then he said, 'Where *is* Simon?'

'At Bella's.'

'Until she screws him over, I suppose.'

'Ryan, please. I know I deserve it, but please, please stop.'

He shrugged. 'Forget it. Tell him I'll see him tomorrow. I'll take them all away for the night, if you don't object.'

I didn't object. I'm better alone.

I saw him out, then crept shivering into the kids' bedroom. Evie was sprawled untidily on top of the duvet. I tugged it from under her and cocooned it round her. She grunted but stayed asleep. I knelt by Benjy's bed and looked with remorse at the damp lashes, the cherry mouth. I pulled the covers neat about him, kissed him on the cheek, stroked back his hair.

'Good night, darling,' I whispered.

He opened his eyes, closed them again, nuzzled into my hand.

'I'm sorry I was grumpy,' I said. 'I love you and Evie so much. I always will.'

Benjy snapped both eyes open. 'Yazzie says *she* loves us best,' he said. 'She says she'll always be there.'

Jesus. I gaped into my son's bewildered face. 'Benjy,' I said, at last. 'You know that's not true, don't you? Yazzie is a nursery teacher. I mean, perhaps she does love you – I can see why anyone would – but of course she doesn't love you more than I do, or Daddy does.'

Benjy shrugged, turned his face into the pillow. 'Yazzie said it,' he said, like a much older child. 'I love you, Mummy.'

Yes, I thought. *But do you love me best?*

I kissed him again, walked back onto the landing. I scooped up the soiled clothes, carried them down to the washing machine. If he still did, I wondered, did I actually deserve it?

26

Laura

31 December 2018

It was 4.45 by the clock on the oven; 4.50, then, in practice. Ryan was making a steak pie. A celebration piece, ornate as a cathedral, pastry cornicing and carved holly leaves. For his parents' benefit? Our children's? Or because he was not, after all, about to have another dead wife?

I was prepping dessert, longing for space, crashing into him whenever I needed anything. In the sitting room, Simon, Jean and Benjy were playing snakes and ladders. Malcolm was forcing his eyes open, reading to Evie.

I opened the drinks cupboard, gave a perfunctory glance inside. I said, 'You forgot the cognac.'

Ryan frowned. 'You didn't ask for any.'

'I suppose I'll have to go out.' I gave an exaggerated sigh. If it all went wrong, perhaps I could run away and get a job as a bad actress in a daytime soap.

Simon called from the sitting room, where Benjy was revving into a tantrum because he'd lost the game.

'I'm away to see Bella. When do I have to be back?'

Simon's mellowed since Christmas, talking openly to his grandparents about his girlfriend, even showing Jean a photo on his phone, which is more than he's done for Ryan and me.

'Tea's at eight,' I said. I peered round the door. The board was upside down, counters littering the rug. Jean was cuddling Benjy.

'I'll be back soon,' I said.

'There's brandy in the cupboard,' Ryan said, behind me.

'Not the right one.' I cut off his response, ran upstairs for my fleece.

Back in the hall, pulling on trainers, I could hear Malcolm saying he'd drive Simon, then Jean reminding him that he'd be over the limit. Thank God, or he'd have offered me a lift too.

Ryan followed me into the hall. 'If you wanted a run, why didn't you just say?'

I tugged my down jacket from the hook in the porch and waved it like a proof of honour. 'I'm not running,' I said.

I did run, though. I ran to Blackford Pond, away from the main road, away from the shops. I passed Christmas lights and windows with the curtains drawn back and trees and families who stayed in and were happy together. Outside, all was still. No poltergeist tonight. Or not yet.

I stopped just inside the black gateway, waiting for Alexis.

Earlier, cold families would have weaved in and out of these gates, moaning about missed *Paw Patrol* and too many mince pies. Later, the hill above would be thronged with celebrators, coats and scarves over party clothes, drinking out of hip flasks, stamping feet with the cold, waiting for twelve. We'd done it ourselves before the little ones were born. We'd stood hand in hand, the three of us, and watched the fireworks that exploded around the castle.

Now, it was empty. The city hung winter dark between the street lamps; the road opposite stretched straight away from me. Behind me was space, and the gathering trees. Dark as midnight. Without thinking about it, I started to sing. 'Memory'. The wrong musical. But then I will never sing *West Side Story* again. Nor listen to it, if I can help it.

Alexis's footsteps sounded quick on the hard stone. I kept singing as he reached me. I would have stopped then, but he shook his head, gripped my bare hands in his gloved ones. I sang on to the end, for him and for myself, looking up into his face. The lyrics came to me as though the city itself was whispering, prompt side, in my ear.

At the end, my toes were numb and my lips were cracked. Alexis's face was shadowed and beautiful, sharp with pain. He let go my hands, put both his to my face and kissed me. His mouth was cold, then warm; the wool of his gloves scratched my jawline. It was the most loving kiss he had given me, and the least passionate. And something inside me stretched and snapped, because I knew in that moment why I remembered the words.

We had done T. S. Eliot for A level too, Claire and Jem and I. And Hope. It hadn't just been *The Mill on the Floss*.

I walked with him through the darkness towards the water, holding hands, tracing our steps of six weeks since.

'You still sing,' he said.

'I don't really,' I said. *Not since that night.* 'Just to the children and sometimes to myself.'

'Me too,' he said. 'I only sing to Gracie.'

'But your voice is beautiful,' I said, because it was true and because it seemed suddenly terrible that amid everything else, that too had been lost.

He said, 'In Graz, I had a friend who persuaded me to do an audition. A light opera, university am dram. You know the kind of thing.'

'And?'

'I was offered a part, got to the first rehearsal, and walked straight out again.'

I said nothing. We skirted the pond, keeping back from the edge, barely lit by the waning moon. The ground was icing over. We moved without speaking, stepped off the path. Between us and the road were bushes and trees; behind us the black water, the hill.

'What did you tell your friends tonight?' I asked.

He stood still, looking away from me. 'I told them Gracie wanted me to wish her a happy new year in person.' He pulled his eyes back to mine, jet in the darkness. 'Laura, sometimes I hate myself.'

'Perhaps you should hate me.'

'That's impossible.' He said it sadly. 'Besides, I make my own choices. You didn't ask me to lie.'

'I'm not sure I *do* make my own choices,' I said. 'Not any more.'

He didn't answer. I shivered, stamped my feet up and down. 'Do you want to go?' he said.

'No,' I said. 'Not yet. Not without you.'

He drew me against him, my cheek on his shoulder. 'I wish we could go back to mine,' he said.

'I wish we could go anywhere warm.'

He chuckled. It felt forced.

'Are they nice?' I said, into his coat. 'Your friends.'

'Very nice, but I shouldn't have asked them to stay.'

I looked up. 'Why? I thought you were close.'

'That's why,' he said. 'They keep asking if I've met someone.'

I laughed, only it was halfway to a sob. I asked just how well they knew him.

'Not quite well enough,' he said. 'Not well enough to guess the someone is you.'

I reeled in his arms, freed my own, pressed cold fingers on the back of his neck. I pushed myself against him, feeling the warmth of him through his jacket. He unzipped it and I sank inside, pulled his mouth down onto mine. It wasn't cold now, nor passionless. His teeth nipped my lips, his tongue traced the tip of mine.

'Oh God,' I said. 'Alexis.'

I had not felt like this, this need that overcame place and cold and fear of discovery, not since he and I had made furtive, laughing love behind trees and benches, in the park by school. I thought of that, twisted with memory. I pulled with numbed fingers at his clothes, felt his hands stripping through layers. I wanted to scream with wanting him, felt him moaning beneath my hands.

I drew him back against a tree, he pulled me sharp up so my legs were round his waist. Gripping, twisting, gasping, moving fast and hot in the cold air, crying out together. Laughing as our breath eased.

Through the trees, a car flashed by, then another. A dog yapped, somewhere in the darkness. I didn't care.

Then we heard it, a stone cracking, loud as a gunshot. We saw the white arc of light, moving, dipping, going out. Then nothing.

Silence again. Stillness more complete than it had been before. I clung to Alexis, my fingers biting his shoulders through his coat. My breath was a long shudder. I thought for a moment that he wasn't breathing at all. Then he put his mouth to my ear, whispered through my hair, 'It was nothing. Someone on the road. A light going on and then the curtains being shut.'

'It was a torch,' I said.

'A dog walker, then. We heard a dog. Come on . . .' He prised my fingers off his coat, pulled up clothes. 'Let's get out of here. God, your hands must be frozen.'

He peeled off his gloves, made me wear them, kept his arm around me as we skirted the pond, and went out through the gates onto the road. The ground was slick with ice.

'I'll walk you home,' he said.

'You can't,' I said. 'You know you can't.'

'I'll walk behind, then, and watch from the end of your street.'

'You said it was nothing.'

'I'm not quite sure enough.'

I said nothing after that. I kissed him, a deep, quick kiss, then walked sliding-fast along the wide stretch of Cluny

Gardens, up the steep hill of Braid Avenue, past trees with branches like silhouettes, and hedges where watchers could hide. Higher up, it was even colder, and the pavement was black. I knew he was behind me. When I reached my own door, I turned, once, and looked at him. I didn't wave. He stood at the corner, waiting. Like the cab driver, he wouldn't leave until I was safe inside.

In the hallway, Evie launched out of Ryan's arms and into mine. He said, 'Where's the cognac?'

'They didn't have any,' I said. I squeezed Evie, held her warm face against my cold one. 'I tried all the way up the hill to Waitrose, and even they failed me. I'll have to improvise.'

In the sitting room, Ryan's dad was asleep on the sofa. His mum was reading to Benjy. They looked up with almost identical expressions, though Jean tried to hide the reproach.

Benjy said, 'You were gone ages.'

'I know, darling. I thought I might as well run the long way back.' I looked at Ryan. 'I know it was stupid of me. It was so icy, I ended up having to walk most of it.'

Ryan rolled his eyes. 'You're incorrigible,' he said.

I smiled back. I wanted to run upstairs, slam doors behind me and hate myself in peace.

The evening progressed inexorably. At midnight, Malcolm kissed his wife, perked up by his nap and quantities of Talisker. Ryan pulled me to him and kissed me too. I turned my face away, turning it into a hug, not thinking of him.

27

Hope

16 February 1999

In theory, the sixth-form locker room is for anyone; in practice, it opens directly onto the girls' toilets, so it is ours: a space where you can lurk unmolested or get things out of your bag without comment. Even the popular girls use it when they have tampons to change or a difficult boyfriend day. I'm there all the time, but then for me, life is a bad period. The boys stay well clear.

Rick knows all this, but he shoves the door open as though it's his best mate's house and stands slick and alien against the grey sky.

Cue minor chaos. Make-up bags are shoved to the side. Two girls make noises like cats who've seen a dog. Claire rolls her eyes. Stacy is there, unusually, stowing a bag of clothes and singing along to Britney Spears on her Discman. She fakes outrage, then turns down the music and asks if Rick was looking for her. Jem looms behind her, the knock-off version to her Platinum Barbie, looking as though she'd like to ask the same thing.

'Not this time, Stace. I'm after Hope.' I don't think he even notices Jem. He scans the room, spots me in my corner. 'There you are. Ready?'

I walk the narrow room, followed by a score of female eyes. Rick turns to go, indifferent or oblivious to the sensation he has caused.

'What about registration?' I ask.

'Someone can explain.' He glances round again. 'Laura, just say she's seeing the police, will you?'

Laura nods. I wonder, passingly, how he knows she's in my class. Then he's outside again and I'm following him, and I can almost hear the pandemonium as the door shuts.

Rick marches me across the grounds. 'I thought we'd go to Old Flop first,' he says.

Dr Flopworth: unfortunately named headmaster.

I wish he would go more slowly, so I could figure out what exactly I'm going to say. Perhaps I can leave it all to him.

I can, at first. In the headmaster's office (odour: citrus air freshener; decor: self-consciously erudite), Rick gives a succinct account of what he saw on Friday.

'The bike stuck on the door, sir,' he says. 'Mark had to give it a proper tug. I do a lot of cycling, and if it was the brake calliper that went, it could easily have happened then.' He pulls a face. I wonder if he's going to repeat what he said to me about wishing he'd stopped Mark. He doesn't. He says, 'We thought we should tell someone,' and leaves it at that.

Old Flop is looking as solemn as Mr Appleby tried to. I stare at the shelves of leather-bound books, the photos of cricket games and opening nights, like he's trying to pretend this is Winchester. Does he really care about Mark? Or does he just mind for his precious school?

'Quite right, Richard. Quite right,' he says.

'Riccardo, sir,' Rick says. The headmaster gives a little jump, shuffles a heap of newsletters on his desk.

'Of course. Sorry. Did you see the same, Hope?'

I swallow, tell him yes. 'I was leaving then too, sir. I saw the bike jammed in the doorway, though I couldn't see which bit of it.'

Five minutes later, he tells us the police are coming. We wait in the outer office. Rick refuses tea, so I do too. The secretary's computer keys click constantly, except when the phone rings. Then it's her sweet, modulated voice, offering reassurance without information. They're all asking about Mark.

Neither Rick nor I speak, but our silence carries a feeling I did not expect and hardly recognise. I think it's companionship.

A panda car creeps up, slow as a pedestrian. It wouldn't do for the investigating officer to hit a pupil. The secretary goes to meet them, straightening her blouse. Rick looks at Flop's closed door.

He says, 'Do you think I'm to blame?'

I know what he means, though it's hard not to laugh, under the circumstances.

'No,' I say. 'Or if you are, I must be too. I never thought of stopping him.'

'Why would you?' he says. And then, '*I* should have. I was just a bit distracted.'

I'd like to ask by what, but I can hear a door opening down the corridor. Then there are feet heavy on the laminate tiles, voices crisp with authority. Should I pat Rick on the arm, as if he were Isaac?

I don't.

'It wasn't your fault,' I say.

The police ask more questions than Flop did, and they ask us separately. I didn't expect that. Rick goes first, and when he comes out, he gives me a weird half-smile. Perhaps it's meant for reassurance.

In the study, the headmaster is still behind his desk, with one police officer crushing a plastic chair and the other standing by a pot plant, crinkling her nose as if she'd like to open the window.

I sit down. Old Flop says he thought it would be reassuring for me and Rick to have him there. I say thank you, since he clearly expects it and also because it *is* actually helpful not to be alone with them. I didn't think I'd be scared, but I am.

The woman officer takes me through the whole 'incident', as she calls it, from when I left the hall after rehearsal. She has a primary teacher voice and the eyes of a vulture. I tell her exactly what Rick and I told the headmaster. I add, for good measure, 'It could have been the back wheel that jammed, but I couldn't swear to that.'

The man writes everything down, the notebook creasing on his elephantine knee. The woman waits for him to finish. Then she asks, 'Were you good friends with Mark?'

I tense up. I can't help it, though I try to help showing it.

'Not especially,' I say. 'I only really knew him in the show.'

'Did he seem like himself to you, that day?'

'I didn't notice. I suppose so.'

'Did he talk to you at all?'

I bite my lip, as though I'm trying to remember. 'I think he said something in the break, when he was on his way out for a . . . for some fresh air. Just something about where I was meant to be in the scene we'd just done.'

'Isn't that the director's job?'

I squirm, trapped in my own lie. 'I don't mean that,' I say, and it comes out like I'm sulking.

'What don't you mean?' she asks.

'That he was trying to direct me. He was just joking about. That's what he was like.'

She seems to accept that. 'And when you left together? Did he say anything then?'

'We didn't leave *together*,' I say. 'He and Rick just came out after me.'

She nods. 'But he spoke to you? Said goodbye?'

'Yes, of course.'

She smiles, as though I'm a baby who has finally grasped their own spoon and now has to get it to their mouth. 'Can you remember what he said?'

'Nothing particular.' Another stupid lie, when she's just spoken to Rick. I try to correct myself. 'It was probably something silly.'

She's already looking at her colleague and he's paging through his notebook. He says, 'We were told he said, "See ya, wouldn't want to be ya."'

At least they didn't get the 'Hopeless' bit.

I shrug. 'Like I said, Mark mostly tried to be funny.' I attempt to look the right amount of concerned. 'He seemed totally as normal.'

They let me go after that. Rick has long gone. I go to the loo on my way to history and lean my face into my favourite mirror. I think three things.

Number one: my spots are so reduced that there are one or two students in the school who look worse than I do. Boys, admittedly. But still.

Number two: Rick treated me like a normal human being. This might be because I look less like a science experiment gone wrong. But to be fair to him, I don't think it is.

Number three: whatever I might have had a chance of being before Friday night, I'm not normal now.

28

Laura

8 January 2019

We're both scared. I hear footsteps everywhere I go. I spin to bland nothingness, to strangers walking and chatting and leading their lives. We talk, but not about what we are really afraid of. I tried today and Alexis closed his face to me, said it was nothing to do with the past.

'You know it can't be,' he said.

'What is it then?' I said. 'Do you think Diana is watching us? Do you think Ryan is?'

Alexis said Diana wasn't his girlfriend, hadn't been for years, didn't care what he did. I doubt the latter. He said nothing about Ryan. But lying next to him in the dour midday light, I thought about my husband.

It made a change: usually I lie by Ryan, fantasising about Alexis.

Ryan is not the stalking type, if there is such a thing. But even if he were, I am almost sure he has not guessed. Each day, I pile lies on lies, stretch out on them like a fake princess on her mattresses, waiting to be toppled off. But it's amazing how much you can abuse someone if they trust you.

This morning, he asked again if I was OK. I told him I was tired, watched him writhe. He said he was sorry, knew he was working too much. 'We'll try to get you a break.'

Then it was me who writhed.

'It's not Ryan,' I said, against Alexis's chest.

'It's not Diana,' he said.

I smiled. 'Well, do you have another ex? A dangerous one. One I should know about.'

He frowned. Then he rolled towards me, hand on my waist. 'Laura,' he said. 'You were the only ex that mattered. You know that.'

'Mattered to you,' I said. But I said it quietly, and I pulled his body in to meet mine.

Afterwards, while Alexis showered, I lay on my elbows staring at my phone screen. I listened for the sound of the water falling, thought of him naked, turning his face up. Then I did what I had for so many years *not* been doing. I searched for her name. The phone took a long time to refresh and I felt that I was making a terrible but unavoidable mistake. But it told me nothing, not even what I knew already. Several Hope Mitchells, living their blameless lives in unexceptional parts of the globe. Nothing that could refer to her.

I tried her brother. It took me a while to remember his name. A slight child, hiding in corners. Isaac. That was it. Again, nothing. I closed the window. When Alexis came in, I was listening to the wind. I didn't tell him what I had done.

*

In the office, the first thing I saw was Kai's blue glance, dropping to a puzzled frown. Danielle looked censorious, but I had told her I was going to the gym; she disapproves of that on principle. Also, her brief walk-out with the guy from HR has ended and she finds solace in dispensing ill-will.

Also, the customer campaign starts this week. And I was late.

Another thing I didn't tell Alexis: I worry how much Kai knows, or guesses, after my failed joke at the Christmas party. There's nothing explicit, just endless questions. How was my weekend? What did I get up to last night? How is Ryan? How are the kids? How was our *family* Christmas? It could be innocent. My head says not, but then my head says a lot of things.

Today, Kai wouldn't shut up about the gym, which one I go to, what equipment it has, how I get there. I sat at my desk, examining our website, and lied. I do that so well now that I should put it on my CV.

Danielle interrupted. 'Take your time over your fitness chat, why don't you? It's not as though our real work is important.'

If sarcasm burned calories, my boss would look like Gigi Hadid. But I was glad all the same. The last thing I wanted was Kai trying to join my fictional gym. Then Graham went out, Danielle summoned me to his empty office, and I wasn't so glad after all.

'Look at this, please.'

I looked. It was an email I'd drafted earlier, desperate to get away. Danielle squashed her finger against the text. The nail still wore the remnants of Christmas nail varnish; the screen stretched in a distorted circle around the scratched red.

'Well?' she said.

'It's not the usual wording?'

'It's not the *agreed* wording.'

I hadn't checked. 'I thought it was close enough.'

She looked at me as though I'd committed treason. 'I'm sure it is,' she said, 'if you want to get us fined.'

I said nothing.

'You're lucky,' she said, 'that I spotted this before it went to Legal.'

I thought that was why we have Legal.

I swallowed. 'I'm sorry,' I said.

Her face became slightly more conciliatory. 'Laura,' she said. 'Is something wrong?'

First Ryan, now her. I stood with a hand on Graham's desk. I stared at veneered wood, at my own fingers, then at hers. 'What do you mean?'

'I *mean* that you're not doing your job properly. You were always quite efficient. Reliable.'

Thanks.

'Graham and I had high hopes for you.'

If so, that was the first I'd heard of them.

'Now you're all over the place. I don't know where your mind is, and I don't need to, but it's not here.'

My mind was in Alexis's bed, tracing his collarbone, his spine, the dip at the bottom of his back. Breathing love. 'I'm sorry,' I said, again.

Danielle sighed. Heavy is the head that has to answer to senior management. 'I'm afraid,' she said, 'that's not really enough.'

'Is this a warning?'

'It's a friendly chat,' she said. 'For now.'

When she let me go, skulking in her borrowed sanctuary, Kai's questions started again. About Ryan this time. So I went on the offensive and asked, compounding my lack of professionalism, about my colleague's love life. 'It's got to be more interesting than mine.'

That was a low blow, given the bedridden aunt. Beauty is nothing if you spend every night emptying bedpans.

'I did think about it for a while,' Kai said, manicured fingers flicking, then settling on the desk. 'Internet dating, you know. But it was never going to work.'

After that, at least, we were quiet.

29

Laura

9 March 2019

Alexis was alive in my sleep. Alive and young again, and I was too, a girl to his boy, lying close in wild flowers. Security flooded me like honey, heart to fingertips. As I woke, I fought my own consciousness, clinging as he was dragged away. I lay thinking I would pay any price – pay my own life – for the drug that would keep me in that dream. Then I reached out and felt the furry exterior of Evie's onesie and knew that I could not. I waited with my hand on her stomach, rising and falling, reminding me that I must breathe too, until the breath was all.

When I woke again, it was light and Benjy was standing like a phantom beside me, crying because he'd wet the bed. I pulled off wet pyjamas, pulled him in wee-sticky beside me. I hoped I'd sleep a third time, but I didn't.

*

There's still washing, even in desolation. I was hanging out Benjy's sheets, dropping pegs, when the police rang. Sergeant Morse, telling me to come to the station.

'I have the children,' I said. 'My husband has left me.'

She didn't comment on this revelation, only pointing out that I could leave them with someone else. 'Their brother, for example.'

She rang off and I stood mute with a pillowcase in my hand, looking at the unpruned apple tree. I wondered if Ryan would prune it. I wonder it still. I wonder if he will live here, or I will. But I cannot deal with any of that today: the weight of now is too much for me.

In the end, I did get Simon off his computer and downstairs to keep an eye on the children. 'What do the police want?' he said. But I hadn't even bothered to ask. I knew they wouldn't tell me until I got there. And even then they'd keep me waiting.

I was wrong about that. Esme Morse retrieved me from the foyer almost before I could sit down, and Capaldi was waiting in the interview room. It was the same one as before. I recognised a coffee stain on the wall. At least, I hope it was coffee.

The inspector looked rougher than usual. Maybe she'd run out of her usual shade of lipstick; maybe she was working too hard to bother. She greeted me perfunctorily, gestured to a chair. The sergeant did the 'do you want a lawyer?' spiel, then offered me water. I didn't rate tea this time.

'We know about your previous relationship with Alexis,' Capaldi said. 'We know you were boyfriend and girlfriend at school.'

Of course they did. Something else I should have predicted. Who had told them? Diana, probably.

I said, 'It was twenty years ago. A schoolkid thing.'

'From what we've heard, it was pretty serious.'

I tried to smile. 'Don't you always think that, at seventeen?'

She didn't smile back. 'How did it end?'

'He went to Paris,' I said. 'How can this matter now?'

Except, of course, I felt certain that it did.

'We heard . . .' the sergeant pretended to read her notes, 'that the relationship ended and *then* he moved away.'

'Maybe,' I said.

Capaldi sighed, stretched out narrow feet. 'Something more decisive would be helpful.'

'I'm sorry,' I said. 'It was a long time ago.' I frowned, as though I had to try to remember. As if I could ever *not* remember. I heard his voice, husky from days of crying. *I'm sorry, Laura. I'm so sorry.* I heard his footfall, ghost-quiet, on my parents' lawn. I smelled the damp soil. I heard my own screaming sobs into the turf.

'He ended it,' I said.

It was a game now: tell the truth but conceal everything.

'And that upset you?' Capaldi said.

'Jesus.' I started to laugh. 'So I tracked him down after nearly two decades, never mind that it was *his* daughter who joined *my* children's nursery. I entrapped him into a relationship purely in order to kill him, and I did this all because he dumped me when we were teenagers. That's quite some story.'

'Your story, not ours,' Esme Morse said.

Capaldi flicked invisible dust off one fuchsia claw. She said, 'He might have wanted to break up with you again.'

I stopped laughing. '*I* tried to end it,' I said. 'I tried, and I couldn't do it.'

I realised I wasn't helping myself, began again. 'Alexis and I were . . .'

I thought what I had thought once before. *More myself than I am.* But these were erudite women. I already knew that. No playing smart to distract myself.

'I loved him,' I said, at last. 'We loved each other.'

I swear Capaldi rolled her eyes. The sergeant said, 'Why did he terminate your relationship at school?'

Terminate?

'I don't know,' I said. 'I told you. It was a long time ago.' So much for telling the truth. 'It was different then. We were younger. I think his mum wanted him in Paris. And it was *Paris*, for crying out loud. What seventeen-year-old wouldn't rather live there than some nondescript Midlands town?'

I ached with the disloyalty.

Capaldi said, 'Laura, Alexis died for a reason. Don't you want to know what that reason is?'

Morse said, 'Unless you already do.'

Another silence. The sergeant said, 'We'll be speaking to his parents tomorrow.'

I shrugged. *How much do they know?* A bit, probably, from his grandparents. Not everything. Nothing from Alexis himself. And they never met me.

Still I said nothing. They let me go after that.

Walking along Melville Terrace, I searched for churches on

my phone. I couldn't name the one the Mitchells attended, but I could find it on a map. It wasn't huge, our town, and Hope had pointed out the tower once as we walked about. I can still remember the expression on her face.

Later, Alexis had pointed it out too. Later still, I had gone the long way round to avoid it, just as I did the bridge, or her house, or his grandparents'.

I stopped and stared at the number on my screen, willing myself to press the dial button, until someone walked into me and swore. I apologised, found a bench and sat on it watching a poodle taking a crap among the spring flowers, until I could make myself put the call through. After two rings, I cut it off. My hand was quivering.

The dog owner stooped with a bag over her hand, gave me a defensive look as though I was the 'bin it' police. I suppose I looked like I was, holding my phone and gaping. I got up and ran.

I ran along and down, past the towering tenements and parked cars of Marchmont, the mansions of the Grange. I didn't stop until I was by the gates to Blackford Pond, shins jolted, breath stinging. Then I moaned aloud, because I hadn't meant to go that way.

I pulled the phone out of my pocket, watching the path that Alexis and I had walked. I touched the dial button again, not giving myself time to reflect. It rang a long time, then went to voicemail. A woman, middle-aged, capable. I heard my own voice, stretched with suppressed sobs. I left my name, my number. Would they please call me? I needed to contact one of their past parishioners.

When I rang off, I was shaking again.

25 September 2018

From: Khaleesi8690

To: AlwaysHaveParis

Subject: Tonight and other things

Morning!

I was just laughing, cleaning the toilet.
That never happens. I blame you :)

Also distracted because there's a job
I want to apply for and I can't decide
whether to do it! Can we talk it through
tonight? (If we have time ;))

xx

30

Hope

19 February 1999

The hall is crammed with plastic chairs, rows so tight that they tangle when you pick them up. (I know because we have to stack them afterwards.) The teachers stand to the side like armies lining up. Claire is on my left, forced close so I can feel her arm hot through her jumper. The boy to my right keeps an inch between us, but I can still smell him.

On the stage, Old Flop is trumpeting his eulogy on Mark. He's made an effort. He's wearing his graduation robes, which usually look stupid. His shoes shine like black boiled sweets.

'A GOOD friend,' he proclaims, 'a BRILLIANT student, a WONDERFUL actor . . .'

None of it is true and no one thinks it is, though two girls punctuate his sentences with sobs. One of them is Stacy; I can't see the other.

We listen, though, because we're on edge for what he will say next. Speculation shifts, flows. Was the lorry driver drunk?

Was Mark? Was he doing stunts? Have the police been back in secret?

I would like to know that last myself.

Rick and I were everyone's best mates for a day or so. Until we failed to get arrested or put the driver behind bars.

Flop disappoints, too. He glides mid-sentence from Mark alive to Mark dead. The phrase 'tragic accident' is uttered and the atmosphere of expectancy dies with it. He lets falls the orator pose, assumes one of loving concern. He mentions the family, gives details of the funeral. It'll be heaving, since anyone going gets a day off school.

He jumps tone again, paternal-fond to paternal-reproving. His new theme is cycling safety, road safety, Taking Proper Care. The school has asked the town's one and only bike shop to run maintenance workshops. More times are given, more dates. Some pupils yawn, others open diaries or write times in biro on their hands. Some of the teachers exchange looks. Too soon, I suppose. Or not soon enough.

Poor Mark, to have this last word a reprimand for a carelessness. Or almost the last word, since when Old Flop is done, he summons Mr Balmore onto the stage for an announcement about *West Side Story*.

Balmore doesn't try to top the eulogy. He knows the moment has passed. He insists that Mark will be missed by cast and crew, then slides straight to the 'but'. The show will go on. He says he's talked to the other teachers, Mark's parents, the principals.

I look for Laura and see her two rows ahead, her head tilting upwards to Alexis, then straight again. Her ponytail hangs like a plumb line down her spine. She didn't say anything to me. But then I've hardly seen her.

Balmore goes on. Riff will be recast. He's confident they've made the right decision. I remember him at the first rehearsal: *Nobody is indispensable.*

Old Flop nods, like a judge pronouncing a verdict. 'I'm sure that's what Mark would have wanted.'

I'm not.

Balmore goes on, with a little cough. There will be no auditions. He still has his notes from last time. He and Mrs Henderson will discuss the new casting over the weekend.

No Miss Pendleton, I notice. She's at the end of my row, face turned down. I wonder if she's angry, but there's no time to stare, because the assembly ends and the teachers tramp out. We sit fidgeting until they are gone, then rise in rows to fight the chairs.

At the back of the hall, I find Rick beside me, arching his chair onto a wobbly pile. There's a piece of chewing gum fused to the leg; he swears in Italian when his hand grazes it. Then he takes my chair from me and pitches it up on top.

I stare at him.

'What?' he says.

He's the only boy in the school who would do that for me, but I can't say that. 'Nothing,' I say. 'Thanks.'

As we squeeze out of the hall, he tells me, 'You should be Riff.'

I don't know how to react. From Mark it would have been an insult; from Rick, I'm pretty sure it's not. I jerk my school bag up my arm.

'I don't have the qualifications,' I say.

'You've got the best voice of all the extras. Better than poor Mark's, come to that.' Rick winces, then turns it into a grin. 'Much better than mine.'

He's making a decent job of Bernardo. I should tell him so, but I'm trapped by this new idea.

'I'm a girl,' I say.

'So?' We're in the corridor now, by the rows of lockers. Rick edges round two first-years, stretching up for their books. 'They've cast girls as Jets; why not the gang leader? The songs could be transposed.'

His voice is casual. He has no idea what vistas he is opening up for me. 'Nice idea,' I say. 'But Balmore would never go for it.'

'Ask him.'

I shake my head. I'm sick with excitement and with trying to hide it. But Rick is looking pensive. 'Yeah, I suppose that might count against you. *I'll* ask him, if you like.'

As I walk away, I'm still dazed by the kindness.

Outside, I put my hands to my face, trace the ridgelines of spots. Still there – still the first thing anyone will see – but so much better now. Five in a line along my chin; a few dying half formed on my forehead. I think of the scenes Riff has with Tony. The extra rehearsals. I let imagination pull me close, wrap me in its deceitful hold. I see myself on stage with Alexis, hands clasped, sharing applause. It only takes a minor revision of my original dream. I see him bending his head to kiss me, in the wings.

In the vision, Laura is not there.

I don't have long with my cloud castles. I see Rick two

classes later, when I'm walking with Jem from history. I'm going to the locker room; she's looking for a better offer, eyes flicking about like a hungry lizard even as she answers my question about concealers. Rick is striding in the other direction, his face redder than usual.

He stops when he sees me. 'Sorry, Hope.'

'No go?' I'm not surprised. If I want to puke, it's not shock; it's because I'd fabricated a future on this plan I never thought would hold.

'He said it was none of my business,' Rick says. 'Bastard,' he adds, gesturing back up the corridor.

'It was kind of you,' I say, plucking truth from my crashing citadels.

He shrugs. 'Pointless, though. Sorry. Maybe try yourself. He can't say it's not *your* business.'

He can say worse than that, I think. Then I see that Mr Balmore is still by the staff room door, where Rick must have cornered him, and Miss Pendleton is with him. Rick probably wants rid of me now, embarrassed by his own anger. Jem is giving him sideways glances like he's the fat fly she's been tracking but is too timid to swallow.

'OK,' I say. 'Thanks.'

I don't look back to see if Jem makes her move. I'm watching the teachers. I can't see Balmore's face, but his shoulders are rigid. I can see Miss Pendleton's and it's as pale as Rick's was ruddy. As I get nearer, I hear my name.

I think I expected it. I step back, hide behind a screen of sports photos. Miss Pendleton is talking very fast. Cross-casting, innovation, fairness, courage. 'People would sit up and listen,' she says.

They'd sit up and look.

I hear the words, in the long silence, as though he had said them. Balmore shuffles his feet. I hug the pain tight against me.

Miss Pendleton says, '*Well?*'

The feet snap still.

'I've already made my decision,' he says. 'And to be honest, Shaina, I don't welcome your interference.'

Shaina. I consider this. It suits her. But it can only distract me for a moment

She says, 'Hope is the most talented singer we have.'

It's true, but it makes me like her. Balmore gives a theatrical sigh. 'This, if you'll forgive me, is why I'm the director. There's such a thing as stage presence. I look for that too.'

I think of Stacy, of Laura, of all the Shark and Jet hangers-on with their good legs and pretty faces and perky boobs in low dresses. Miss Pendleton – *Shaina* – says sharply, 'Is that what you call it?'

You can tell a lot from the back of a head. From Balmore's, I'd say he wants to hit her. Maybe she sees the same from the front, because she changes tack. 'Just let her audition,' she says.

'She already did,' Balmore says. 'She shouldn't be Riff.'

She looks him in the eye. I can tell because of her voice, and because his feet are doing their shuffle dance again.

'No,' she says. 'Hope should be Anita. We both know that.'

Her outrage is like Rick's kindness: it succours and sears me at the same time.

I don't hear Balmore's reply. I see him stamp past and hear the staff room door thump shut behind her. A crowd of younger kid pass by and I slip among them, let myself be drawn along the corridor. Above their heads, I watch Balmore's fake thatch out of view and hear Miss Pendleton's last words, over and over, as clear as if they came through headphones.

I *should* be Anita.

I hate him now too.

8 October 2018

From: Khaleesi8690

To: AlwaysHaveParis

Subject: I got the job!

I'm over the moon! They want me to
start next week, which will be a bit
of a challenge to organise, but I'm too
excited to care.

Thanks for all the support; it made a
big difference.

Celebration later?

xx

PS You must be my lucky star. I feel
like everything is falling into place.

31

Laura

9 March 2019

The house was empty. The children's coats were stripped from the hooks by the door; their voices sounded in my mind like ghosts. Simon's school shoes had fallen from the rack and lay askew where they had landed. I checked my phone, found a message from Ryan.

> I'll bring them back tomorrow afternoon.
> Text if any problems.

No kiss. I sagged to the floor, my back bumping down cabinets, sat heavy on the hard tiles. The heating had gone off, but my coat was on. I could stay there all day and all night, and no one would know. I closed my eyes, felt the cold seep up through my thighs. I was hungry, but it was too hard to move.

My phone beeped. Simon. He'd sent me a picture of Benjy and Evie in what looked like an adventure playground.

Evie was wearing Ryan's hat. I stared at them a while as though they were someone else's children. But they got me out of my still despair.

I messaged him back with thanks and kisses. I kept my phone in my hand, redialled the last number: Hope's church. This time a man answered. Middle-aged, at a guess. Accented, possibly Caribbean. I'd expected the woman from the answerphone, and for a moment I lurched off course, wordless.

'Hello?' he said, a second time; and then, 'Are you all right?'

Perhaps he was the vicar. Perhaps he remembered Hope.

'My name is Laura Reville,' I said. *I'm not all right.*

When I told him who I was looking for, he said it was before his time but he'd ask. The phone was muffled. I heard voices. Another man, a woman – the answerphone woman, I think. It took a long time. Then he was back, his voice muted.

'Were you close to the family?' he asked.

What a question. 'My parents were,' I lied. 'But they lost contact. I promised my mum I'd look them up.'

'Well . . .' he said. Then he began again. 'It's rather a sad story. My colleagues have been filling me in. They say there was an accident.'

Cold nausea, launching in waves. I shrank into the cabinet door. Why hadn't I anticipated that he would try to tell *that* story?

I flailed for words, found them, threw them out. 'I know. You don't need . . . I know that bit already.'

God only knows what my voice told him. It was, after

all, the truest thing I could have said. I put a hand on the cold floor, breathed in to my fingertips. 'I was wondering what happened afterwards,' I said. 'I know they left.'

'The boy was sent away to relatives, somewhere south.'

I hadn't known that. But it made sense.

'John Mitchell died,' he said.

'How?' I asked, and I felt the reluctance, of this kind man, as though it was a visible thread down the line.

'He hanged himself,' he said at last.

'Oh God.'

'Yes. It is very sad.'

'And Mrs Mitchell?'

The vicar went off to ask. When he came back, he said, 'My churchwarden has an address for her somewhere. Can we call you back?'

'Please.' I gave my number, forgetting it was on his answerphone.

I thought he would ring off, but he didn't. He said, '*Are you all right, Mrs Reville?*'

No. 'Yes,' I said. 'Thank you.' My voice sounded like it came from my own grave.

'Well then,' he said. 'You take care of yourself.'

'Thank you,' I said again, and I sat staring at my silent phone, crying without a sound.

32

Laura

17 January 2019

I crave time with Alexis, the way some people crave pain. I fumble through the days, hunting minutes, snatching at them, watching them pulled away from me. My lunch breaks are swallowed by meetings, extra tasks, endless reminders of regulatory rules. Danielle is implacable as concrete; Graham, behind her, is a mute threat. Ryan works all hours and Simon goes almost nightly to Bella's.

Am I a bad parent, to let him? Probably. But Ryan doesn't stop him either. He sees, as I do, the boy who came still-eyed out of counsellors' offices, a solitary waif, stuck in time, who could not forgive himself for what he could not help.

I *am* a bad parent, but not because of Bella.

For days, I've been angry with Ryan, angrier because I know all this and because the alternative is to be furious with myself. I have snapped at him for working the hours we once agreed together, chided him for abandoning me with the childcare, the chores. Yesterday Benjy heard me and his face blanched as though I had rejected him. I held him to me, daubed him with endearments, hissed over his head at my husband as though this too were his fault.

Then I carried on anyway.

I've asked Mhairi to have the kids, more often than I can count. Last Friday she said yes to an hour after school, which became three because I couldn't get out of the office, and then Alexis's bed was warm, and he kissed me on the collarbone as I was trying to leave. The next time, Monday, she said no. Even that didn't stop me. I went out in trainers in the bitter dark, waiting by the door when Ryan opened it, just after nine.

'I need to run,' I told him, as though he would object if I let him. 'You've always known that.'

But I ran only to the main road, sprinting, hearing things that were not there. Or probably weren't. I hailed a cab. Half an hour with Alexis, so eager for each other that we barely pulled off our clothes, hardly had time to speak. Then another taxi back. I've started to wonder if the drivers are watching me.

Today I worked from home, defying Danielle. Alexis came to me in the afternoon, pushed two doors hard shut behind him, held me in his arms. I felt his chin on my cheek, curled myself into his coat.

'Christ,' he said. 'I've missed you.'

I wriggled back, tilted up my face. 'How did you get out of work?' I said.

'Dentist.'

I laughed, touched a finger to his mouth, waited to be

kissed. But he wasn't laughing, and he didn't kiss me. His arms had loosened as though a lever had been pulled. He was looking round.

After Evie was born, Ryan's sister had a collage made for us, with the names of the five of us engraved on a silver tree. For my husband's fortieth, I'd given him a print: one of those montages in a brazen font of all the places that matter to you both. In the middle, *EDINBURGH*, in giant letters, shouted its significance to the life I had forged without Alexis. The one we were stealing from Ryan.

Alexis slipped from my hold, walked from one framed picture to the other. I watched him, knowing I shouldn't have asked him here. Another line crossed, unforgivable to contemptible. In a minute, I thought, we would go upstairs to the bed where Ryan still tries, intermittently, to caress me – the bed where I had conceived my babies – and we would consume each other there.

We'll make ourselves sordid.

Alexis turned to me with opaque eyes. I went to him, took his hands. I wanted him still, so much my body was screaming. But for the first time I wanted – really wanted – not to want him.

If he looked past me now, he would see holiday photos stretching up the stairs. Wedding pictures in the sitting room. The other way, the kitchen, my children's artwork on every cabinet door.

He gazed down at me. 'Not here, Laura,' he said. 'Whatever we are, we're not so bad as that.'

He kissed me on the forehead, lips as hot as that first night in Advocates Close. On his way out, he picked up the letters lying where they had landed on the porch floor. *Mrs Laura Reville. Mr and Mrs R. Reville.* He looked at the envelopes, handed them to me, went without another word.

I did not try to make him stay. I went back and traced the names on our tree picture with the finger that Alexis had not kissed. Ryan and me on the branches, the three children on bright leaves. When it arrived, I had worried that Simon would be upset by this erasure of his own mother. But he had held the picture to the light and showed me a shadow tree behind, so pale it almost vanished into the white background. 'She's there,' he had said. His aunt had talked to him. This had been his idea.

'Why aren't you at work?'

I jumped. Simon was coming into the hall, school bag already sliding to the floor. I hadn't even heard him open the door.

'Jesus,' I said. 'You startled me. What are you doing back?'

'Free period.'

'Aren't you meant to stay at school?'

He shrugged. 'No one does. Anyway, you haven't answered my question.'

'I'm working from home.'

He scowled. 'Looks like it.'

But he stood next to me, studying the picture. I put an arm around him and for once was not pushed off. My mind spiralled with what-ifs. I looked from Simon's face – Ryan's face – to his name in cursive on a leaf.

I thought how I had held him, that long-ago day, giddy with love and relief. How he and I had stood in this exact spot together, Evie sleeping in her sling on my chest, while Ryan took Benjy on his balance bike to the park. How Simon had hammered the nail into the wall, hung the picture carefully straight, and kissed his sister on her fluffy head.

I thought, *I cannot hurt you.*

'You hadn't shut the door properly,' he said, sounding like Ryan. 'You should be more careful.'

'I will be,' I said.

33

Hope

22 February 1999

The spots are down to three this morning, last men standing. In the bathroom, where the door has a lock, I open the concealer. I got it on Saturday when I was allowed out to run an errand for Her. We get birthday money from Father's parents, and occasionally he gives me some. I think he knows that other girls my age can buy things for themselves. He doesn't tell me not to get anything She would notice. He doesn't need to.

The concealer isn't perfect. The way my face was before, it would have been nothing, a shower cap in a storm, but now it's enough. I step back from the gaudy cabinet light, turn my face one way and then the other. I have not seen it unmaimed for so many years that I cannot stop staring. I am not beautiful, but I'm not hideous.

I am made foolhardy by success.

Isaac is at the table when I get down, eating porridge with his head bent. She has her back to me, arranging cutlery. My brother looks up, then down again. It's warning enough. I murmur good morning, try to sit down as though I wasn't there. I know She has heard me, though She doesn't say anything. I look for Father, but he has left.

We eat in silence, wincing at every clang of spoon on bowl. I hear myself chew. When I am done, I take my bowl to the sink. She looks at me and the wincing becomes a curl of fear.

She says, 'What have you done to your face?'

'Nothing,' I say. I think of the pills, twist inside. I tell myself that acne must sometimes get better on its own.

She cannot prove it, I think. *She cannot prove anything*. But She never cares about proof. Besides, it's not the missing blemishes that concern Her today; it's what I have done with the ones that remain. She pushes a finger under my lip, rubs it hard along, pressing the spots so I jump with pain. She stares at Her finger, grips me by the ear and yanks me under the light.

'Make-up,' She says.

Isaac stops in the doorway, then scuttles into the hall as though he will be contaminated by my crime. She pushes Her finger against my chin again, until I squirm away. I don't cry. It wouldn't do any good.

'Take it off,' She says.

I run upstairs. My handiwork is already destroyed. The spots, angry at ill-treatment, are redder than ever. With a flannel, I rub away the remaining concealer. Downstairs, She says, 'Give it to me.'

I hand over the silver tube. She holds it between two fingers, plunges it deep into the bin. I wait. She takes my wrist between Her two hands. Sinewy fingers. Red knuckles. Nails cut to the quick. She twists them, opposite directions, until I scream. Then She goes on a bit more.

I can get another concealer. But I'll have to be more careful.

By lunchtime, my wrist has stopped hurting. We gather in the hall to get measured for costumes. Four mums, roped in by Balmore, are chatting in a corner, notebooks and tape measures in front of them. I knew this was happening, but I wish it wasn't today.

Balmore sneaks the new Riff in between fulsome thanks to the mums and instructions to us. Mark's replacement is a hefty fifth-year, upgraded from the Jets. There's some logic to it. He looks every inch the gangland thug, and to be fair, he's not as bad at dancing as Mark was. Balmore presents him without conspicuous rapture, which could be because of me but is more likely because of Mark.

Rick rolls his eyes.

One of the costume mums is Laura's. She smiles when she gets to me, hugs me to her, smiles again when she sees my face.

'Hope,' she says, 'you look wonderful.' A serious exaggeration. But the words, or the embrace, almost bring tears to my eyes. I say hi, then lift my arms for her to measure chest and waist.

Close to, she says, 'I'm so glad you found something that worked. I know it was troubling you.'

I say thank you. At least I think I do. She looks at the tape measure, writes something down. 'We haven't seen you for ages,' she says. 'I hope you'll be round again soon.'

I don't know what to reply. I look at Laura. She's already been measured and is waiting with Alexis, watching as Rick stands off against the new Riff. Her hair touches Alexis's shoulder; their hands are knotted together. I turn my face back, but Laura's mum has seen.

'I've been busy,' I say.

She finishes measuring in silence, but hugs me again before she lets me go. There's a crinkle in her forehead, like she wants to say more, but in the end she just tells me, 'Don't be a stranger.'

I walk away across the hall, wondering what she'll say to Laura. Or if she'll say anything at all.

I open my sandwiches alone at the back, unfurl my own mother's words of love.

> *Charm is deceptive, and beauty is fleeting; but a woman who fears the LORD is to be praised.*
> *(Proverbs 31:30)*

She's never warned me against beauty before. It's almost a compliment.

I'm still thinking about Laura's mum as we practise the Dance at the Gym. I don't realise I'm getting the steps wrong until Mr Balmore yells at me. I don't realise I'm still doing it until the whole group stops.

'Hope Mitchell,' he says, 'are you in a different show? You do know the point of being a team is stay *in* the team?'

The mums look up from their lists. Even Mrs Henderson seems surprised. My face blazes. Laura stops mid-spin with Rick, glances over her shoulder at me. She's surprised too. But I'm not, and I know Rick isn't.

176

Obsessed

I don't know how Rick feels, but I'm angry.

I wait all afternoon, enduring classes. Then I stand outside Balmore's classroom, out of sight, until I see him strutting off to rehearsal.

The corridor empties and I dive in. The room is as the students left it, chairs akimbo. I skirt desks, heading for the cubbyhole at the back. It's unlocked, like I hoped it would be. Maybe he was in a hurry. Or perhaps he thinks his students love him too much to pry. Well, he can think again.

Inside, I flick on the light, push the door shut and look around. It's barely more than a cupboard. Lots of books. Plays mostly, but novels too. A pile of essays. A smell that I trace to a bowl of apples, browning by the essays. Coffee and a mug, clean. A chair, which I stand on to scan the upper shelves.

I don't know what I'm looking for. Something incriminating, I suppose. Pictures of Laura's bum or Stacy's breasts, snapped furtively in rehearsal. He spends enough time looking at them. Or, failing that, actual porn. But there's nothing like that. There *are* two photos, but they're on display on a lower shelf. One is his wife. Thin, like a pretty ferret, simpering in a yellow dress.

She picked him up from rehearsal once. She's just as skinny now, and even more ferrety. Less pretty, though.

I'm more interested in the other photo, mainly because it's old and hopefully irreplaceable. It was black and white once, I suppose, but now it's brown and bumpy behind the glass. It's a family – two boys, a woman and a man – on a park bench. The smaller boy is on his mother's knee. The father has his arm around the older one. They're all beaming.

I stare at this a long time. I don't know which of the boys is Mr Balmore. Technically, I don't know if *either* of them is. But I feel sure it's the younger one, smug against his mother's breast. I knock the frame, sweeping it with the back of my hand, jump when it hits the floor.

It lands face down. I lift it by a corner, but the glass is unbroken.

I hear footsteps. For an instant, I am held still. Then I move, quicker than I thought I could. I stand against the door, holding the handle. It's a flaky ruse, but it's all I've got. I think of Mark, breathing rancour and cheesy crisps, calling me a peeping Tom. But whoever it is, they just come into the classroom, take something, go out again.

I wait some more. Nothing. I slide to my knees and turn the picture over. The mother is smiling down at the boy in her lap, like Laura's mum smiled her goodbye earlier. I stand up again, hands unsteady. There's a paperweight on the essays, a glass lump with a model theatre inside it. I pick it up, enjoy it heavy in my palm. Kneeling again, I bang it into the picture. The glass breaks. I do it again, just hard enough that I don't cut my hand. It takes a third go, pushing the broken glass inward, before I get what I want. A clear shard cuts through the boy and his mother, slashing the old print, piercing them head to heart.

I'm shaking.

I clasp the paperweight, afraid and excited. Then I wipe it all over on my grey skirt and put it back on the essays. I take another look at the photo, turn it over, and wipe the edges of the frame.

*

I don't go straight home. Instead, I walk to Laura's house and stand on the street outside. Buds are starting on the tree by the gate. Snowdrops are out in the garden and daffodils just opening in pots by the front door. Laura is out, rehearsing. But her mother is in. I see her moving about the kitchen. I can't hear, because the windows are shut, but I've been there so often, I know she'll be listening to the radio.

She looks so like Laura.

I wait, thinking she'll look up and see me. If she asked me in, perhaps I would go. Perhaps I would tell her everything, or almost. But she doesn't. She pours herself a cup of tea, takes something from a tin on the side, reaches out to where I know the radio is. Then she goes out of the room. I watch for five minutes, but she doesn't come back. I walk almost to the front door. I see my finger, pressing down on the bell. I see the door opening. I see a future expanding from that widening doorway. Social workers and questions, and Her word against mine, and everyone at school looking and talking about me.

Isaac wouldn't say anything; my father would pretend he doesn't know.

I walk backwards down the path, along the pavement. Then I run.

34

Laura

23 January 2019

Today I asked Anja to stay longer after bringing the kids home. I told Benjy and Evie at drop-off. 'Mummy loves you,' I said, piling kisses, lavish with guilt, 'but I have to work late.'

They like Anja: they were excited. I don't know if that made me feel better or worse. Yazzie glared at me, but that was nothing new. I messaged Simon and Ryan from the bus to tell them, added that I'd left the cash out for Anja. I told myself it was OK because I was paying her. It wasn't like making Mhairi do it or keeping Simon from Bella. Although doubtless I'll do both of those again soon enough.

I did work late. I had little choice. Danielle tracks our every move, then darts into Graham's office with a checklist of what we haven't achieved. Kai's lovely face is gaunt-edged, which might be stress – or might just be an unsatisfactory home life.

I met Alexis late, at the Pear Tree. A student pub, alive and noisy, even on a Wednesday night. I picked it thinking there would be no one we knew there. But I wondered, standing close to Alexis, what the students made of us. Two lecturers, maybe, having an illicit drink.

'They probably think we're parents,' Alexis said, handing me a gin and tonic, 'visiting students.'

A sobering idea. We could have been. Just. If things had been very different.

Some of those kids drinking beers and artisan spirits tonight were almost as young as we were then. A couple sat near us, fresh-minted lovers, hands held in the middle of the table, heads close. Her hair was the copper of a new penny; he had a narrow, dark face, gravely beautiful. I stared at them, poleaxed by self-pity, until Alexis put a hand on my back and steered me to a free table. I don't know if he saw them.

We met there because I wanted to make a point, after last time; to reclaim our relationship. It is about the sex. It always has been. But it's not *all* about it. It's about a thousand clichés, stripped of their Hallmark triviality. It's about the fact that we can hardly breathe without each other.

Only it didn't work, if that was what I was trying to prove. In that pub, chaperoned by strangers, with students pushing and laughing and eating chips, I longed to touch him, to feel him, to hold him, close inside me. I wanted to tell him that. I wanted to ask him if he had seen the thin boy and the girl with the brilliant hair, who gripped each other as though they had found paradise on a January night. I wanted to ask him what he remembered most about the way we were before.

Instead, I asked, 'Do you ever go to church now?'

He started. Beer swelled in the glass, trickled onto his hand. 'No,' he said. 'Not for years. I went last for my grandparents' funerals.'

I'd known they were dead, had held his face in my hands and kissed him when he told me, weeks since. Now, I let my hand brush his across the table.

'The same church?' I said, and he nodded with his face closed.

'That can't have been easy,' I said.

We had only one drink, then walked through the cold dark to his flat. Leaving the pub, I looked back at the couple near the bar. They were kissing, joined across their empty drinks. His hand was in her hair, nails showing through the metallic strands.

Nothing seemed wrong, until we reached the flat door. The stairs were dull and empty, doors shut. But Alexis frowned with the key in the lock.

'What is it?' I said.

'I don't know. It feels . . . different.'

He yanked out the key. The door swung open. In the muted light from the stairwell, I saw the floor strewn with objects, heard Alexis's quick inhalation, saw his hand go to the switch. Then the disorder lay before us in merciless light. Coats and shoes were on the floor, the row of hooks pulled half out of the wall, hanging by clinging screw-ends, plaster in crumbled piles below. Further in, pictures lay face down on the floorboards.

'Jesus,' he said.

We tiptoed, stretching feet over tumbled garments. The sitting room was the same, worse even, with books swept off the shelves, spine-open on the floor. The TV was on the ground, wrenched off its stand. The kitchen was worse again, cutlery scattered, glasses smashed. In the study, the drawers had been tugged from the desk. The laptop was open, its screen a mosaic of cracks. Papers lay everywhere. Alexis lifted his passport, pulling it open from a pile in a corner. He stood with his hands unmoving, his face white as the wall behind him.

I stood close to him, looked down. The picture page had been cut, straight across his face.

In the bedroom, I started coughing, then retching. The blinds had been pulled off the window; books covered the floor. Pillowcases were ripped. The duvet huddled half empty on the floor. Sheet and cover, cut to pieces, were scattered on the bare mattress. Down was over everything. As we went in, it shifted, feathers floating in clouds towards us.

The blanket, sky grey, had been cut into four pieces. They lay now with the massacred sheet, unravelling at the severed edges. Alexis picked up one of the quarters, held it to his face. 'My grandmother made this,' he said.

The scissors were on the floor, still open. I bent to pick them up, stopped myself, started coughing again. 'We should leave it,' I said, when I could speak. 'Not touch anything.'

But I touched him. I wrapped my arms around him, kissed the pulse in his neck. 'Oh God,' I said. 'I'm so sorry.'

The door to Gracie's room was shut. I felt Alexis's fingers tighten in mine. Then he pushed it open, flicked the light. I closed my eyes, opened them, gripped his hand.

But the room was untouched: books on the shelves, characters from *Moana* dancing round the walls, yellow curtains closed. The bed was made, toys piled up on it, waiting for her. Alexis dropped my hand. He pushed back the toys, peeled back covers, checked under the pillow, then under the bed. At last he stood up, smoothed the cover flat, arranged the toys again. One of the bears fell over and he picked it up, held it, settled it as though it were his daughter he was resting on the pillow.

I didn't help. I had never been in that room before and I didn't think he would want me in it now. It was not my space.

He came back to me. Something had eased in his face. 'They had that much decency,' he said.

Or they were disturbed.

Neither of us said it. He held me in the ruined hall, so tight I felt the breath in his chest. He said, 'Tomorrow I can ask the neighbours. They might have seen something.'

'The police will do that.'

He waited: a long, taut pause. Then he spoke with his face in my hair. 'I'm not telling the police.'

I wriggled free, made him look at me. 'You have to. You'll never feel safe here. *Gracie* won't be safe here.'

'And if I called them?' He looked down at my hands, held them up to his chest. 'Laura, your fingerprints are everywhere. Do you want me to tell them you were here, and how often – and why?'

'Tell them I'm a friend from overseas. I came for dinner once.'

He looked at me. In his desolate eyes, I saw my hands

gripping the bed frame, my feet kicking out, my body turning under his.

'Tell them it was a one-night stand,' I said. 'Tell them I stayed the night, stayed for breakfast. You threw away my number. Anyway, I haven't touched that.' I pulled him towards the study door, gestured at the desk, split and pouring paper. 'There's plenty I never touched.'

'No,' he said. 'I'm not bringing you into it. I won't risk that.'

I watched his jaw and stopped arguing. I asked myself what he wasn't saying. I thought about what I wasn't.

'It's coincidence,' he said. 'And they'll never catch them anyway.'

We surveyed the broken flat, venom in every scattered sheet.

'I'll change the lock,' he said. 'I'll use the mortise lock, get bolts. If they had touched Gracie's room . . .' He let the sentence fall, seemed to realise the inconsistency of his arguments. 'There's no point,' he said.

I went to him, slid hands round his waist, waited word-less for his kiss. But later – much later, as I lay sleepless by my sleeping husband in a house that had not been sacked – I thought again of that little room with its yellow cur-tains, pristine behind a closed door. Reassurance? Perhaps. Or a warning.

35

Laura

9 March 2019

When Simon sent another photo, I got up off the floor. Benjy and Evie chocolate-mouthed in a café. She was in a highchair, marshmallow halfway to her lips. Benjy was eating milk froth with a spoon. *Babycinos*, Simon had captioned it, with a heart emoji. I sent three back, one for each of them. I plucked an apple from the fruit bowl, took a bite, felt it mealy in my dry mouth. I spat it into the sink. Upstairs, I pulled on running kit, shivering. Loud music on headphones, trainers tight-laced.

I ran fast. One foot in front of the other. Breathe. Breathe again. Into Braidburn Valley Park, where the path lies smooth and grey beside the burn and the grass stretches up, unthreatening, either side. Behind me, where I would not look, the stream dips below the road. A dark tunnel, promising adventure, which the children beg to explore.

I will never take them there. We would come out with the water in the sharp cuts and wooded shade of the Hermitage.

I slammed down my thoughts as though I were banging my finger on a remote control.

Ahead of me, the stream was innocent. Trees arranged like dancers on a stage. Little bridges where my children play Poohsticks. Dogs romping in the water. A girl Benjy's age, careering on a scooter. I veered off, ran steeply out of the park, past the sprawling bungalows of Greenbank, past iron fences and rhododendrons, sedate modern houses, and the clock tower, curved and lovely and incongruous, of what had once been a Poor House. I crushed thought with music. Lady Gaga. Modern and vivid and unreal. I made my lips mouth the words.

I went up Craiglockhart Hill because I thought it could not catch me with memory. Stumbling on roots, slipping on ground that had gone from mud to ice to mud again. Past an old wall, thick with ivy. Up and round and up, through trees – living and dead – and into open space and claggy sky. A child ran towards me, feet bright in scarlet wellies. I stopped to let him pass, finding a dead smile for his mother's thanks.

I looked left to the Pentlands, cloud-tipped, with their ski-slope scar, right to Corstorphine Hill with its pylon towers and the flash of the Forth bridges, white on grey, behind. I rotated, slowly, found the castle on its rocky peak. Calton Hill. Arthur's Seat. Blackford Hill. The Braids.

I have loved these Edinburgh hills, collected them like charms on a bracelet. Maybe one day they will comfort me again.

I found the Meadows, green among the grey roofs. I dipped south, and south again. I realised I was looking for Alexis's flat.

There is so much space in this city, but nowhere to hide from myself.

I ran on, on rock and mud and grass. I leaned gasping on the trig point and stared down through heavy tears. I thought, *I will never stop crying.*

Someone was talking to me. An accent, German perhaps, or Dutch. Irritated, and escalating. I looked round to see tourists bulky in winter jackets, arms around each other. The man was holding a phone at arm's length and scowling at me.

'Sorry,' I said. I fumbled aside, tripping, catching myself. The woman looked at me: dimly compassionate, a visitor at a zoo. I said it again – 'sorry' – although her companion had been rude.

I went down, legs wobbling, eyes salt-sharp, sliding on the treacherous path, catching at tree branches. I went on by the pavements, stopping with deep, sharp breaths at the edge of the main road.

You have to eat.

My own voice? Or my mum's? I had no idea.

In the shop, I threw bread and cheese into a basket and thought of my parents. I will have to tell them that Ryan, whom they trust, has left me. I will have to see my mother, shutting down the questions that she wants to ask. Tiptoeing round me again.

I added a bottle of wine. If exercise failed me, this was what I had left. At the till, I waved my phone at the reader and found the battery just dead. I pressed the power button, searched empty pockets for cash or card.

'I'm sorry,' I said, stilted, as though it were all I could ever say. 'I don't seem to be able to pay.'

The man shrugged and took the basket from me. I thought, *I've been in here a hundred times. Couldn't you trust me, just once?* In the doorway, a woman moved aside, shiny boots over new jeans. Glowing red hair. She didn't meet my eye.

I walked home, too drained to run, quickly cold. Outside the church, people crowded on the pavement. Laughing, calling kids back. There must have been a party. I walked on with my head half turned, listening to their joy. I pushed open our low gate, still not looking, tripped on the path edge and fell hard onto my knees.

I didn't call out. I curled there, where I was, forehead on stone, sobs jerking my ribs. It was easier that way.

I felt hands on my shoulders, heard a voice I recognised but couldn't place. I opened my eyes and knew that I was very cold. Mhairi was leaning over me, her scarf, soft as cotton wool, kissing my cheek. Behind the fence, her boys watched me with matching eyes.

I tried to speak, found myself gulping for air. Mhairi crouched on the path, warm hands finding mine. 'God, Laura. You look awful. Should I call an ambulance?'

I shook my head. I tried to say *I'm fine*, failed, and stared over the silence into her face. Her brows were perfect arcs.

'I'll call Ryan,' she said.

I shook my head again. The words came, stuttering. 'He's left me.'

'Shit.'

She looked across the fence at her sons, back at me. Then she hauled me to my feet.

She took me to her house, made me drink tea, then have a hot shower. It was like waking in a dream: my home, but not my home. She went off with my keys, brought me clothes, wrapped me in a shawl as soft as the mohair scarf. She sat her boys in front of a film, me at their kitchen table, fed us all pizza. When she put them to bed, I lay on her sofa, playing spot the difference, and afterwards she gave me wine. I talked. I told her what I had told the police. I watched her face, waiting for the sympathy to slip. It never did.

On the second bottle, her face blurred, coming back intermittently, distinct as a professional photo. She had gold studs in her ears, blusher that stayed on her cheekbones. I examined the tidy room, boys' reading books stacked with today's *Guardian* on the coffee table. Roses in a vase on the side, cat curled like an expensive cushion.

I said, 'I wish I were like you.'

For the first time, she sounded irritated. 'We all want love, Laura. Some of us just hide it better than others.' Then she grinned. 'I could tell you about my dating adventures some day. Only not now.'

I finished my glass, reached out for the bottle, remembered this wasn't my home. 'Help yourself,' Mhairi said. But when I cried again, curled like a foetus in her mother's shawl, she changed her mind and poured me water.

'I had a love,' I said, and then I said it over and over again, words falling into sobs, the mantra that had not saved me. Mhairi slid towards me along the sofa, unwound my hands from my knees, fixed them on the water glass. The cat got up, glowered amber-eyed, stretched, and left the room.

'You have to stop,' Mhairi said.

I took a long slug, then choked.

'Laura,' she said, when I had coughed myself to silence. 'You need professional help.'

15 October 2018

From: Khaleesi8690

To: AlwaysHaveParis

Subject: Thank you . . .

. . . for the flowers! That was
incredibly sweet, and sent me in for my
first day with a smile on my face.

It went well, I think. (Or hope, but
I'll fill you in later.)

xx

PS Confession time. I said something
about 'my boyfriend' today. You don't
mind, do you? That was all I said, but
I couldn't resist.

36

Hope

2 March 1999

We see Alexis after English. Laura darts to him like they've been separated for years. He spins her towards him and they stand close and still, dancers after a pirouette. It's as though they've been painted with light. Alexis looks through the glow at the rest of us. He acknowledges me, then Jem and Claire. His smile is beautiful, but it's not the one he gives Laura.

They turn away, going to the common room. Laura rotates her head, still ballerina-smooth, as his fingers settle on her waist. 'Coming?' she says.

That's enough for Jem. She scampers after them, levelling her hair with one hand, pulling her skirt over her bum with the other. She has no pride. Claire refuses, saying something about an essay.

'Hope?' Laura says.

If she meant it, everything might still be all right. But I know she doesn't. Her gaze touches me, her lids drop.

I shake my head. She shrugs, then moves away with Alexis. I feel sick.

I'm still watching when a group of first-years push past them, making for the classroom we've just left. Closer to, I see Isaac in the throng, with a friend from church. He's looking over his shoulder as he walks, to where Alexis and Laura are visible only as disembodied heads above the descending stair rail.

I duck my own head and follow Claire, pretending I haven't seen him.

Rehearsal is boring. I've given up waiting for a reaction from Mr Balmore, so I suppose I'll never know how he explained his smashed picture. I should be relieved, but I'm not.

I wanted to see his pain.

I stand among the extras, waiting unneeded for the new Riff to get his lines right. After the fifth attempt, Balmore roars at the rest of us to sit down. Rick lies across three chairs at the back of the hall and closes his eyes. Alexis stays on stage, getting flack himself when he tries to cover for the other boy's mistakes. I sit on the edge of my plastic chair and learn, at length, that Stacy has dumped her boyfriend and how painful this is for her. She's not telling me, of course. She's telling Laura, but I'm nearer than they realise. For Stacy, now that I don't even have horror-show value, I don't exist.

After rehearsal, I follow Laura and Alexis out. They shout goodbyes to Stacy, stepping into her mum's fancy car.

Laura shrieks, 'Take care of yourself,' so you'd think Stacy had suffered a searing grief instead of inflicting it.

Rick goes off fast. He waves me goodbye. None of the others even notice that I'm there.

I expect Laura and Alexis will go home together, but they don't, so I lurk by the wheelie bins to watch.

They snog in the dim orange circle of the automatic light. The bins are to one side, a fire escape to another. Gritty romantic, I suppose. Balmore should be setting *West Side Story* out here. I stand on tiptoes, getting a better view. It's not like Mark is going to jump out and stop me.

This close, the rubbish smells disgusting, fish and sour milk. I gag, but I don't move. Beyond, my ex-friends gleam like a billboard of a better life. In profile, Alexis looks like Jimmy Dean.

When their mouths unfuse, he says, 'I'll walk you home.'

'No,' she says. 'You'll be late already.'

Late for what? I wonder. He lifts his wrist. The watch screen is a blue patch, briefly bright. 'Oh God,' he says. 'You're right.'

'Of course.' She clings close, kisses him again. He says something into her neck, and for answer she laughs. 'Oh Alexis, I've been doing this walk since I was eleven years old. What is this? *Scream*?'

More kisses, more muffled argument. Then he goes. Steps quick, now he's given in. She picks up her bag from the floor, calls after him, 'Wish your grandpa a happy birthday from me.'

Mystery solved. He calls something back. Then the sound of his feet is absorbed in the traffic, and Laura thinks herself alone. She puts her rucksack on. She's humming as she does, only it's not Anita's song, it's Maria's. 'One Hand, One Heart'.

She sounds so happy.

I pull the bin, let it go. It lurches, pivoting on two wheels. Then it thuds back down. Laura jumps so hard her bag falls with another bang to the ground. I crouch, breathing the adrenaline.

She says, 'What was that?' Her voice is high but trying to be calm. 'Who's there?'

I could show myself now, as though I'd just come out from the building. I could act as surprised as she is. I could be shaken and friendly and walk home with her. I could build bridges or burn them.

'Who's there?' she says again.

Her fear slides into my stomach like a hot, sweet drink. I touch hard plastic to keep myself steady. I can see nothing now, just hear the cars buzzing and Laura's quick breath. Then there's a scrape and a fumbling. She must be picking up her bag.

Running feet. I wait a moment before I slip out. She's almost out of the far gate, stumbling, her rucksack lurching on each step like the bulge on a hunchback.

Not so poised now, I think.

After supper, when we're at the kitchen table with Bibles open, Isaac watches me. At last, the phone rings and She leaves the room, and he asks, 'Are Alexis and Laura going out?'

I don't look up. I want him to think I'm bored.

'I saw them today,' he says.

'Did you?' I say.

'They looked quite . . .'

I wonder what word he will find, but She has trained him well.

'. . . inappropriate,' he finishes.

I almost laugh, thinking how inappropriate I would like to be with Alexis. I do smile, since he's still looking at me. Then I stare at Revelations again.

'Something like that,' I say.

From: Khaleesi8690

To: AlwaysHaveParis

Subject: Your daughter is adorable

It was wonderful to meet Gracie at last! She's such a cutie. (No surprises there.) And yes, she's shy, but I really think we clicked.

Am I right? I hope I am.

xx

37

Laura

10 March 2019

I woke fuddled, reaching for the children. My hand found the cold pillow. Something else was wrong, too: I was still in my clothes. I pushed up, stomach spinning stale alcohol, then flopped back and reached for my phone. 4.30. Christ. There was a pint glass of water half drunk by the bed. I swallowed a little and the evening revealed itself to me, frame by merciless frame.

I lay hating myself. In that eviscerating loneliness, I almost called Mhairi, begging her to come round. Or my mum, to drive hundreds of miles, wrap me in clean sheets and feed me toast and boiled eggs. As though time had turned back, twenty years and more, to when she could still help me. I imagined phoning Ryan, begging him to take me back. I hungered for my children, for normality. Perhaps if I went to the doctor, if I took enough drugs, I could forget it all.

I couldn't, though. Alexis was in my bloodstream. Nor would Ryan forget now, even if he could.

I fought the long hours for sleep and lost. At seven, I showered, drank cold water and black coffee. My face was old as a gargoyle in the bathroom mirror. I wandered the house, picking up toys, wondering when Ryan would bring me the kids. I stared at a fused bulb in the kitchen. Then I went out because I could no longer bear to be at home.

I walked, too fragile to run. The city was quiet, taking its Sunday-morning ease. On the street, in the stillness, I heard something snap, loud as a gunshot and as unexpected. I screamed, jarring loud, and whirled round. Nothing, no one. I moved again, shrinking, and felt the broken twig under my own foot. I kicked it away as though it had wronged me, then rested my hands on the cold fence, my lungs forcing air in and out, waiting for my neighbours to appear.

None did. Not a sound, even from Mhairi. Perhaps she was still asleep. I went on, half walking, half jogging, every sound a footstep behind me, playing interlocutor in my own head. *Are you watching me now? Do you want me as well? Or is it enough that you have taken him, and turned my own mind against me?*

I turned with every sound on the damp air. *Who are you? Who the hell are you?* Each time, I found only the houses and the gardens and the empty road.

Mhairi was right: I needed help.

I headed north, then east, knowing where I was going but not admitting it to myself, finding reassurance in other people. An old man walking a dog, a woman on a bike, a student in high heels and last night's make-up, shouting into her phone. I slipped past them, insignificant. The phantoms fell away.

*

I went to Alexis's street because it was where my body took me. I walked past his flat without looking up, turned at the end of the block, went back, stopped opposite, forced my head to tilt. Grey stone and the bay window, like a thousand Edinburgh windows. Glass facing blindly out. Behind it, nobody.

Memory clutched me, visceral, so I hung forward, bent at the waist, head hanging, hands reaching for nothing. I rocked there for I don't know how long. When I stood up, I spotted the red BMW parked outside the building, with someone in the back seat. It must have been there all along. *Shit.*

Legs, fusing. I thought, *I should go.*

I didn't. I held my phone, fiddled with it, thought about photographing the car, *then* running. Then the door to the building opened.

For one incredible instant, I believed that Alexis would walk out, casting back time. A second later, I thought of Capaldi and Morse. Scornful eyes and accusing questions, dispelling ghosts. Only then did I remember the other flats, the living. I scolded myself, turned away.

Two paces on, I heard a child's cry, looked back – and saw Gracie.

A man held her, silver-haired in a long coat, gripping her as though unaccustomed to the task. A woman of the same age was fussing and trying to pull her from him. The door shut heavy behind them. Their voices carried, acrimonious as gulls.

'Why the hell did you bring her? Obviously she'd be upset.'

'She wanted to come. They're her toys.'

'For crying out loud, she's *three*.'

'What does it matter whose fault it is?'

'It never did to you, when it was yours. You haven't changed, have you?'

'Jesus, Geraldine. There's a time and a place . . .'

She paused child-wrangling, swung so fast I thought she wanted to hit him. But she only glared.

I knew them, though I had never met them. Clear as the present, I heard Alexis's voice in my ear, felt him close-fitted to me in an armchair at my parents' house. Across from us, on the sofa, my mum and dad had clung together, crying-laughing at a film. Alexis had disentangled himself, gone out, and I had found him in the hall with his forehead on the wall. I put my arms round him, hands sliding into his waistband, lips on his neck, waiting without asking.

'My parents hate each other,' he had said.

Apparently, they still did.

His mother said, 'Fine. You can explain to Diana.'

The man recoiled and she dragged the child from him, holding her like a plank to her own chest. 'Oh God, Gracie,' she said. '*Chérie*. Please. Stop crying. You just tell us what toys you want and Grandad will get them. Then we can go from here.'

'Daddy! I want Daddy.'

The little girl's wail whipped through me, as I had thought only my own children's could. I ran across the road, not seeing the cyclist until she swerved past me, shouting. I didn't apologise. I rushed to Gracie, called out her name.

They all looked at me, the grandparents surprised, then

hostile. Gracie twisted herself towards me in one violent contortion.

'Evie's mummy,' she said, and shoved out her arms.

I saw Alexis's mother's face, realised my stupid, tactless mistake. She let me take the child, but her hands dropped afterwards, like dead weights. I cuddled Gracie like I hug Evie, felt her little chest leap. If thoughts could transmit, mine would be sounding in her brain.

Oh Gracie. I miss him too.

'I'm sorry,' I said. 'I'm so sorry. Gracie is at nursery with my daughter. I heard her cry. I heard about her dad. I wanted . . . But of course she's with you. I shouldn't have interfered.'

The man said, 'Did you know my son?' His face was so like Alexis's that I could have screamed as Gracie had.

'*Our* son,' the woman said.

How much did they know? How much would Diana have told them? Or the police? How much would *they* tell that snooty cow Capaldi?

'A little,' I said, tears hot and flowing. Shit. Shit. *Shit.* 'I'm so sorry,' I said again. I took a hopeless gulp, pulling back a sob. 'I'm so sorry for your loss.'

Gracie was snuffling into my neck now, water and snot on my cold skin. I wanted to take her home. Alexis's father turned from me, as though he thought me distasteful. The woman said to him, 'You get the toys from the flat. I'll stay with Gracie.'

'I'm sorry,' I said again. I started to detach the child. Her fingers gripped and I gave up. Besides, they were no longer attending to her, or me.

'Why don't *you* go up?' he said.

'Because I can't bear to go back in there.' I realised she was crying, felt my own tears start again. 'I can't bear it,' she said. 'I can't bear any of it.'

'And you think *I* can,' he said.

I jumped at the car door opening. I had forgotten the man inside. He was very tall, unfolding from the low space. He took the crying woman in his arms, murmured endearments. Alexis's father gave him a glance like a swipe, then went back to the door and let himself in. After a moment, the newcomer detached himself.

'I think she will come to me,' he said, and I realised he was addressing me. His voice was accented, gentle as pouring sand.

Gracie did go. He held her like a baby, her head on his shoulder, his face to her hair. He brought her to her grandmother and put his other arm around the older woman, crooning to them both in French. He smiled at me without judgement, and I went away without a word.

No spectre then, and no plain-clothes detective. Only a stepfather who had been kind, once, to a broken seventeen-year-old boy.

38

Laura

26 January 2019

Alexis hasn't called the police.

We stood side by side in the Meadows while he told me this, while Benjy ascended a metal ladder, feet placed with concentrated care, and Evie shot down a slide, wailing joy. Below them, Gracie squatted among the woodchips. Her little hands moved like birds, gathering, pressing, making a heap.

Our children, who thought this meeting coincidental. Our children, who are Ryan and Diana's too.

I said, 'How is the flat?'

'Better,' he said. 'Not right, but better.'

I nodded. A breeze snapped under my jacket, pulled at my hair. Promised rain clung to the air. It wasn't the weather for this. Our children, in ski suits, were almost the only ones there.

I said, 'Has Gracie seen it?'

'Not yet. She'll come back with me tonight.' He answered

the question I hadn't asked. 'I've changed the lock. It was old, easy to slip. I've asked my neighbours not to let anyone in they don't know.'

'Is Diana OK with that?'

Have you told Diana?

'Yes,' he said.

Benjy had come down the slide, met Gracie amid the woodchips. Evie stood shouting at the bottom of the ladder. I helped her up and watched her down, plaits sticking out like horns. I thought how little I knew of Diana. I thought of Gracie's room, untouched amid carnage. I've done that a lot this week, whenever I've tried to convince myself that this is not about the past. Our past.

I said to Alexis, 'Does she know about us?'

'Of course not,' he said.

I hesitated. 'You've never told me much about her.'

'No,' he said. He looked away from the children, flashed a glance at me, turned back to them. 'Just as you've never talked to me about Ryan. Because we are people who want to be decent, even while we're behaving indecently.'

Not so decent now. I looked past my children to a couple standing silently together, holding steaming cups; a woman with a baby in a carrier. How far we had sunk, even since last week, when we had still had principles, kept back from our lines in the sand. But Ryan was working all weekend, Simon was evasive, Mhairi away. What choice had I had?

I said, of Diana, 'I was wondering how she took your break-up.'

Alexis looked at me. 'Laura,' he said, 'you cannot imagine . . .'

He stopped while Evie ran back to me, was helped up the ladder again. On the damp ground, Benjy listened to Gracie's instructions.

Alexis said, 'We've talked about this before.'

Not really, I thought.

He said, 'You don't know her. I do. Besides, I thought you thought . . .'

He stopped again. All we had not said these past months hung over us like the rain clouds, bloated. I waited. But he would not say it. Nor could I say more. I was studying Gracie, her leaping hands and her eyes as they followed Benjy. I was betraying my children already, in a thousand ways. I couldn't watch that little girl and suggest that her mother was capable of vindictive violence.

Evie squealed. Benjy had hold of her shoulders, keeping her from demolishing the mountains of woodchips. I caught her up, swore under my breath as a rogue foot provoked an avalanche and Gracie began to cry.

Later, we pushed our daughters on the swings, Evie unrepentant, Gracie still tear-stained. I tried to remember how it was, not being always on edge.

I said, 'Do you still wish you'd sent Gracie to a different nursery?'

Alexis paused, mid-push. 'What a question.'

'That's not an answer,' I said.

'Laura . . .' he began. The moment stung, then fizzed. Our daughters swayed away from us, then back. He looked sideways at me. My body spiralled inwards, wanting to weep, wanting him.

'If I do,' he said, 'it's not because this isn't real.'

No, I thought. The rain started, almost sleet, spitting at us. I called to Benjy, let the swing slow. As I hauled Evie out and squeezed her, indignant, into the buggy, I studied Alexis. He was holding Gracie to his chest. His face was a boy's face: beautiful, unfathomably sad.

It's because you don't think we deserve to be happy.

39

Hope

7 March 1999

In church, I am at the back of the choir. I can't see Alexis unless I turn my head, which I cannot do without Her noticing. Instead, I contemplate the stained-glass window. It needs cleaning and has a crack in the corner, so St Francis is preaching to half a deer. Still, it has always soothed me. I don't listen to the service. I gave up doing that a long time ago, though I say all the responses. The vicar's God may be kinder than Her God, but he hasn't done anything to stop Her. But I still like that picture. I like St Francis.

And the hymns. I like them. In the singing, I am part of something.

Afterwards, I do see Alexis. It's the only time in the week I can speak to him without Laura, and it's the thing I look forward to most. We stand about in the church hall where I used to attend Sunday school, amid drawings of sunbeams and Jesus and Adam and Eve. Tea and coffee are laid out on a checked tablecloth and there's orange squash in plastic cups that crack if you hold them too tight. The milk is warm and smells like goats, and there are biscuits baked by very old members of the congregation.

You can tell that Alexis's grandmother is his grandmother. She's what Victorian novels would call a handsome woman; he is a beautiful boy. His grandfather is round-faced and balding and nothing like him.

His grandmother is on speaking terms with Her, which is the closest She gets to friendship, so when they find themselves near us, they talk. Alexis grins at me, like he always has. My face warms, as it always does. But then it goes wrong. His grandmother greets my parents, turns her smile (his smile) to me.

'Why, Hope,' she says, 'you are looking well.'

She means I'm looking like an actual human being. She's so pleased for me, she's almost shining with it. Like Laura's mum was. Like *Laura* was. Any other time, I'd welcome the compliment, but not now, not with Her scrutinising my every mumble. I say almost nothing, and then Alexis's grandfather is speaking, and it gets much, much worse.

'How are you enjoying the show?' he says. 'All coming together now?'

There's a moment of stillness. I see Alexis's stricken face and know that Laura has explained the situation to him but he has not explained it to his grandparents.

She says nothing. My father says, 'What show?'

Alexis's grandmother is frowning, weather-vane quick, but her husband has missed the signals. He puts an arm round Alexis, says, '*West Side Story*. Our boy is playing Tony. I knew he sang well, but not that well.' He smiles at my parents, assuming shared pride. 'I'm told your Hope has an exquisite voice.'

An instant's joy, spinning through fear, that he told them that. Then just the fear. My father says, 'Yes. Yes, she sings nicely.'

He looks at Her, as though he can't help it. She says, 'We didn't know Hope was taking part.' She grins like a Hydra. 'She must have been planning to surprise us.'

Alexis's grandparents stand with smiles held, then faltering. They turn in relief to friends bearing tea. Alexis hovers, his eyes all apology. I try to smile at him. Then he follows them away. My father retrieves Isaac, who's with a group of boys at the other side of the room. I stand by Her, wordless, my insides freezing, then thawing to pain.

She drinks her tea to the last drop, before we walk home.

No one speaks. Isaac goes straight upstairs, my father to the garden. They do not look at me. I leave my shoes by the door and follow her into the sitting room as though I am on a string. Not a cushion out of place. Bible on the coffee table, ready for later. She snaps the curtains shut and the bright morning is lost.

'Tights,' She says.

I stand on one leg, then the other, rolling them off while She goes into the hall to get the belt. I fold them and put them on a chair.

She strikes the back of my legs, once, twice, countless times. At first, every one is a new, clean agony. Then they blur so that each stripe is a wave, rising and dropping in the ongoing, crashing muddle of it.

I do not cry, though I know She waits for me to do so. Something has shifted in me, though I do not know yet how seismic this will be. For now, I can win only this minor victory. I focus on the tiny gap between the curtains, the line of light feeding onto the brown carpet. I am silent – wincing, yelping inwards, but silent – and she goes on hitting until we hear the back door open.

It shuts again immediately, hard. My father doesn't come into the room, but it is enough. She stops.

'I'm waiting,' She says. She means for me to apologise. I hear Father adjusting a chair in the kitchen, low sobbing from Isaac upstairs. I stand upright and look into Her face.

'I'll quit the show tomorrow,' I say.

I leave the room. I can feel the blood dripping down my legs. My heart is pelting. But She doesn't follow.

Isaac gets Savlon from the bathroom and rubs it on the cuts. I lie on my front on a towel, eyes watering at the clumsy touch. I clench my fists so my nails scrape the skin, irritated by his watery sniffs. I think about Mark. I think about Her.

40

Laura

29 January 2019

I met Diana in the toddler room, when I'd almost given up thinking I would. I spotted Gracie first, swerving out of Evie's dynamic embrace. Then, when my lungs were tight with anticipating Alexis, I saw Diana. I gripped my wriggling daughter by the hand, looking, pretending I wasn't. Fair as wheat, this woman who had loved my lover, leaning over her now sobbing child. A face taut-planed, mascara-lashed. Dressed like she thought it mattered. She didn't look like a stalker.

Yazzie lifted Gracie. 'Let's go to the window, shall we? Wave goodbye.'

I let Diana ahead of me through the stair gate, stopped to bid Evie our usual farewell. My daughter touched my fingers, scampered from me to the sand tray. Yazzie turned on her way to the window, eyes inscrutable.

'I heard about the play date on Saturday,' she told me. 'Evie and Gracie were full of it. But wasn't it very cold?'

Impossible not to feel the words as malicious. Impossible, too, not to realise how ridiculous that was. Behind me, Diana paused, then stepped onto the stair.

I smiled. 'It *was* cold, though it was hardly a play date. It turns out Gracie's dad and I have the same insane approach to all-weather outdoor play. We ran into them at the Meadows.'

Too much. I stopped myself, went out fast. Outside, Diana was folding a buggy. I said, 'I'm Laura, by the way. Evie and Benjy's mum.'

She looked up from the buggy, face pink now, hair falling in strands from its French pleat, eyes like Gracie's, too large for her face. 'I know who you are,' she said.

I started, felt myself redden. She closed the buggy with one fierce movement, stood straight again. 'I'm just glad I'm not with him any more,' she said.

I watched her carry the buggy to the store cupboard, shove it into a minimal gap. Then I turned from her, scurried away. When I paused at the corner, she was at the front gate, one hand in the air. Gracie was in Yazzie's arms at the upstairs window, crimson with woe.

At lunchtime, I skipped a meeting, went out for a sandwich, made Alexis meet me in Princes Street gardens. The benches, clogged in summer, sat barren. The trees were winter-bare. We walked side by side, knuckles brushing, fingers aching with not holding each other.

I said, 'You told me Diana didn't know about us.'

He looked sideways at me, half stopping, walking on. 'She doesn't.'

'That's not what she said this morning.'

He didn't speak. I told him, in short sentences, what Diana had said. I realised, as I went, that I was angry with him. Almost for the first time. Rage pivoted like a spun nail, hurting me instead.

He said, 'She knows we were together at school. Not about now.'

'It didn't sound like that.'

'She meant . . .' He waited, let a woman push a pram past us. 'She knows it mattered, you and me. More than it normally would. She knows *you* mattered.' He looked away. 'She knows I was screwed up, for years.'

I wanted to kiss him. I wanted to claw at him and remind him that *he* had parted us, not me.

I said, 'How could she know?'

'Laura, Diana and I were together. We have a child. Are you telling me Ryan knows nothing of your past?'

An empty lager can lay discarded on the path. I kicked it out of the way. 'He knows a bit,' I said. 'But that's—'

He interrupted, so uncharacteristically discourteous that I knew he was angry too. Or defensive. 'Diana doesn't know what really happened, so she thinks it was *all* you, the hurt.' He paused, sighed. 'She was always threatened by it.'

'That's not what I meant.' I knew it sounded petulant; I didn't care. 'How did she know that *that* Laura was me?'

'I thought perhaps you could tell me that. Apparently one of the other mums said something about us knowing each other at school.'

I had never heard him so sardonic. 'Heather,' I said. 'Liam's mum. Shit.'

'Diana put two and two together and asked me outright.'

'Shit,' I said again. We reached the end of a path, turned, swooped down with the dropping grass. It was a loch, once, that gulf between the nine-hundred-year-old castle and what is now a shopping street. Now the grass stretches down and up, prettifying curves that the water hid.

Alexis said, 'That's all she knows. I swear it.'

I glanced up at the castle, perched on its cliffs, unwelcoming as a prison. 'You told me she knew nothing, the other day.'

'I didn't want to worry you.'

'I worry more that you lied.'

He said nothing. The accusation dragged the air between us. 'Besides,' I said, 'it seems relevant to what you wouldn't let me discuss.' *One of the things you wouldn't let me discuss.* 'She obviously still cares. She might be angry.'

Alexis groaned, stood still so suddenly I almost tripped. 'Diana had Gracie with her last Thursday,' he said. 'She wouldn't leave her.'

I found the words I had set aside before. No Gracie there now, a dancing sprite to shame me. 'I wasn't suggesting she did it herself,' I said. 'Only that there are people you can pay.'

I thought perhaps I had gone too far, that he would crack and snap at me. But he was walking again, uphill now, taking us back to the street.

'It wasn't Diana,' he said. 'Trust me.'

I glared at him. He said, quickly, 'If you *did* know Diana, you'd laugh at the idea. I've never known anyone so resolutely, kindly middle class. And there you are suggesting she's in league with some criminal underworld.'

I said sulkily, 'She wouldn't have to be in the Mafia. Just capable of an internet search or two.'

Alexis shook his head. But quite soon he stopped smiling and let his fingers touch mine. 'We can't scapegoat them,' he said. 'Diana or Ryan, or anyone else it seems convenient to blame. They're not the wrongdoers here.'

My fingertips curled into his. I felt watched: a sudden, irrational certainty. *Talk then. Talk to me about what we really believe, and how illogical that is.*

He released me, so quickly he must have felt it too. I said, 'Perhaps I'm clutching at straws. But if I am, you know why.'

He didn't answer. In silence, I examined his profile, wondered when we could next be alone together.

We were at the gate to Princes Street now, crammed with shoppers. Alexis kissed me quickly on the cheek, as he might kiss any friend goodbye. I tilted my face so his mouth brushed mine. I heard the pull of his breath, felt my body veer towards him. He swung from me as though I had hurt him, walked quickly into the crowd. I stood a long time in a queue of bus passengers, pinned and swaying and wanting him.

Safety in numbers. Except that was irrational too.

When I got back to the office, my head was a lunchtime drinker's, troubled, inclined to sleep. Danielle looked up at me, unforgiving as a boulder.

'Long line, was there?' she said. 'In Pret.'

41

Laura

10 March 2019

I remembered to buy food before going home. Holding Gracie had impressed on me how much more I had to lose. When I got in, my children were there, real and immediate, watching *Toy Story*. Benjy sat hunched with one hand gripping his brother's leg. On the other side, Evie was curled against Simon, her chest on his arm. The boys barely glanced up from the TV when I came in, but Evie slid from the sofa and ran to me.

I caught her up, my vital girl. Warm as Gracie, and more solid. I kissed her until she wriggled away. I slid her back by Simon, hugged Benjy to me, leaned across him to kiss Simon on the cheek.

'I've missed you all,' I said.

Benjy looked up, then back to the screen. 'I wanted you, Mummy,' he said.

'You had Daddy,' I said, kissing him. 'Where *is* Daddy?'

'Gone,' Benjy said.

Simon detached himself, followed me into the hall. He looked as tired as I felt. Would he always have to play the adult now?

'Dad said he'll get in touch,' he said. 'About arrangements.'

'Thanks.'

I was staring about me, jarred by something I couldn't place. 'What's changed?' I said, and before Simon could answer, I saw for myself. The tree print, with our names on it, had gone. I went to where it had been, touched the darker patch of paint.

'What happened?' I said.

'Dad took it down.'

My phone rang, brash and clamorous. I flicked it to silent without looking at the screen. Simon was still watching the shadow square on the wall.

'It's in the cupboard now,' he said. 'I tried to stop him, but he said that's not who we are any more.'

I put my forehead on the paintwork. God, I needed to sleep.

'He's not coming round,' Simon said. I heard panic in his voice, felt the guilt and worry rising. 'You'll have to talk to him,' he said. 'He'll forgive you, but you'll have to ask.'

I squeezed him to me, felt his trembling breaths. I wanted to make promises, to take that old look from his eyes. But they would only be lies. As I walked upstairs, feet like stones, I thought of Alexis's parents, unable to be in the same space as each other. Even after decades, even in despair.

Dear God, may Ryan and I never be like that.

Sitting on my unmade bed, I saw my phone ringing. Mhairi. 'I wanted to check you were all right.'

Clouds of embarrassment. 'I'm fine,' I said. 'I'm sorry about yesterday.'

'I don't need apologies,' she said. 'I'll help, if I can.'

'The kids are back,' I said. 'I'll be OK.'

'I know they are,' she said. 'I saw Ryan on his way out.'

Oh Christ. 'You didn't tell him? About last night.'

Visions of custody battles like fast shadows on my mind. *Unbalanced. Incapable.* I shoved fingertips into my temples. *Stop it, Laura. Stop it.* All I had done was get pissed. And the children had been miles away.

'No,' Mhairi said. 'No, of course I didn't. But Laura . . .'

'What?'

'You will see a doctor, won't you?'

'I will,' I said.

I looked at the wallpaper, wondering if I was lying. Lilies on water. Ryan had never liked it. I said to Mhairi, 'Did you call me a few minutes ago?'

'No,' she said. 'Take care now.'

The other call had been the vicar from Hope's church. I recognised the area code, sat quaking before I could press play. When I did, the man's rich voice was unexpectedly comforting.

'I have the address you were asking for.' He gave it twice, articulating as to a full congregation. I stopped shaking, perched ice-still on the edge of the bed. 'Look after yourself,' he said, and I heard Mhairi's voice again, in his. Then I heard myself, responding to the recorded voice.

'Thank you,' I said. 'Thank you so much,' before I let the phone drop from my fingers and land with a hushed thud on carpet. I put my thumb to my mouth, pressed the flesh up into my teeth until the pain made me gag.

Abigail Mitchell lives in Penicuik, barely eight miles south of here.

2 November 2018

From: Khaleesi8690

To: AlwaysHaveParis

Subject: Maybe next time

Hi love,

You OK? I was kind of assuming we'd
spend last night together . . . But
I suppose it made sense to get some
sleep. School night, good impressions to
make and all that!

I'll see you tomorrow, anyway. Can't
wait ;)

xx

42

Hope

8 March 1999

I go to Mr Balmore's classroom at the start of break. I can't bring myself to tell him before them all. I walk slowly because moving my legs tears the congealing sores. Tonight, when I take off my tights, it will be like ripping off a plaster.

Balmore is at his desk, picking his nose with a biro. I am quite close before he sees me, and when he does, he whips the pen into a drawer. He stands and faces me with cheeks already red.

I tell him straight. 'I can't do the show any more.'

He's relieved, I could swear it. It gleams a moment in his eyes. Then he frowns, covering unprofessionalism with anger. 'What do you mean, Hope? It's less than a month away.'

'I'm sorry, sir. My parents say it's interfering with my schoolwork. They're not happy.'

'*I'm* not happy.' He looks at me. I stare back at him. He's purple-faced as a baboon now, dyed hair spiking round his forehead like fur. I know he's lying, even if he doesn't. But he can still bite. 'You need to rethink your attitude, Hope. I know you didn't get the part you wanted, but nor did lots of others. They all live with it.'

Anger, like a black fist. I drag it back, repeat in the same lifeless voice, 'My parents are worried about my work.'

He lifts his shoulders, arranges exercise books on the desk. 'Very well. I'm disappointed in you, Hope, that's all.' He stills his hands a moment, glares at me again. 'And don't go thinking you can change your mind and come back, because you can't.'

'I won't, sir.'

I stump straight-legged out of the room, leaving him to his bogeys. Hopefully he's wondering what Miss Pendleton will say.

There's a rehearsal at lunchtime, and when I am in the locker room, unpeeling my sandwiches, Claire asks why I am not there. I don't say anything. I screw up today's strip of paper, not wanting her to see it.

Blows and wounds scrub away evil, and beatings purge the inmost being. (Proverbs 20:30)

I'll remember it without learning.

Claire asks again and I tell her I've quit. She frowns at me like she wants to say more, but I get up and put the piece of paper in the bin, and then Jem comes in, her bag undone, moaning that she's lost her T. S. Eliot.

It's harder afterwards, when I see Alexis and Rick and Laura outside, buoyant and chatting. They stop when I would pass them. Three comely faces. Three lives going well. Blocking my path.

I know they know, because they all sober up their expressions and Rick tells me he's sorry. 'I get why you'd had enough, though,' he says. 'You were wasted as an extra.'

'It's not that,' I say. 'It's my parents.'

Silence. Rick looks unconvinced and slightly disappointed, which upsets me more than I expected. I suppose this is what everyone will think, but I don't care about most of them. I shift on my feet. Pain springs and spreads behind my knee.

'It's true,' I say.

Laura says, 'Hope's parents are super-strict, Rick.' She grins. 'Not like yours.'

There's a stillness. Rick pulls a face. He knows there are things none of us are saying, but he doesn't ask. He makes an excuse and leaves us to it.

Alexis says, 'I'm so sorry, Hope. I could have kicked myself.'

I could have kicked him too, if it had been anyone else.

Laura says, 'Was your mother very angry?' She speaks as though she cares. There's a moment – a switch I could press – where things between us might change direction, even now. But Laura's hand is in Alexis's even as she spouts her concern for me. Their pity trickles through radiance, and that seems the worst thing of all.

'She was angry enough,' I say.

I try to smile at them and can't. I feel as though the scabs on my legs will burst open, pouring blood over my grey tights, my straight calves, my plain school shoes. I stare at their joined fingers, and I want to scream.

15 November 2018

From: Khaleesi8690

To: AlwaysHaveP@ris

Subject: Celebration?

Hey boyfriend,

So, I was thinking, next time you
don't have Gracie, we could go away
together. Call it a belated celebration
of my amazing new career prospects.
(Exaggerating? Much?!) Or just of us.

I didn't want to suggest it before, with
you all preoccupied with Gracie's big move.
(Yes, I could tell you've been worrying.)
But you said yourself she's settled
beautifully. JUST LIKE I SAID SHE WOULD!!

xxx (the extra one is for her)

43

Laura

11 March 2019

Danielle has run out of patience. I woke to a text message checking I would be back in the office.

> Crunch time for us, as you know. If you're too ill to come in, you'll need a doctor's note. Otherwise it's another warning. Sorry.

The 'Sorry' made me want to punch her.

I could demand compassionate leave now. *Marriage breakdown.* No need to tell them the rest. Instead, I tugged on creased work clothes, kept my options open. At breakfast, Benjy spilled milk and cried. Evie launched her porridge bowl to the floor, cackled like a jackal cub. Simon picked it up for her, fed her spoonful by spoonful while I swirled black coffee in a chipped mug and wanted to weep too.

On the way, Benjy said he hated me, because I wouldn't detour to look for trains. At nursery, Yazzie would have taken Evie if I had let her. I didn't. I left her with arms outstretched, helped my daughter out of her coat myself and sent her to her peg. Then I looked Yazzie in the eye.

'I would appreciate it,' I said, 'if you didn't tell Benjy you love him better than I do. That crosses a line.'

She didn't deny it. I'd thought perhaps she would. She looked at me, iron-faced.

'Benjy is going through a difficult time,' she said. 'It's important he has people he knows he can trust.'

Bitch. *Bitch*. I felt her words in my ribs, recoiled, stared at her. 'He can trust me,' I said.

She looked me up and down. 'I'm just doing my job,' she said.

Behind her, I saw Gracie alone at the round table, lifting handfuls of Play-Doh, squeezing, dropping them again. Then Evie was back, coatless and hugging my legs. I knelt before her, kissed her hair. I looked up at Yazzie, wanting to slap her, biting on the words.

'My children are loved,' I said.

When I went, Yazzie had her back to us. Evie came to the child gate, arms up and hands splayed, and Gracie ran up too, reaching out her fingers, looking past me. Tears started, streamed down my face. I put out a hand to each of them, brushing fingertips. Evie's hands were hot, sticky with porridge; Gracie's were ice cold. When I left, they stood together, watching me. Outside, I put my hands to my hot cheeks. I thought how angry I had been with Yazzie. I thought how angry Diana might be with me, if she knew.

My bus was approaching. I watched it slow, stayed

motionless, saw it gather speed again. I thought the driver looked oddly at me. Perhaps he could see my face. Perhaps he, too, was just having a bad day.

I crossed the road without looking, walked through the Grange, implacably beautiful, and trailed passive work-day streets to Morningside, where I could get another bus, to Penicuik.

The houses in Hope's mother's street are pebble-dashed, flat-faced, the colour of oatmeal. Gardens face the road, some lively with flower beds, sprouting yellow and white and purple, others gravelled into torpid order. I stared as I walked, toes pinching in my work shoes, absorbing details without curiosity. Not wanting to get there. Beyond, grey clouds slumped on the Pentland Hills.

The number leered at me from the low metal gate. I tried to remember the house Hope had grown up in, but I had never been welcome, had gone as little as I could. I thought the door there had been the same mud brown as this one, but the garden, front and back, had been neat with grass and shrubs. Her father's work. This square was paved over, with only two pots, sprouting daffodils, pushed back against the wall. Path and steps had been replaced with a railed ramp, institutionally bland, running from pavement to door.

The gate screamed like a banshee when I opened it, sending me jumping back onto the road and plunging a pack of dogs into a concerto of leaping barks. Their walker cursed, then shouted. I recovered myself, started up the ramp. Through the window, I could see a room lit dim orange. Beige walls and a huge sampler over the dead fireplace, clearly legible even from outside. *CHRIST LOVES YOU*. And close by the window, the back of a head like Norman Bates's mother, spine straight and shoulders sharp in what seemed like a standard chair, until I saw the curve of the wheel. A table, close enough to reach, with a glass of water and two books. I'm sure one was a Bible.

She was watching someone in the room, visible only as a blue movement, a swinging door. A moment later, the front door opened, and a woman came out wearing a puffer jacket over a uniform, carrying a bag. She looked glad to be out of there.

Her expression shifted, at sight of me, to surprise and competent cheer. 'Hello, hen. Have you come tae see Abigail?'

Without waiting for an answer, she twisted her neck, called back into the hallway. 'Visitor for you, Mrs Mitchell. Won't that be nice?'

I was processing the wheelchair, the nurse, the impossibility of my suspicions. I thought of what Capaldi would say if she found out. I shook my head, like a nodding doll.

'Sorry,' I said, backing up. 'I think this is the wrong house.'

But Abigail Mitchell had seen me, recognised me even after twenty years. Her face, yellow-white, mouth gaping, pressed against the window, neck and torso contorted in the unmoving chair.

'Harlot,' she screamed.

The nurse sighed. 'Oh dear,' she said. 'One o' her bad days.'

I took another step back. The voice followed. 'Don't think I don't know you. I know you, and the Devil will know you too.'

'Jesus,' I said, inaptly.

The nurse turned back into the hallway. 'Now, now, Mrs Mitchell. This lady came here by accident. You don't know her.'

'Laura Gregory,' the voice said, oddly detached from the distorted face at the glass. 'Jezebel. Slut.'

'I'm sorry, hen,' the blue woman said. 'She seems tae have taken a dislike tae you.'

She did that long ago.

The nurse was still speaking, over the continued shouts. The dog walker, almost at the end of the street now, had turned to listen. Mrs Mitchell's vocabulary was sliding, biblical to obscene. The nurse yanked at the door, clicked it shut behind her.

'Best get away,' she said, 'before she gets intae one o' her states.'

It was as though she had turned off the volume. The face continued, furiously mouthing, squirting spit at the window. Abigail Mitchell got a thin wrist up, hammered with her fist on the glass. I turned, ran jolting on my awkward shoes, the sound hitting the pavement like stones.

44

Laura

4 February 2019

I'd forgotten our work retreat until Kai mentioned it today. A weekend in some golfing hotel in Fife, trouble-shooting the website and enduring PowerPoint presentations from Legal on everything I do wrong.

'It looks beautiful,' he was saying. 'Are you coming?'

The poor kid knows nothing.

'God, no,' I said, eyes on my computer screen. 'I have small children.'

Of course, I should go, even for shared bedrooms, cardboard sandwiches and death-by-legalese. Danielle and I had another little chat on Friday, complete with Graham and her former fling from HR. *Not* a convivial atmosphere.

'They also have a father.'

I looked up. Danielle was behind Kai, wreathed in acerbity. So much for my get-out-of-jail-free card.

'He has to work,' I said.

'I see,' she said.

I really should go. But I knew I wouldn't, because I'd had an idea.

In the evening, when Ryan finally got in, I presented it as a fait accompli. 'I have to go on this thing. My job could depend on it.'

My husband was sitting down to cold toad in the hole. He was tired, the burden of working all hours showing in jaw and temples. The bit of me that still felt guilt was squirming with it.

He said, 'What about the kids?'

I welcomed the flip to irritation. 'I don't know, Ryan. Maybe their sodding father could look after them for a change?'

'That's not fair, Laura. You know I didn't mean . . .' He stared at the lumpen plateful, pushed his chair back and himself out of it, and shoved the plate into the microwave. I sidestepped, watching him. He said, 'You know what it's like. I'll never get the weekend off.'

I said, 'You worked all this weekend. I never complained.' Not strictly true, but I had cared for the children.

In the end, he gave in. I sat hugging my purloined hours, frantic to contact Alexis, watching, as though through a screen, what I was doing to my husband. Regret without willpower: is that what addicts feel?

We sat a while in chill silence. When he'd finished eating, Ryan made an effort, produced a grin, which tightened my ribs.

'I've news on the girlfriend front,' he said.

For a moment I didn't understand. Then I did – and smiled too. 'The elusive Bella. You've met her?'

'Mhairi has. She saw them choosing pizza in Waitrose.'

'How domesticated.'

'Aye. Simon was decidedly shifty, Mhairi said.'

'So Bella's real.'

'Did you doubt it?'

'Of course not. What's she like?'

'Standard teenager, apparently. Looked shocked at having to speak to an adult at all, then said hello nicely enough.'

I nodded, one minor worry off my list. 'When did you see Mhairi?' I said.

'Just now,' Ryan said. 'She was putting the bins out. Shite, I suppose—'

'Don't worry,' I snapped. 'I'll do ours.'

I dragged the big bin onto the dim street, set the glass crate clanking alongside, came back with the food waste. I did it without thought, because to think was to allow guilt. I stared along sets of matching bins, phantoms lining the street. As I bent to put the caddy down, I heard a sharp sound.

A heavy stone. Or a lid, dropping.

The caddy fell from my chill fingers, tipped, slid on its side into the gutter. I waited, rammed by fear, bent like a pivot lamp. I heard breathing, loud in the darkness. I held my own breath, heard it still. I was seventeen again, afraid in a deserted playground. Wanting Alexis, whose kiss still warmed my shaking lips. Terrified of being alone, and of not being.

Another movement. A footstep? Or a bin, shifting. I twisted, ran still bent towards the house. I yanked open the door, slammed it behind me, pressed my back against the heavy wood.

Ryan looked up. 'What's up wi' you?'

'Nothing.' I took a breath. Another. 'Just cold.'

He dropped his eyes, back to emails. 'Thanks for doing that,' he said. But he was already reading.

I looked at him, hunched over the table. My husband. Stymied by his own decency. I told myself I could go on the work retreat after all. Or not go at all.

But later, while Ryan lay dressed on the bed, still gaping at his phone, I messaged Alexis.

> You don't have Gracie this weekend, do you?

He replied immediately.

> No. Why?

> Because I've got a free pass.

I smiled, imagining his face as he read it, envisaging whole nights in the same bed.

> And we're going away together.

45

Hope

15 March 1999

Now, when it can do me no good, my skin is clear. Only a few scars linger, puckering the dent below my mouth, the periphery of my nose.

I gaze at myself, first in the bathroom mirror then in the loos near the locker room at school. Two months ago, I would have paid almost any price for this bland normality. Now I want Stacy's straight nose and curving mouth. I want Laura's lashes like spider's legs. Isaac, my brother, has a kind of tentative good looks. Perhaps I hoped to find the same under my pustular mask.

I want to be stared at for the right reasons. But now I am no longer a figure of nightmares, I am not stared at at all.

The show goes on, in a parallel universe. I know rehearsals are happening, but the only sign is when Jem cannot sneak into the common room as Laura's plus one and sits fidgeting and painting her nails in the locker room instead. She never mentions *West Side Story*. Claire doesn't either, and I wonder if Laura has said something to them about why I'm not in it any more. If she did, she didn't say it here. She barely comes into the locker room now, and never to stay.

I see her in class. I see Alexis only when I avoid Claire and follow them home. I don't see Rick at all.

Today, though, I see Miss Pendleton. She spots me in the corridor, smiles her bright, solicitous grin. She stops and her eyes skim my face. Brown eyes, they are, speckled with copper. Beauty again: unbuyable, separate. But she is kinder than Stacy, kind as Laura used to be. She smiles again without the distraction. Her teeth are white and perfectly neat.

'How are you?' she says.

'OK thanks, miss.'

I step to the side, hoping it'll appear polite but also make her go away. It doesn't. A frown pivots round her mouth. She says, 'How's the show going?'

So she doesn't know. I'm even less important than I thought.

I say, 'I'm not in it any more.'

The frown spreads, wrinkling her cream forehead. She moves an arm, letting someone by, and I see the flash of a red stone on her ring finger. I don't know if it's new, or if I never noticed it before. I like her a little less.

'What happened?' she says.

I can tell she thinks Balmore threw me out. I could let her go on thinking it. Maybe it would provoke a row. But what's the point?

I say, 'My parents insisted.' I cross one leg over the other, scratching the scabs. Then I see her see me. I stop. 'They're worried about my grades.'

Miss Pendleton puts a hand on my arm. The ruby stares up at me. 'Is there anything wrong, Hope?' she says. 'Is there anything you'd like to talk about?' She looks about her, students pushing along the corridor, a teacher grumbling over dropped papers. 'We could go to my classroom,' she says. 'I have the time.'

I shake my head. 'There's nothing the matter, miss. Thank you.'

She looks at me. The bell rings. I say, 'I've got English now, miss.'

'OK, Hope. But remember, the offer is there.'

'Thank you.'

I hurry away from her. *What would you understand, miss?*

That night, while my father is out and She listens to hymns on the CD player, I take the book of children's Bible stories from the shelf in my room and let it fall open at my forbidden foil packet. The page has a picture of Moses in the bulrushes, colours garish, the princess's dress imprinted with circles from the remaining pills. I smooth the leaf, take out a tiny tablet and swallow it.

When I am replacing the book, Isaac says, 'What are you doing?'

I jump and the book falls, but I grab it again before it hits the ground. My brother is standing by the door. Did he open it, or did I forget to shut it?'

'Nothing,' I say. I put the book back.

'I saw you. You took something.' He shuts the door behind him. 'It's not dangerous, is it?'

'Of course not, idiot. It's just something for my skin.'

'Oh.' I think how slight he is, like he could turn from us one day and disappear between two walls. 'It does look better,' he says.

'Thanks.'

'Does She know?'

I shake my head. 'Please don't tell Her.'

'I won't.'

He's looking at the floor. I go towards him and get hold of his school shirt, shaking him gently until he meets my eyes. His are periwinkle blue, expressionless as the sky. It usually makes me sad to look into my little brother's face, but now I'm too worried to think about that.

'Promise, Isaac,' I say. 'It's important.'

'I promise,' he says.

I let him go. I shut the door behind him and take the pills from the book and slide them under my mattress. I hear Isaac moving around in his own room, getting ready for bed.

I don't trust him. In his place, I wouldn't trust myself.

46

Laura

8 February 2019

Neither of us has a car, so Alexis hired one. I was late to meet him, jolting through the wind with my weekend bag, carrying my guilt. Ryan was still at work, texting apologies. Simon was with Bella, ignoring frantic calls. I yelled at Ryan's voicemail, then left the kids with Mhairi. She didn't say it wasn't convenient, but she didn't say it was either: I gave her no choice.

Evie cried, arms like pincers round my neck. I sat down with her on Mhairi's sofa, Benjy's hand on my knee, counting the minutes. Mhairi's boys proffered TV, still in their school uniforms. When I left, one of them had Evie on his lap. The tears were drying in streaks on her face. Mhairi was in the kitchen, slamming pots. Benjy looked at me with his mouth tight shut.

I slid into the dark car without speaking. Alexis leaned over, kissed me, pulled back, stared black-eyed through dimness, finding my face.

'What's wrong?' he said.

I couldn't complain of Ryan to him. It might seem strange that I have any standards, in my consummate disloyalty. But I do, and Alexis has them too.

'Nothing, I said. 'Just . . .'

'Everything?'

I nodded, told half a truth. 'I feel like the worst parent in the world.'

'Oh Laura.' He made the word a sigh, held his palm against the curve of my jaw. I turned my mouth into it. 'You know you're not,' he said.

No. Only the worst wife.

I kissed his hand, then pushed it from me. I turned in my seat and kissed his mouth, lips opening, jarring with longing. His fingers gripped my shoulders; my hand pulled on the back of his neck, kissing deeper. Headlights blared, catching us, passing by, and I sank back, lust-lorn as a teenager, breathing deep and shuddery.

The hired car smelled of chemicals. The engine sounded sudden and loud, promise and threat. The radio came on with the ignition: Radio Forth, playing, unaccountably, Britney Spears. Alexis shoved his finger on the button, cutting it off, and pulled the car out, sliding along the street. Outside our bubble, the wind teased branches and flattened hedge tops. An old woman carried shopping home. A cyclist spun into a driveway with a child on the back. Blameless lives.

I saw the car draw out behind us, but it didn't matter then. Not until we'd weaved through side streets to the main road, heading south in Friday traffic, and the same car was still there. A silver Renault. I looked over my shoulder, then back to the road. I saw Alexis, eyes on the mirror, flicking away. He was frowning.

'You don't think . . .?' I said.

'It's the main way out of town,' he said.

He pulled out to pass parked cars, then back in again, slowing down, letting the car behind past. It didn't pass. It dipped in behind us, then out and in again, hugging the line of pavement and cars. We moved together, like slalom skiers, along the long incline down to the roundabouts, out of town.

I craned my neck round. I could just see the driver, nondescript below a dark cap. Not looking at me. I couldn't tell if there was anyone in the back.

'Perhaps they'll take the bypass,' I said. But they didn't. Another car got between us, tucking in on the roundabout, but still the Renault clung. Our route took us off the main road shortly afterwards, forking across country. Alexis indicated at the last minute, took the exit fast. It was dark and the road twisted again immediately, abruptly rural. But we both saw the white of the lights as the silver car took the turning after us.

Alexis didn't say anything. He let the Renault follow us along the shallow sweeps of the road, wait behind us at the Easter Bush traffic lights, ease with us onto the southbound A701. I rotated my head again, but the driver was unrecognisable in the dark.

At the Gowkley Moss roundabout, Alexis took the left into Roslin, fast and from the middle lane. 'Now we'll know,' he said, yanking the wheel down. And we did, by the violent hooting of the car in the inside lane when the Renault tried to follow us.

'He's had to stay on the roundabout,' I said, watching contorted in my seat. I realised I was laughing, wondered if this was what hysterics felt like.

'He'll go round,' Alexis said.

That gave us maybe forty seconds. Alexis used it, driving fast for a few hundred metres, then spinning into a housing estate, stopping the car and turning off the lights.

We watched, twisting necks, while lives went on in the houses around us. Lights flashed at intervals down the road towards Roslin. One, two, a third. The first was too dark to be the Renault, the second was as close a match as we would get, in this light. The third slowed a fraction, tightening my chest, then went on. We waited another minute, then Alexis turned the car and pulled out of the estate.

Back to the roundabout, onto the main road again, then off it immediately for the sharp drop into Auchendinny. I kept my head at its painful angle, suspecting everyone behind us. Alexis took a hand from the wheel and touched my thigh, his eyes unmoving on the dipping road.

'We've lost him,' he said, and I straightened with a yelp.

But I didn't believe him until after Auchendinny, after Howgate and Leadburn when the cars spread along the wild stretch to Peebles. I held my nerves close to me, speculation pointless, and studied Alexis's profile. It was the first time he had driven me since we were seventeen, and then it was someone else's car too. His grandfather's, on loan and very much on sufferance. He had driven well even then, focused and not flashy. Now, watching him, I felt desire spark through fear.

*

We'd booked dinner for eight but arrived late, roads shrinking and turning until there was only the long, sweeping drive, the country house hotel, shadowy as a film set. We were late again when we'd flung bags to the floor of our room, pulled at buttons and zips, made love fast and hard and half undressed against the wooden dressing table. Afterwards, he carried me to the shower and we did it again, very slowly. Hot water on wet skin, cries sharp and sweet at sliding fingers, tiles like wet marble against my back.

Drugging ourselves, to forget.

We ate under cupids and chandelier, still wet-haired, faces flushed and clothes cleaving to damp skin. Alexis's collar was half in, half out of his jumper. We looked like what we were, illicit lovers. The rings on my left hand marked me out. Badge of respectability; blazon of deceit.

'I should have left them off,' I said, spinning the diamond.

Alexis put his hand on mine, gripped the fingertips. 'I wish I'd given them to you,' he said.

The waiter took our starter plates. I smiled to stop myself crying.

We drank red wine, velvet in deep glasses, and talked about Edinburgh and Paris, about running and films and books we had forgotten we loved. About everything but the reason my fingers shook on the stem of my glass and Alexis jumped at the drop of a knife behind him.

47

Laura

11 March 2019

I got to the office for eleven, lying without contrition.

'Smear test,' I said, loud enough that Graham, lowering behind Danielle, had no choice but to hear me. 'Sorry I'm late.'

Kai looked up, said, 'Poor you.' Graham gave an 'I'm-not-embarrassed' grunt and vanished into his office. Danielle looked as if she wanted to call me out for lying.

I sat at my desk, readjusting ideas, pulling myself out of the past, casting round the present. I was remembering Gracie's mother, her eyes like stones: *I know who you are.*

Ridiculous, Alexis had said. But Alexis thought the best of people, always. And he couldn't know how hard he was to give up. Was Capaldi interrogating Diana, whom he had rejected, like she had drilled me, whom he loved?

'How are you doing?' Kai said.

I jumped, then realised Danielle had left the desk. We were alone. Kai smiled, added, 'I guess you had a nasty bout of it.'

It took me a moment to realise the *bout* was of my supposed flu, not my alleged gynaecological ordeal.

'I'll be OK,' I said.

I didn't look it, but then Kai didn't either, now I'd got round to noticing. The sunshine glow had ashen undertones; blue eyes gaped from purpling bags.

'What's up with you?' I said, too worn down for circumlocution.

'Nothing. A rough weekend.'

'I know how you feel.'

I checked myself, remembering the sick aunt, clocked how self-absorbed I must appear. How self-absorbed I was. But Kai merely nodded and said, 'Kids playing up?'

'Something like that.'

'Oh well.' A smile, a flash of the old Aussie brilliance. 'Let us not become weary . . .'

Kai checked, laughed a little oddly.

'What's this?' said Danielle, wedging herself back behind the computer and slamming at the keyboard. 'Inspirational quote of the day?'

Kai stared through the monitor. Unease wrapped me, layer on layer. I couldn't say why.

At nursery, I asked to see the manager, was ushered with formal surprise into the tiny office. I refused tea. I wanted gin, imagined her face if I said so, and choked back a yelp of hysteria. Then I took another breath, sat on the edge of a chair, and told this middle-aged, blonde-streaked American what Yazzie had said to Benjy and what she had said to me.

'I don't want to complain,' I said, and it was true that I

hadn't wanted to. 'But they are my children. I won't have them told I don't love them.'

I don't know what I expected. An apology, perhaps. A promised inquiry. Instead, the manager scrutinised me as though I was the one under investigation. I became aware of my hair slipping from its band, make-up barely scratched on this morning and untouched since. I thought of Abigail Mitchell mouthing 'whore' through spit-stained glass. Of how Kai had studied me; of how Danielle had rolled her eyes. My hands shook, and I gripped them tight to still them.

'Laura,' the manager said, almost as Mhairi had said it on Saturday night, 'I'm glad you stopped by. I've been wanting to speak to you. You see, sometimes the children say things, and we don't know if they are true or not.'

Laura, you need help.

'This isn't about me,' I said. I unclenched my hands, pushed hair behind my ears, then gripped them again. 'This is about your staff being unprofessional.'

'Of course, you don't have to tell me anything,' she said. 'But it can be very difficult to support the children if we don't know the full story.'

'For Christ's sake . . .' I stopped myself, grasped at calm. 'OK,' I said. 'I guess Benjy told you Ryan and I have separated.'

'Yes. We were sorry to . . .'

I don't care if you're sorry.

'It's true. OK. It's true, and yes, please help the kids through it if you can. That's what Ryan and I are trying to do, believe it or not.'

'Of course I will. We all will.' She leaned forward as though she would put a hand on my arm, then thought better of it. She spoke in a voice to reassure a toddler. 'I'm sure that was all Yazzie meant.'

'I'm not,' I said.

Walking home with Benjy sullen and Evie wriggling in the buggy, my head full of Yazzie and Kai and Diana, I thought of something else. If housebreakers were for hire, so were killers. If Diana could have paid one, so could Abigail Mitchell.

18 November 2018

From: Khaleesi8690

To: AlwaysHaveParis

Subject: Rain check

Hi you,

Doesn't matter about the weekend idea.
It can wait. I'll settle for dinner
in on Friday and a lazy morning in
bed afterwards. But that bit is non-
negotiable ;)

xxx

PS Truth of the day. Sometimes I wonder
if you're a bit freaked out by how quick
and how perfect this all is. You know
what? It IS freaky. But everyone should
have a shot at happiness. We just got
ours now! Stop worrying and enjoy it.

48

Hope

19 March 1999

Laura's parents are away. They've gone to London to visit friends and 'catch a show'. The show is *Chicago*. When I hear this, I try to imagine my parents doing anything of the kind, and fail. For one thing, they don't have any friends.

Laura and Alexis will have the house to themselves.

I know all this because Laura tells Jem on the way to English and neither of them thinks of me, behind them like a hunting dog. Jem laughs, a salacious, jealous laugh, and says she won't ask what they'll be doing with their time.

In class, I sit alone at the back and watch the crack in the ceiling, saying nothing. Ms Barnard tried to engage me for a while, after the Maggie Tulliver episode, but she doesn't bother now. We're done with *The Mill on the Floss* anyway, and are on to *Hamlet*. Today, she has Laura read Ophelia dropping into madness. 'Our stage star,' she says, and Laura laughs and shakes her head and delivers the lines straight, not even trying to act them.

Ms Barnard should have had her play Gertrude, sex-addled. *Honeying and making love.*

I laugh, thinking this, and they all look at me like I am the mad one.

I walk home with Claire, not needing to follow Laura and Alexis because they are twenty meters ahead of us, fingers meshed like wire. When Claire leaves me, I don't join them. I don't follow them either, beyond where our paths part naturally. It's daylight and I cannot count on my invisibility.

Besides, I know where they are. I know where they'll be.

Tonight is Her prayer meeting. She leaves straight after tea, so when I've done the washing-up, I ask my father if I can go out.

'To Laura's,' I say. 'Just for an hour or so.'

He lets me because he's still feeling bad about last weekend. Obviously he doesn't say this, but I can tell. He's been quieter all week. Greyer, pinched.

Also, he's relieved I still have a friend.

Isaac frowns at me as I put on my coat. 'I didn't think you and Laura were so close any more,' he says.

'What would you know?' I reply.

It's nearly dark, the air wet, waiting for rain. Laura has drawn the curtains at the front of her house, pulled down the kitchen blind. I go round the side, letting myself through the gate as I was always encouraged to do. There's a window into the kitchen from there, a yellow rectangle, spilling light. They never remember to cover that.

Inside, there is only a side light on, and wine and candles

and pudding bowls on the table. The candles are in the silver holders I saw last on Laura's sixteenth birthday. They're listening to music, though I can't tell what it is. Alexis's face is towards me, candlelit, perfect. Laura's hair is down, dark and straight and halfway to her waist. She leans towards him and it separates like seaweed on her shoulder blades.

They're out of their school clothes. (How out? In my mind, his hand twists in that mahogany hair, lifting it cleanly from milky flesh.) Alexis wears a jumper I have seen him in at church: dark wool, like a crofter. Laura is in cream. A bride.

The rain starts, sharp as winter. They hear it at the window, look across. I know they can't see me, but still I shrink. Looking in again, I see his hand across the table and her wrist, ivory-blue, turning into it. They kiss across the plates, so near the candles I think her hair will turn aflame. She gets up, comes round to him, tugs him to his feet. His face, tender and excited, snags like a knife in my throat.

They blow out the candles and go out, hands fast. I suppose they will go upstairs now, to Laura's bedroom with its lilac walls and white shelves. They'll screw each other under her rose-flecked duvet, with Sleeper crooning on the CD player and the cast of *Dawson's Creek* watching from the wardrobe door. I know that room almost better than my own, because I like it better than my own. And I've pictured this often enough.

But they don't go there. A light comes on at the other side of the hall. I edge round the house and my foot hits something as I go. I bend, hands flailing in the dark cold. I touch metal, then plastic. Laura's mother is a tidy gardener, but today she has left trowel and gloves and secateurs propped up against the side of the building. In too much of a hurry for her night away.

I smile. I think of Mark, who died because he was too lazy to wheel a bike around the school. I slip my fingers into the handle of the secateurs, play them open and shut. The blades are sharp as ice.

The sitting room curtains are almost shut, but not quite. I stand pressed under the jut of the roof, barely sheltered. I put my nose to the French doors and see a narrow slice of the room, palely illuminated. I see Alexis's back, Laura's hands lifting jumper and T-shirt, jeans dropping to the floor. I see Laura smooth and pale and naked, fingers gripping. His hands turn in heavy hair, exactly as I imagined them.

I close my eyes, sick with desire and despair. Rain runs down my collar, seeps up through thin soles. I am shaking with cold. I open my eyes and they are on the sofa, legs twining, horizontal. Laura's toes, lilac-nailed, glint like wet petals as she twists. I lean sideways, seeking more. His mouth on her breast, her hands where I cannot see them, but where they make his face contort. Then she is turning, shifting, on top of him, with her hair in his face and her legs bent under her, and I cannot watch any more.

I step back, kick something hard. Plant pot, stone, I don't know. Whatever it is, my foot slips with it and I fall to the ground, dropping the secateurs.

Stillness, after the crash. Then I hear Laura's voice, high, and the sounds of someone getting up. I crawl to the side, squeeze against the wall beside the window. The gap in the curtains darkens. I hear Alexis's voice, reassuring; Laura's saying something about a key.

I reach out a hand and hold back a yelp of pain. I'd forgotten the rose that climbs this wall. Golden in the summer, dazzling as Laura's lamp-glossed face. I lie almost flat, groping for the secateurs. Inside, I hear locks clicking.

I cut the plant through the stem, close to the earth. I take the handles in both hands and squeeze them together until the thick living thing breaks and gives.

I hear kicks against the door: a few seconds' grace. I hold the secateurs a moment against my chest. I imagine them swiping at Alexis's long fingers, Laura's hot face. Another kick. The door squeaks.

I cannot do it. Not yet. I wipe the plastic handles on my wet school skirt. Then I drop them and run.

23 November 2018

From: Khaleesi8690

To: AlwaysHaveParis

Subject: See you tonight!

I'm knackered! And you're a hard man to pin down right now. If I didn't know exactly who the other girl in your life is – and how gorgeous she is – I might be getting jealous!

I need a BIG glass of wine and a giant bed. But I'll settle for a pub, just this once.

Innis & Gunn at 8?

xxx

49

Laura

11 March 2019

The police have been digging. They showed up tonight when Benjy and Evie were asleep, moving toys and plumping bums down in my sitting room as though they'd been coming here for years.

I sat on a chest, pointlessly full of Ryan's vinyls.

Esme Morse said, 'Why didn't you tell us everything?'

I said nothing.

Capaldi said, 'Laura, we're tired. I'm sure you are too. Please answer the question.'

She may have been tired, but she had remembered her lipstick today and her suit was crisp and clean. I studied her with a dislike so strong it surprised me.

'I told you everything that mattered.'

Morse said, 'Not about the accident.'

'What accident?'

They looked at me the way I look at the children when they lie too blatantly. Then we heard feet on the stairs, a shout of 'Mummy!' Seconds later, Benjy was in the room with us, reprieve and reproach. He stood in his pyjamas at the door, glaring at the strangers. Then he ran to me. I hauled him onto my hip, held him like a shield.

'This isn't a good time,' I told Capaldi.

'It will have to be.' She eyed Benjy, unsmiling. 'Sergeant Morse is good with kids,' she said. 'She'll look after him.'

The sergeant approached, holding out a hand. 'We'll read a story, will we, pal?'

Benjy shook his head, grabbing my shoulders. I waved her away, carried him to the door.

'I'll come back,' I said.

Upstairs, Benjy gripped my hand like one of us was drowning and screamed when I tried to leave. I lay beside him as he quieted, wondering how long it would take for Capaldi to march up and interview me there. But it wasn't the inspector who appeared, minutes later. It was Simon, still in his school coat.

'Why are the cops here?' he said.

I eased myself over the edge of the bed. Benjy snapped an eye open, flung out a hand. 'Shh,' I said, and then, to Simon, 'Did they speak to you?'

He shook his head. 'What do they want?'

His eyes were as scared as his brother's. In her toddler bed, beneath her mobile of dancing bears, Evie grumbled and turned. Guilt settled into my stomach.

I got up. 'Hush, Benjy,' I said. 'I won't be long.' I hugged Simon. 'It's OK, darling. They just have a few more questions for me. Nothing for you to worry about.' I stepped back, pulled his chin down and round to look at me. 'It'll be OK.'

He gripped my hand. 'Promise?'

'Promise,' I whispered, and left him with Benjy.

Downstairs, the officers had spread a printout on the coffee table, weighed down at the corner with Evie's milk cup. The headline sprang out from across the room: *SCHOOL TRAGEDY*. It was the newspaper story, decades old, that I had read on my phone on Thursday.

I picked it up as though I'd never seen it before, skimmed it with my back to them.

'Congratulations,' I said at last, dropping it on the table. 'You can use Google. But this has nothing to do with me. I wasn't there.'

That was a mistake. Capaldi, who had been scrutinising her now-red nails, flicked me a glance of piercing appraisal. 'I wasn't suggesting that you were,' she said. 'But Sergeant Morse isn't just a dab hand at internet searches. She's also been asking questions.'

Alexis's parents. *Hell.* I knew Alexis had told them nothing, but not what his grandparents had told them.

Capaldi picked up the paper, returned it to her bag. 'Tell me about Hope Mitchell,' she said.

I didn't reply.

'You were good friends once,' she said.

'It was a long time ago.'

'Was she close to Alexis, too?'

'They knew each other.'

The edge of the chest dug into my thighs. I slid forward. The women watched. I said, 'We were all at the same school.'

The sergeant said, 'They were at the same church.'

'If you already know, why ask me?'

Capaldi said, 'How did your friendship end?'

I reached behind me, tweaked the curtains tighter shut. 'For Christ's sake,' I said. 'How do you think it ended? You've read that thing.'

'Was Hope jealous of your relationship with Alexis?'

'Maybe. I don't know. He and I were . . .'

'Were what?'

I wrapped my hands together. 'Absorbed in each other,' I said. And among all the lies, that was the absolute truth.

'Too absorbed to notice what was happening to your friend?'

Her voice was even, steady, as if she was discussing the weather. I squeezed my fingers until they hurt. 'What exactly is this in aid of?' I said. 'Apart from trying to make me feel bad.'

Capaldi let me wait without an answer. Then she began again. 'Tell me about Hope's parents.'

I groaned. 'Her mother was a religious nutcase. Well, you know that. We didn't know at the time, though we wondered sometimes.'

Though we should have done more to find out.

'We?' said Morse.

'Hope's friends,' I said. 'It came out afterwards. I don't know if her father was a zealot too. Probably just weak. He's dead now, either way.'

Morse stopped making notes. Capaldi said, 'How do you know that?'

Shit. 'Christ, I don't know. You just hear these things somehow. From my parents, maybe.' I dropped my head, forehead to hands, made myself look up at them again.

'Please don't ask me any more. This has nothing to do with anything.'

'The thing is, Laura, I don't think you really believe that.'

'Aren't I the best judge of that?'

'Right now, you may not be the best judge of very much at all.' She sounded almost gentle.

I didn't speak. Capaldi looked at the sergeant again, and it was the older woman who spoke. 'Mrs Reville,' she said. 'Laura. Are you sure no one was on to your relationship with Alexis?'

'I told you, I thought Diana had guessed. You should be asking her.'

Capaldi didn't quite roll her eyes. 'Thank you for the suggestion.'

I fiddled with my finger, barren without its rings. 'Ryan didn't know,' I said. 'I'd swear to that.'

The sergeant said, 'Anyone else?'

'I don't know. I told you. I don't know any more.'

Capaldi uncrossed her legs. Morse put away her notebook. The inspector leaned forward, watching me like a priest, speaking like an oracle. 'Laura, you need to understand how serious this is. If Alexis was killed because of your relationship, there's every possibility that you could be in danger too.'

I stared back at her. 'Do you think I don't know that?'

Do you think I care? But I could hold that thought only for a moment before recollection rebuked me. I relived my own fear; I saw the three children as I had left them upstairs, Evie buried in the duvet, Benjy curled round his teddy bear, holding his brother's hand.

I care for them. I do not want to die.

Besides, it's one thing to think something yourself, another to have the police confirm it.

50

Laura

9 February 2019

This morning, I awakened in the right place for the first time in my adult life. Alexis slept like he had as a teenager, one hand under his pillow, the other on my hair. He stirred when I moved, smiled when he opened his eyes. Later, torpid after lovemaking, he said, 'What were you thinking, when you woke?'

I shifted, twining closer to him. The ceiling sloped above us, walls white and flecked with blue. It felt safe, airy, under the eaves together. I said, 'If we counted up all the times we've slept the whole night together, we'd still be in single digits.'

'It didn't feel like that last night,' he said.

'No.' I turned my head into his throat, kissed the damp skin. 'I love you,' I said.

After breakfast, we ran together, feet on worn paths and slippery grass, through woods and out of them again, to the sparse, spacey landscape. We were well matched still, lungs tingling with the chill Borders air. High above the hotel, we stopped, hands held, breath scrambling, looking east to the Eildon Hills and north to the Pentlands, until we were too cold not to move.

The quarrel came later, after showering and sex and lunch in a Peebles café where I wore sunglasses and a scarf wrapped high on my neck; after we had abandoned a nature trail because it was full of families. We paced the walled, wintry gardens, gloved hands clasped, and paranoia grew in me. That middle-aged man by the gate. Why was he alone? Why was he watching us? The elderly couple passing under the arched trees. Their glance that could have been disinterest, or could have been suspicion.

'Can we go in?' I said, and we returned in silence to our room. I sat on the bed the chambermaid had made, my hand in Alexis's, thinking of his wrecked flat. Torchlight through trees; a silver car on night-time roads.

I said, 'I should have taken the number plate.'

He let go my hand, turned to face me. 'For what, Laura? So we can go to the police? We've already had this conversation.'

'Maybe we should,' I said. 'Maybe you should have two weeks ago.' I stopped, tasting irrevocable words, forcing them out. 'Maybe we should have told them everything twenty years ago.'

'Maybe we should,' he said, surprising me. 'But we didn't.'

'We still could.'

He watched me, pity in his eyes. 'Do you want your children to know? Or Ryan?'

'Of course n—'

'Or that stepson you're terrified of losing?'

'I never told you that.'

'You didn't need to.' He studied me, thrashing on truth. He said, 'I sure as hell don't want Gracie to grow up knowing what her father did.'

I sat beside him on the bed, my head close to his, seeing Benjy's eyes, Evie's. Simon's. 'OK,' I said. 'OK. Never mind the police. But *we* have to talk about this.' I floundered for words, found only a cliché. 'We have to forgive ourselves.'

'Not for some things,' he said.

I put my hand on his leg. 'It w—'

He pulled back. I remembered how those eyes had once watched me crying, and still he'd left.

'Have you?' he said, like he was accusing me.

'What?'

'Forgiven yourself.'

I shivered. Then I tried for truth. 'I have tried to forgive the girl I was then.' I paused. It seemed important to get the right phrase. 'We were so young. I want to have compassion for all of us. Me, you, her most of all.'

'Her,' he said.

I put my arms round him, my mouth against his ear. He let me, but did not respond. I said, 'Have you talked to anyone about this?'

'A therapist, you mean?'

'Yes.'

'I had one in Paris, but what could I say?' He pushed my arms away, gently, as though they hurt him but he would not hurt me. 'How much would *confidential* mean, when we'd lied to the police?'

I said nothing, waited. At last, words fell from him.

'My stepfather suggested it. He was just my mum's boyfriend then. I didn't give him credit for how nice he was trying to be. Mum was desperate to mend me, throwing money at it. So they found one who spoke English and I went every week for two months and talked about my parents' divorce and how it had made me feel, and I suppose that might have been useful, except that by then the divorce was the least of my problems.'

'Alexis. I'm—'

'I couldn't even talk about you – how I was starving for you – because that would get us to why I wasn't with you.'

He stopped, half smiled. 'How melodramatic I make it seem: our great love. I know we were children. But it felt real.'

I said, 'It was real.'

His face flickered, went still. I wanted to reach for him, but it seemed impossible.

'I made an appointment once,' I said. 'At the university counsellor. I couldn't go through with it.'

I remembered how I had stopped at the door of the building, listening to the London traffic. How I had turned and run, instead, to the bar, where a boy from the morning's lecture had said he might be. I thought of how I had self-medicated. Alcohol, sex. Those university terms that felt like I was acting a part: giving my body, freely, as if it was no longer mine, but never yielding a scrap of myself. Then the lost London years after graduation. Shared flats, temporary jobs, crowded pubs, mind kept deliberately blurred. Until one flatmate, less chaotic than the rest, pulled me hung-over from my stained bed and took me running along the Regent's Canal.

I probably never thanked her. I soon lost touch with her – deliberately, as I did with everyone – but I owed her almost everything. The 'proper job' I got next. Edinburgh. Ryan.

I said, 'We have to do something. We're keeping ourselves in limbo.'

'You mean I am?' Alexis said.

I thought of Ryan, to whom I really *did* owe everything. Ryan, who had made me feel whole, in treating me as such. Ryan, who would be right to hate me.

Alexis said, 'You asked me once if I wished we hadn't met again.'

Coldness settled in my chest, tightened my breath. He said, 'I wish I could wish it.'

I nodded. It cut me, but it was only the echo of my own thoughts, swelling with shame, a few weeks since. It was only what I ought to feel now.

He broke the gap between us, put a hand behind my neck, pulled me in. He kissed me so we both shook with it. 'Ask an alcoholic,' he said, his lips so close I could still taste them, 'if he would rather not have the drink at his mouth.'

51

Hope

22 March 1999

I want to see fear in Laura's face, to hear her confide the collapse of her night with Alexis. I watch her at registration and all through English, but she says nothing. She's pale, but then she's always pale. Skin so fine you can see the veins underneath. But there's a new mauve gleam round her eyes today. It could be anxiety – or eyeshadow. I test for jumpiness, nudging a chair until it topples backwards with a bang. They all start, but she leaps high from her seat, and I think for a moment that she'll bolt from the classroom.

It is enough. I apologise to Ms Barnard, pick up the chair, open *Hamlet*. I hear Jem whisper to Laura, 'What's the matter with you today?'

I do not see her with Alexis. At lunchtime I skulk closer to the hall than I would normally go. I yearn to see them changed, severed from one another. But Laura is not with Alexis. She is with Rick, just outside the hall, dancing.

It's their routine from the Dance in the Gym. Rick is humming the music and they're practising straight-faced, Rick throwing her about with rough sensuality while keeping one eye on an imaginary Riff. Balmore was hassling them to sex it up even before I left the show. Maria and Tony are young love, passionate and innocent. Anita and Bernardo, by contrast, are pure sex. Or supposed to be.

I watch them. Rick moves without corners, as though he's made of plasticine and steel. Laura keeps time, but she moves with the music, not as part of it. I wonder if I would be better if they'd given me Anita. I wonder if Laura would be if she were dancing with Alexis.

They see me and stop. Rick comes over; Laura leans against the wall where she is. 'What do you reckon?' Rick says.

I shrug. 'Very nice.'

He looks at my face as though he's got to learn it for an exam. 'How's it going, Hope?'

Another shrug. 'OK,' I say. 'How's the show?'

I guess Laura's listening, though she acts like she's too out of breath to do anything. 'Coming along,' Rick says. He grins. 'I still think you'd be a better Riff.'

'Thanks. But perhaps it was for the best.'

'Ah yes.' He gives me that look again. 'With your family and everything.'

And everything.

There's a silence. We can hear the official rehearsal from inside the hall. Stacy's voice, saccharine as a Disney princess; Alexis's warm and rich, twisting into it. It's the duet Laura was singing when I freaked her out outside school. Pure love song. I wonder if she's remembering that now.

She's very still, and she's listening. Her eyes are like blank screens. Rick looks puzzled. I realise I'm smiling.

'Better go,' I say. 'Good luck with it all.'

In the locker room, Jem is lying flat on a bench, Discman buzzing, staring at the dank ceiling, fiddling with the edge of her skirt. Claire is reading *Middlemarch*, which isn't on our English list, but she likes to go above and beyond. Jem rolls upright when I come in and asks if I've seen Laura. She pushes her headphones back on her head but doesn't stop the music. The Corrs lodge in my ears, tinny but persistent.

'By the hall,' I say. I think about telling her that Laura is with Rick, but she doesn't deserve it. She too obviously wants to get away from us.

Claire turns a page. Jem scuttles out. She pauses as she passes me and pulls a curious expression. It can't be because my spots have gone. She'll be used to that by now.

'Are you OK, Hope?' she says, and I realise that I'm still excited from watching Laura squirm. My heart is thudding, like I'm being punched inside my chest. Perhaps it shows in my face.

'I'm fine,' I say, and she's out of the door, headphones back on, before I've finished saying it. I sit down across from Claire, then wish I hadn't. She isn't looking at her book any more; she is looking at me.

'What is it?' I say. I dig in my bag for my lunch.

Claire is always direct, when she can be bothered engaging at all. 'Are you sure you're fine?' she says.

'Of course.' I pull out the sandwiches and uncurl the cursive slip. It's the first commandment today, a failsafe when She doesn't have any particular axe to grind. I shove it back and take a bite.

'Only,' says Claire, 'you've been acting a bit weird recently. If you're upset about something, it might be better to tell someone. Me, or someone else.'

I swallow the mouthful. The cheese tastes sour, like it's been at the back of the fridge too long. I wonder if it's deliberate.

'Who?' I say, because I'm curious. Claire knows me well enough not to suggest my parents.

'Well, one of the teachers? Or your doctor? Or if there was someone at your church . . .' She says the last bit tentatively, treading on unknown ground. I try to imagine showing up at the vicarage with the tale of the last few months. I try not to laugh. Claire frowns again.

'There's nothing wrong,' I say, and take another bite.

'OK,' she says. 'If you say so.'

She opens *Middlemarch* again and is immediately lost. I make myself chew and swallow. Then I decide I'm not hungry and put the rest back in my bag.

52

Laura

10 February 2019

An owl woke me. I reached for Alexis, heard him moving, speaking my name. We made love like it was a ritual, drugged and unknowing. I screamed at the sweetness of it, gripped him as if he would turn into a memory in my arms.

We should have had the day together, only in the end we didn't. Nor did we talk about anything that mattered. I tried, but only once. In the car, on the edge of Peebles, bells burst on us, brazen and sweet, and I said, 'Does it take you back?'

He replied with his gaze on the road. 'It reminds me of my grandparents,' he said.

In the car park, emerging to a brisk February wind, the exchange rang in my mind. Truth, yes, but only part of it. We walked side by side along the John Buchan Way, from town to openness, tended paths to grassy slopes. We swapped smiles with hikers and cyclists and dog owners, as though we were allowed to be together. I took his hand, tightened glove on glove, thought of his grandparents' funerals. I remembered his face, lines and planes in the dark pub when he told me that was the last time he'd been in a church.

Hope's church. Had she plagued him then, surrounded by his family, slithering between him and the loved ones he wanted to mourn? They were more his parents than his parents were.

I said none of this. We struck off the main path, climbed Cademuir Hill in sporadic sun and biting breeze, and talked of other peaks. Of Scotland, and places we loved. Of the Iron Age fort, just traceable in bumps and stones.

Not of each other. Not of her.

At the summit, feet crunching on frost, out of breath from the last steep slog, I looked at my phone for the first time. Six missed calls and a message from Ryan, two calls from Simon. I stripped off my glove, opened the message.

Call me please. Soon as you can.

Thoughts crashed into my mind. I struggled, cold-fingered, to return the call. Alexis said, 'What is it?' but I shook my head.

I got my husband's voicemail, calm, professional. I left a jumble of words. 'Oh God, Ryan, answer your phone. What is it? Benjy, Evie. Please tell me they're OK. Ryan, please call me.'

I took a breath, phoned Simon. 'What is it?' I said. I pushed my phone against my ear, covered the other one with my still-gloved hand. 'What's happened?'

'Evie had an accident,' he said, his young voice strident, despite the elements. My intestines froze. 'We couldn't reach you,' he said.

'Jesus.' I put out a hand, felt Alexis hold it. I yelled over the wind at Simon. 'What happened? Where is she?'

'Dad took her to Sick Kids,' he said.

The children's hospital. Shit. Ryan isn't one to overreact to minor injuries.

But if he took her, she wasn't in an ambulance.

Simon's voice went on. In the background I could hear Benjy, overexcited. Simon shushed him, started again. 'She tried to climb onto Benjy's bunk. She slipped at the top and fell. She banged her head on that little wooden chair.'

'She was crying,' Benjy shouted. The words were a comfort. I slid against Alexis, felt him holding me up.

'She wasn't knocked out?' I said.

'We don't think so,' Simon said. 'If she was, it was only a few seconds. She was screaming her head off by the time Dad got in there.'

I heard Benjy again, almost cheerful. 'She had a big bump.'

'We tried to get you,' Simon said. 'She wanted you.'

Behind the worry, I felt the guilt start. 'My phone was on silent,' I said. 'Meetings.'

I stared down the ridge. Rocks and frozen grass. The breeze spun into a flurry, hissed down the line. Simon said, 'You sound like you're in the middle of nowhere.'

'Fresh air break,' I said. 'I'll come back now.'

'Won't your colleague mind?'

'No.' My mind blocked with Evie, I couldn't remember if

the colleague I'd invented to drive me was man or woman. 'They'll be fine,' I said.

I called Ryan again from the car. No answer. I tried again, kept on trying. Alexis drove with one hand on the wheel, the other on my leg. Comfort, rather than desire. After the fifth attempt, Ryan texted me.

> Can't speak. Still waiting.

Twenty seconds later, another one.

> Don't worry.

Typical Ryan.

'I should have been there,' I said, turning the phone in my fingers.

'It wasn't your fault,' Alexis said.

'That doesn't change how I feel.'

'Of course not.' He slid his hand from my thigh, swinging the car north towards Edinburgh. I told myself it couldn't be so bad if they'd kept her waiting. At the traffic lights in Auchendinny, Alexis said, 'I'll take you to the hospital.'

I clung to him a moment before I left the car. *I love you*, I thought. But it seemed a betrayal of my injured daughter to say it out loud.

The hospital is Victorian, intimidating, like an orphanage, the emergency entrance hidden on a side road. I stumbled by the door, stubbed my toe. Tears swelled in my eyes. I ran through the doors, guilt-sped, and a nurse jumped sideways to avoid me. Then, as my mouth formed the request, I heard Evie's voice.

'Mummy!'

Ryan was bringing her out, her bottom on his arm, her arms already unwinding from his neck to reach for me. She thrust against my chest, submitted to my salty kisses. Ryan put a hand on my back, steered me round and out.

'She's fine,' he said. 'I've got a list of things to look out for, but it looks worse than it is.'

I had already found it: the bump on the back of her skull, big as an egg, but more tender. She squirmed. I let my hand slide, felt her hot, solid back. 'Evie,' I said, head in her hair. 'Darling girl.'

'I'm OK, Mummy,' she said, and I quailed with love and shame.

On the cold street, my teary eyes burned. I followed Ryan to the car, said, 'I'm so sorry I wasn't there.'

'You had to work,' he said. 'These things happen.'

If he'd uttered a word of criticism, I could have snapped back, pointed out the innumerable occasions on which he hadn't been there. But he didn't, and I retreated powerless into my own mind.

Later, while the kids watched TV and Ryan poured glasses of wine, I called Alexis from the bathroom.

'Is Evie all right?' he said.

'She is.' I hauled the next words up, resistant, from a throat gone tight and dry. 'But Alexis, we have to stop. You're right. We should want not to want it.'

53

Laura

12 March 2019

Diana knows. I believe that she didn't before, but she's been told now.

We passed her on the stairs at nursery. Benjy was at my heels, Evie behind the stairgate waving with both hands. Diana carried Gracie, head to neck. Her hand, red at the knuckles, squashed the springy curls. Her face was the colour of the plaster, and as impassive. I couldn't see Gracie's. I cringed into the stair rail, pulled Benjy with me. Diana breathed herself in, to make more space between us.

Afterwards, she caught me on the street. She grabbed my arm, pulling me round, almost sending me to the floor. She had expression enough now. 'Keep away from my daughter,' she said.

I said nothing.

'I heard all about it. Sneaking around Alexis's flat. Upsetting his parents. Pretending to comfort her.'

'I . . .' *I wasn't pretending.* In the face of this derision, I couldn't say it.

'This is all your fault,' she said, like an angry child. 'You've done enough harm already.' And what could I say to that, when in my heart I agreed with her?

A man passed us, buggy handle in one hand, phone against his ear, toddler wailing in the moving seat. I knew both father and child but could not have named them for the world. We stood wordless until he had turned through the nursery gate. Then Diana spoke quietly, almost conversationally.

'I should be mourning him,' she said. 'I should be thinking about nothing but him and Gracie. Instead, I've spent days trying to process this.'

She'd been eating in her grief and her face was puffed out, pale like old cheese. I didn't want to notice, but I did.

'I'm sorry,' I said.

'For God's sake,' Diana said. 'Do you think I care about your apologies? I want answers. How long had it been going on?'

'I don't th—'

'Since he and I were together? Is that why he left me?'

'No.' I found words, when they were the truth. 'Since Gracie started here. No sooner. We didn't even know we were in the same city until then. I promise.'

'*You* promise.'

'It's true,' I said, and I stared so long that it was her who looked away.

I said, 'Did the police tell you?'

She raised a hand, dropped it. 'They told me enough for me to figure it out.'

Heather passed us then, hurrying, dragging a protesting Liam by the wrist, but still managing to stare. At the door, she screwed her head so she could still watch us. Diana strode off in the opposite direction. I went with her because I could not bear to stand there on my own. I saw my bus at the end of the road, thought, *I'll run. I'll run now, and get it, and this will be over.*

But Diana spoke and the bus half slowed and sped up again, and I was still there, out of step beside her. 'Couldn't you leave him alone?' she said. 'You screwed him up enough at seventeen; why come back to do it again?'

I said, quietly, 'We screwed each other up.'

'You're married now. You have children.'

I was married.

'This isn't about me,' she said. She looked at me, suddenly Victorian. 'It's about decency.'

'I can't explain,' I said. 'Not so you will understand.'

Not how, when I saw him again, I could think of nothing else. Not how we needed each other, every moment. How we were so obsessed we let everything else fall. She'd said she wanted answers, but these weren't the answers she wanted.

She said, 'You should be ashamed to look at me.'

I didn't look at her.

'Or at Gracie.'

I flinched. I wondered what would happen if I bent my head back and screamed, there in the road, until she stopped. *Decency*, she had said. And Alexis had said *resolutely middle class*. Would she be embarrassed? Would it shut her up?

'Or your own children.'

I put my hands to my face. We stood still, at the end of the street. She said, flatly, 'He's dead because of you.'

'I loved him,' I said, and she swung her head, quick as a falling axe, and spat at me.

I was so surprised I didn't move at first. I watched the bubble of mucus as it hung on my coat button, stretched, and dropped into the fabric. So much for Ms Respectable.

'You know something,' Diana said, changing tone, quick as a cat. 'What are you keeping secret?'

'Nothing. How would I—'

'Gracie's *three*, Laura. That's a lot of years growing up without a father. Don't you think she deserves the truth?'

'Do you think I wouldn't have told someone, if I knew?'

'I get the impression that's exactly what the police think.'

I shook my head, walked away from her. 'I have to go,' I said.

She came after me. 'Or was it you?' she said. 'Is that why you're not talking? Did you have a row? Did he try to end it?'

Again.

I shook my head. *I thought it was you.* But that had only been a distraction.

She kept going. 'Well? Did you run after him, stab him in the back? Would you rather no one else could have him if you couldn't?'

'I *had* him,' I said.

She looked as though she might spit again, but instead she went very quiet, tightly calm. 'Then tell me what you know.'

'Nothing. I know nothing.'

I went faster, trying to run, only my feet were falling over themselves. Diana marched behind me, drill-sergeant quick. A woman, angry-faced, veered onto the road to avoid us.

'Please,' I said, and I realised I was crying. 'Leave me alone.'

'It's there, isn't it?' She sounded almost complacent now. She had me caught, kicking in my net. 'In the past he wouldn't talk about?'

I half fell into a hedge, reaching for something to hold. 'Leave me,' I said. 'Just leave me alone.'

'Tell them, Laura,' she said. 'You don't have to tell me. But tell the police.'

We stood there, me looking at the ground and her looking at me. I wept without speaking or moving. I saw Alexis, savage-eyed in a hotel room. I heard him. *I sure as hell don't want Gracie to grow up knowing what her father did.*

The tears fell from my drooped head to the pavement and were lost. Diana didn't cry, but her eyes were red and her mouth crumpled.

At last, a man with a dog barked at us to move. Diana jumped out of his way, her back pushing into the hedge beside me.

'That's all I had to say,' she said, when he had gone. She tucked her jacket straight and turned away.

'Diana,' I said, and she looked back. Her face was as dull now as it had been when she carried her daughter to the toddler room. I swallowed. 'I'm sorry. I know you won't want to tell me. But I need to ask . . .'

'What?'

'I would like . . . Do you know when the funeral will be?'

Silence.

'You see,' I said, and I knew my voice sounded brattish, unwinning, 'I did love him.'

Diana laughed. 'God,' she said, 'you're quite something, *Mrs* Reville.' And she swivelled, like a soldier again, and stamped away.

1 December 2018

From: Khaleesi8690

To: AlwaysHaveParis

Subject: Lunch

Yes, lunch works. But why lunch? You
know I'm more of a dinner-and-bed-and-
breakfast girl, and you wouldn't stay
over last Friday either . . .

Should I be worried?!

xx

PS OK, I'll be honest. I am worried.
You've been weird for weeks. Reassure
me. Please.

54

Hope

28 March 1999

Palm Sunday and Alexis isn't in church, for the second week in a row. His grandparents are in their usual seats without him. When the service ends, they are close to us in the bustle for tea and squash and biscuits, and he's still not there.

His grandmother asks me how I am. Asks me directly, I mean: not all of us. I study the streaked floor and squirm. I sense Her expression drilling my skull, even if I can't see it. My father coughs; Isaac shuffles from foot to foot.

'I'm fine,' I say. 'Thank you.'

The silence grates. My father plunges into it, uncharacteristically jovial. 'No Alexis today?' he says.

I see Her give him a look, contempt edged with amusement. She'd have happily stared them out. Alexis's grandmother rolls her eyes. His grandfather laughs. 'No,' he says. 'He'd rather be with his girlfriend.'

I glance up; She's gaping as though he'd said Alexis had gone to an orgy. Alexis's grandfather gives a discomfited chuckle. His grandmother smiles. 'He'll come back when he's ready,' she says. 'I don't believe in forcing these things.'

Walking home, She tells me, 'I don't want to hear any more about you being friends with that boy.'

'You won't,' I say.

She glowers like She's about to take up the ambiguity. I keep my head lowered, and after a while She asks instead if I know his girlfriend. '*The* girlfriend,' she says, as though it was *the disease*, or *the crocodile*.

I say nothing. Ahead of us, Isaac turns his head and answers for me. 'We all know her,' he says. 'It's Laura.'

2 December 2018

From: Khaleesi8690

To: AlwaysHaveParis

Subject: Please think about this

Dear Alexis,

Here's what I was too upset to say today.

I don't know what's going on with you. I know there's stuff you haven't told me about and I haven't wanted to push it. We all have our own skeletons. But don't let it stop something that could be really wonderful. You're making a big mistake.

I know I shouldn't say this. Pride and all that. But that's bollocks when it really matters.

xx

55

Laura

12 March 2019

I was late to work and did nothing there. Danielle watched me, her expression disquietingly serious. Kai, whom I half hoped would cover for me, was off. I went home at lunchtime, promising to work there. Danielle didn't believe me, but she let me go. Her brown eyes tracked me to the door. Their reproach barely grazed me, after Diana's contempt.

I walked all the way. I went through scattered sunshine, thinking of Alexis. I saw him in the Meadows, vivid as life, rushing between trees to meet me. And then he was gone, had never been, and the man before me was a stranger, avoiding my eyes. I lurched, like I would fold into myself, into the stony ground. The man who was not Alexis paused an instant, then hurried on.

I went on. I moved fast, as though I had been wound up and could not stop. I avoided Blackford Pond this time, skirted Marchmont, came south down Whitehouse Loan and Canaan Lane, marched up Braid Avenue with my eyes ahead.

At home, I found stillness. I made coffee, left it undrunk. I moved from room to room as through a stranger's domain. I sat where Capaldi had perched her thin arse the night before, gazing at the wall that still held our wedding pictures. They too seemed somebody else's. Ryan hadn't got round to pulling them down yet.

Ryan's son said, 'Are you in danger?'

I jumped, only just didn't scream. Simon was standing barely a meter from me. He'd taken his coat and shoes off but was in his uniform.

I said, 'You should be at school.'

'You lied to me,' he said.

'What do you mean?'

'The police. Last night. I heard you. Benjy went to sleep, and I came down. I heard them say he might be after you.'

'They didn't exactly say that.' I gave up, afraid to ask what else he'd heard. Also, it *was* what they had said.

Simon folded his arms. 'Why won't you tell me the truth?'

'I am. I was. The police are just . . .' *Just what?* 'Covering eventualities.'

Simon snorted. I got up, straightened books on the shelves. 'Thanks for settling Benjy last night.'

'Someone had to.'

I laughed: he sounded so much like me. I said, 'Why are you home so early?'

'You're changing the subject.'

Someone had to. 'Do you have a free period?'

'Something like that.'

'I'm surprised you're not with Bella.'

His face lost its expression. 'I've split up with her,' he said, as if he was telling me he'd forgotten to do his homework.

I spun from the books, arms out. 'Oh darling. I'm so sorry. Why?'

He looked past me, through the windows smeared with fingerprints. 'I didn't need her any more.'

'That's a terrible thing to say.'

He shrugged. I went to him, took his hands. He wouldn't look at me. 'Simon,' I said. 'Tell me this isn't because of me and your father.'

He said nothing.

'Relationships can work,' I said. 'I promise you. Just because ours didn't . . .' I stopped.

'*You* promise me,' he said, the scorn like a blow, and left the room.

I gazed at the closing door. Diana's words, Diana's corrosive tone. I lifted one of our wedding photos from the wall. Simon in a kilt like his father's, with a buttonhole of thistle and white rose; me kneeling in my ivory dress before him, holding his hands in mine. I had made a vow to him that day, as unambiguous as the one I had made his father.

How long, I wondered, until everyone hated me?

56

Laura

18 February 2019

I've seen Alexis.

I tried not to. I've turned up late for pick-up, sprinting in at five minutes past six, my children flotsam among the tidying-up, their coats already on. Or I've been early, ignoring Danielle's ire. Last week, I got my first written warning, a shark's grin in its white envelope, waiting when I got back from lunch. My gut clenched, security ebbing. I may not like this job, but I need it.

But I could not think about that.

Today I was early, but Benjy had drawn me a picture, and it could not be found.

'We'll get it tomorrow,' I promised, forcing flailing limbs into thick wool. But his mouth widened, his eyes shrank, the crying became screaming. So I waited, too tired to endure the meltdown, while Anja stripped shelves and radiators and Benjy's rage became whimpering and Evie sat straight-legged on the floor and cast off hat and gloves. I closed my eyes, tried to find the resolve I had counted on. To be a better mother, do the right thing.

Outside, we met Heather, garrulous and in no hurry to retrieve Liam. I responded by rote while Benjy hung heavy on my hand and Evie kicked in her buggy. And then there he was, and it was almost like November again, with Heather talking to me, and me only pretending to listen.

He was walking fast along the street, head down. He hadn't seen me. I watched him as Heather pouted endearments at Evie, who scowled at her. Last night, I'd had sex with Ryan. I had initiated it: another box ticked. Only it was faked, distasteful, and I was drawn down by shame. Not for the act alone, but because of his joy in it, the laughter in his eyes when we woke this morning. Laughter snuffed out, almost at once, by my overstated briskness.

Now, that uneven coupling stung like a brand on my forehead, as my very pores screamed for Alexis.

He saw me, looked once across Heather's bent head. My body glowed, inside to out. She stood up, snapped the link, bared her teeth at him. I pulled the buggy aside to let him pass, my eyes on Evie. He gave us the brief thanks of a stranger.

I stood still. Benjy yanked my arm, impatient and confused. Heather watched Alexis to the nursery door, irritated and mildly salacious. She turned to me. 'I thought you knew each other.'

I spoke without thinking. 'That was in another country.'

She frowned as though I was making fun of her. Then, seeing Alexis being buzzed in, she scurried along the street. She caught the closing door, out of breath but smiling. Her voice carried, but not the words. I hoped they weren't about me.

57

Hope

29 March 1999

She is bad today. I know it when we go into the kitchen. Her eyes are dotted scarlet and She raises hands scoured by prayer and cleaning. The room smells of bleach and of something else, unpleasant. Father isn't there. He left early; he knows when to do that. She hooks one finger, indicating first the clock, then the table. The porridge is cold, curling on the plate like something years dead. When I take a spoonful, I taste fishy bitterness.

Cod liver oil.

I allow no expression onto my face. I swallow, put the spoon in again, scoop up another mouthful. Isaac takes one, gags and spits it out. She swings around, quick as a fox, and grips him by the hair. He trembles, then starts to apologise.

She says, 'Put that back in your mouth.'

He struggles with the spoon, gets it halfway in again, then drops it. She tightens her hold. His face folds. He tries again, gets it in, swallows, coughs, drinks water, swallows some more. She lets him go. She'd have struck me for that, but like I said, he's Her favourite.

He eats on, crying in silence, swaying forward like he's about to puke every time he tastes it. But She's not interested in him any more. He's an easy victory. She sits between us drinking her mahogany tea, watching me. I finish the bowl and run my spoon about the edge, getting the last scraps. I feel strange, as though I'm on a platform that's slowly revolving.

I take the bowl to the sink, wash and rinse it and put it in the rack. I look at Her. 'Thank you,' I say, from my podium. 'That was very nice.'

She says nothing. Isaac is half choking, half sobbing, barely halfway through his bowl. She glowers at him. Then, suddenly, She smiles, speaks as I turn for the door. 'Perhaps you'd like your brother's too, since you enjoyed it so much.'

I stop, acid in my throat. I breathe in, bring my shoulders down. I sit at the table and Isaac pushes his plate across. He's looking contrite, but also a bit scared. It takes a moment to realise that he's afraid of me too now.

I eat everything in the bowl. I do it looking down at the table because I cannot stop my mouth from twisting. I take this bowl to the sink too, and wash it carefully. Then I thank Her again. They're both watching me as I leave the room.

I won't let Her win.

Today is the dress rehearsal. Laura arrives with her mum, delivering costumes. They park in the teachers' spaces and lift dresses swathed in sheets from the boot. The same ponytail and the same tilt of their eyebrows and shape to their chin. Laura's face is tight with nerves. Her mum smiles at her.

'You'll be amazing,' she says. 'You *are* amazing.'

I slide out of view. My fingers bend and straighten. I see the severed stem of a rose bush, bleeding sap. I follow them towards the main doors.

Laura spots Stacy and Rick and veers off with her own dress over her arm. Her mum waits, smiling. I press back, behind Old Flop's polished Passat, terrified that she will see me. But she's watching the others, Laura and her new friends. They stand by the rain-dirty windows and Laura peels back the sheet. The dress shows shining red, black-belted. She'll be wearing it for the Dance at the Gym. She does a few steps, holding it to her chest.

Stacy strokes the fabric, says something with a laugh. If she's nervous, it doesn't show. Then she goes over to Laura's mum – she'll be asking about her outfits – and they all walk together into the school. As they go, I see Rick put an arm round Stacy's waist. She turns her face up to him, poised as a mannequin, and rests her cheek on his shoulder.

I freeze a little more.

None of them see me.

The rehearsal is in the afternoon. The cast get time off class and the rest of us sit restless and diminished. In English, we dissect *The Waste Land* while grey rain tips onto the window. Claire is smiling, inhaling the words like she is lying in sunshine. By my side, Jem seems hardly to hear them. She's scowling, and her make-up is scuffed at the edges.

I wonder where they've got to in the hall. Is Alexis singing? Is he holding Stacy by both hands and gazing at her with the look he gives Laura? Is Laura devouring him from the wings, his voice a seduction, memory as foreplay? I bend back the lid on my biro, forcing it down against blistering fingers. It is maimed but it will not snap.

As we put our books away, I say to Jem, 'Are Rick and Stacy together now?'

Jem's voice is as sulky as her face. She doesn't even sound surprised that I'm asking. 'Apparently so,' she says.

She thrusts her books into her bag and follows Claire and me to the locker room with her head down.

58

Laura

25 February 2019

These past days, I have been almost nothing because so much of me has been occupied with *not* calling Alexis. A fortnight of silence, broken by that almost-meeting that was worse than nothing. Fifteen days of vowing each morning to mend my marriage, quarrelling before breakfast. Of always playing helicopter parent, hands out for the tumble.

It's been worse since I saw him. I alternately stifle the children and snipe at them, rigid with shame when they retreat from me. Simon watches me, wary as when he was a small boy. Sometimes he seems on the point of asking something, then creeps into himself again.

At night I will myself to roll into my husband, arm over chest, to be normal with him. In a curious way, I want to. I want him to comfort me. But I am not ready, after that last hollow time, to give him the body I long to give to Alexis.

And now I am afraid that I have betrayed myself. Not to Ryan, but to Kai.

We had drinks after work. It was supposed to be team bonding, in some masochistic City way. Play hard, work hard. All crap anyway, because Graham went home on a transparent excuse and Danielle bailed after one JD and Coke. I stayed for the same reason I'd gone in the first place, because what the hell? Ryan would be home for once, and I didn't want to go there.

We were in the Cumberland, amid the cobbles and stately fronts of the New Town. At least I'd never been there with Alexis. Ryan and I went in our dating days, held hands across the polished wood, found our bubble of laughing solitude in the packed beer garden. Tonight, it was too cold for that. I carried drinks brimming over as I squeezed past strangers, the room flashing chrome and mahogany and pub-carpet red. I tried to find nostalgia for those first days with my husband and found only a spearing sadness.

I thought, *Why am I doing this?*

I drank as though the glass would answer me. I had wine first, then whisky. As the rounds multiplied, colleagues fell away until there were only four of us: Kai and me and two lads I barely knew, who were in the fixed-eyed, hand-touching stage of flirtation.

I gave Kai my phone. It was the last thing I know for sure I did. 'Keep it for me,' I said, staring into the golden face as though I saw four of them. 'I dare not have it.'

Kai took it with a frown, saying nothing. The questions came later, when our companions were thigh to thigh in a corner and I'd bought more whiskies, then more again, and my body, alcohol-flared, cried for Alexis. I do not know what my answers were.

Obsessed

I found my phone in my bag when I woke in the taxi, outside my front door. The driver's 'That's you, pal' had risen on repetition to a shout, and I was forcing open mascara-stuck eyes.

I paid, over-tipping, and peered into the phone screen as I opened the front door. Nothing. I stood alone in the hall, hearing the dishwasher gurgle from the kitchen. I flicked on the light, abruptly, horribly sober. The children's nursery bags were packed and waiting. Ryan had gone to bed. I looked again at my phone. It was only eleven o'clock.

I was sitting on the stairs, scrolling through headlines, registering nothing, when the message from Alexis came.

I miss you

I held the phone with juddering hands as my imagination crumbled one future and formed another. I replied:

Tomorrow

Then I went upstairs, kissed my sleeping children and climbed into cold sheets, listening to Ryan breathe.

59

Laura

12 March 2019

Ryan hates me too. I suppose it's not surprising. He picked up the kids from nursery, took them out for supper. Afterwards, he came in with me, face like clay, stowed Benjy and Evie in front of the TV, and said we needed to talk.

'We have to make arrangements,' he said.

I focused on the word, which grated my nerves, as though it would get me out of acknowledging what it meant.

'Laura,' he said. 'I'm in a hotel. This isn't sustainable. I need a place to stay. We'll have to sell this house.'

I glanced round, oppressed by the weight of possessions, the memories, the impossibility of division. 'OK,' I said. 'If that's what you want.'

The room was full of the retorts he didn't make. I turned towards the fridge, fought off guilt with bravado. 'Would you like a drink?' I said.

That was when I knew he hated me.

'I'll find a six-month let,' he said. 'Then I can have Benjy and Evie half the time.'

'Half?' I said. The prospect skewered me, cracking the cocoon of grief. I thought of those long days and nights without my children, without Alexis.

'Of course,' said Ryan. He sounded impatient; I suppose he was right to. I sat down at the table, shoving aside half-eaten toast. He came closer to me. 'Unless you want me to take them all the time,' he said.

My throat closed, ice-clogged. I opened my mouth, tried to speak. The sound of the TV drilled through the doors. Canned music, American accents.

'You're a mess, Laura,' Ryan said. I examined his face for compassion, found only contempt. 'You look terrible.'

'I'm OK,' I said. 'I'm their mother. I can look after them.'

He sighed. 'Fifty-fifty then. That's fair.'

'And Simon?' I said.

Simon had been with them for dinner. He'd come back without speaking to me, slunk straight to his room.

'That's up to him,' Ryan said.

'He told me . . .' I said, and broke off, for that had been before, when Simon still hoped to reconcile us. Ice again, in my ribs this time. 'I thought he would want that,' I whispered, to the table.

Ryan said, 'That's not the impression he gave me.'

'Ryan . . .' I said, yelping through fear. I swallowed, stared at my stranger-husband. 'He's my child too,' I said, daring him to contradict me.

He didn't. He softened, perhaps at memory. 'I'll talk to him,' he said. I gulped again and thanked him.

Silence but for the *Super Monsters* theme. 'You know he split up with Bella?' I said.

Ryan nodded. 'Another one to chalk up to your account,' he said. So much for softening. I started to cry. He looked at me as though the tears were a ploy. 'Sort yourself out,' he said. 'I'll put the kids to bed, then I'll go.'

I'd bought a bottle of wine for Mhairi this morning. It was easier than apologising properly. While Ryan was upstairs, I opened it myself. I drained my glass, topped it up again so Ryan wouldn't see how much had gone. I didn't want more. I wanted only the passing blur. To drag a film over Alexis, bleeding on a dirt path. To hide the shadows that are everywhere now, even in my own home.

I lay on the sofa, still warm from my children. Eyes closed, I listened to their chatter and Ryan's quiet voice. My phone beeped. Anja. My eyes refused to focus, and then my brain.

> Sorry Laura. Can't do tomorrow. Doctor's appointment. I've arranged cover though.

I messaged back.

> Hope you're OK. Who's the cover?

It was always someone from nursery. Normally that would be reassurance enough, but not this time. She replied straight away, and as I had known in my gut she would.

> Yazzie.

When Ryan came down, I told him I didn't want Yazzie looking after the children. He was exhausted, in a hurry to leave. 'What are you talking about?' he said.

I showed him Anja's text, told him the rest. 'She told Benjy she loved him best.'

'He's four. He misunderstood. Anyway, aren't you glad they care about them there?' He sounded like the manager now, like Yazzie herself. 'Poor wee things,' he said. 'They'll need all the help they can get.'

'I don't like her,' I said. 'I think she's trying to take them from me.'

Ryan looked from me to the wine glass, the rug still twisted from Benjy's den-making, three days since. Coffee mugs on bookshelves and windowsill. Curtains open onto the darkened street. He went over to the window, yanked them shut. 'You're being ridiculous,' he said.

'It's not just what she told Benjy,' I said. I felt like a child, failing to make the grown-up understand. 'She's been weird lately.'

Ryan snorted. 'You've been weird,' he said. I didn't speak. 'Pick them up yourself if you want,' he said. 'I'm not doing it.'

I closed my eyes, opened them again.

'If that's all,' he said, 'I'm going now. Evie was asleep. Benjy probably is now.' He paused for a response, but my phone had beeped again, and I was staring at the screen, eyes clouding. I barely heard him.

'What is it?' he said.

'Nothing,' I said. 'Nothing.'

He touched a photo on the wall, scrutinised it as though he'd never seen it before. I thought he would drop it, or throw it, but he just straightened the frame. He turned away from me and went to the door.

'Oh Ryan,' I said. 'I'm so sorry.'

He left without replying. As the front door snapped shut, I looked back at my phone, reread the message.

> The funeral is a week Thursday. 11 at Mortonhall.
> I'm a better person than I seemed this morning.
> I hope you are too. Diana

Simon stayed in his room all that evening. I sat where I was on the sofa, sobbing and flicking the message on and off, until my phone ran out of battery and the heating clicked off and I was shaking with cold.

9 December 2018

From: Khaleesi8690

To: AlwaysHaveParis

Subject: Well screw you

You can't do this. You can't just not answer my calls all week and then bugger off to Paris leaving me hanging.

Look, I don't need you. I have other options.

But you need help.

60

Hope

1 April 1999

Tonight is the last night of the show. I haven't seen it. I don't want to see it. But I think of it almost all the time. All week, the principals have drifted through the day like celebrities, coming in late, missing from class altogether, or there with a self-conscious, nervy air. I've hardly seen Laura or Alexis. My voice of reason tells me to be glad. But that voice is very quiet now. I barely hear it.

At the end of school, I don't go home. I go to the hall, feet lifting and setting themselves down, as though I have no choice. I expect it to be empty, a set for my daydreams. But they are there, the four of them. I catch voices before I open the door, and I stop where I am and peer through the glass panel.

Rick and Stacy pose like Tony and Maria on the stage, kissing. Her hair, yellow as buttercups, lights the dusky room. Laura and Alexis are on the floor below the stage, his back against the wooden panels, her head on his thighs.

From where I stand, squinting in the distance, her face is a gleaming oval, turned up to him.

Laura calls something. I don't know what, but Rick and Stacy step apart and cross the stage. Rick springs down. Stacy laughs and jumps to him, hands meeting hands, pulled to his chest. Laura rolls over and gets to her feet, tugs Alexis after her. They come towards the door.

I glance along the empty corridor. Then, because it's all I can do, I shrink against the wall. The door pushes open. I grab the handle as it comes towards me, hold it there, shield and camouflage. As they come out, I'm turning my body inwards, trying not to breathe. Rick has an arm round Stacy's shoulders, her hair in swathes against his leather jacket. Behind them, Alexis and Laura walk in step, hands held. Her long hair, plaited, swings like a metronome. They're laughing, but I don't know what at.

What must it be like to feel like that? I'd almost given up thinking *It's not fair*. But I think it now. I hear the joy in Laura's voice, through the pretended nerves, see Stacy snuggling into Rick as they walk. I watch the back of Alexis's neck, his shoulders. I feel my jealousy like a living thing, feeding and growing.

I bite hard on my lip.

I think of Her.

I see them out of sight, tasting blood. Then I creep round the door and enter the empty hall. I tread the centre aisle, between blocks of plastic chairs. The stage is set, but the curtain hasn't been pulled across. An art-class imitation of run-down New York: tall buildings, a fire escape, and a graffiti-daubed wall, red against grey. I touch my bleeding lip with my tongue. I walk straight ahead to the spot where Alexis and Laura were, and slide my back against the hard wood of the stage, until I am sitting on the cold floor.

I close my eyes, imagine it is me there with him, his hands on my hair, excitement in every touch.

I climb onto the stage and stand at the very centre of it. I open my mouth to sing, to recapture whatever it was that filled and sustained me in my audition. But my voice will not come. I see Stacy's hair, and Rick's hands. I see Alexis's bare shoulder, Laura moving over him. I hear a sound in the corridor and dip behind a cardboard tenement. The door opens and the janitor's grey head pokes in, rotates incuriously, withdraws. I wonder how long I have. The show is at 7.30. How many hours to dress and make up, and psych themselves up?

She will be looking for me now, interrogating Isaac as he hangs up his coat, pulls off school shoes and lays them in their place on the rack.

I go backstage, past props laid out on tables, into the classroom. Art studio by day, dressing room by night. And then I see it, as though it was waiting for me. A Stanley knife, on the floor by the desk leg.

Tut tut, I think, smiling. *That should have been locked away with the others*.

I pick it up, slide the blade in and out. I touch it on my fingertips and blood beads on the dry skin. I put that to my lips, too.

If I still believed in God, I would say He had sent me a message.

Sheets hang across one side of the room, an improvised

curtain. I pull them hard, so they slither and settle on the floor. The costumes hang on racks, on coat hangers with labels in someone's careful blue handwriting. Dresses with sticking-out skirts for the girls, jeans and bright shirts for the boys. Black for the Jets, Red for the Sharks. I see Laura's dress, the flared hem showing beside Alexis's shirt. Stacy's Maria wig hangs in a plastic bag, a black mass like a suffocated animal. I'm trembling, with the blade in my hand.

I pick a dress at random, ocean blue. I pull out the skirt, slice the scalpel down. The rip is like a yell of triumph. A pair of jeans next. They're tougher, but the blade is clean. I go back to the end, work my way through. I butcher Stacy's wig through the bag, so strips of plastic and shining black threads pile on the floor. I save Laura's red dress for last, lift it out and lay it on the big wooden table.

It's beautiful.

I imagine her mum, head like Laura's bent over the sewing machine. I imagine Laura, perched on a chair, giggling at the pins. I imagine Alexis's kisses, his hands, crumpling the dress in the wings. Last night, the night before. Not tonight.

I cut the dress from neck to hem so it lies in two shuddering halves, a murdered butterfly. Then I keep on cutting, faster and faster, until it's a heap of red and black ribbons. I start to laugh. I lift handfuls of the coiling strips, drop them. The red is mesmerising, blurring before my eyes.

I go back to the hall. The set is made of plasterboard, and I cannot cut it through. I can scratch it – sharp lines across doorways and stairs and billboards – but that isn't enough. I close the blade, put the knife in my pocket. I get paint from the art room, carrying it through in an open tin. When I throw it, it splashes in dripping scarlet circles, bright as Laura's dress, as the haze in my mind.

14 December 2018

From: Khaleesi8690

To: AlwaysHaveParis

Subject: Tonight

Well hello stranger!

Did you have a good trip to your home from home? Did you have time to think?

Have to admit, I was kind of disappointed not to see you today. I'll pop round tonight, shall I? Then we can grab a drink and talk. I know we can work this out.

xx

61

Laura

26 February 2019

We had an hour. It was all I could get, and that was by feeding lie upon lie to a reluctant Mhairi. 'I have my own children to look after,' she shouted into the phone, traffic buzzing behind her.

'My job is on the line,' I told her. 'I wouldn't ask if I weren't desperate.'

I took a taxi from work, ankles weak on the tenement stairs. Alexis let me in without touching me, pushed the door shut as I passed. The floor was still scratched.

I held out my hands and he pressed them to his face. I touched stubble, put my mouth to his, tasted sweetness and passion and something new. Certainty. Whatever mental scouring he had done while we were apart, he had come to a conclusion.

He read my thoughts. 'I can't come to terms with the past,' he said. 'But I can't do without you.'

'The future, then,' I said. 'Just make peace with that.'

I kissed him again, harder, blotting out ghouls. It wasn't Hope's face they wore now, but those of the people I'd have to hurt. Ryan. Simon. Benjy. Evie. They hung like human sacrifices, ready for the knife, between me and everything I wanted. I closed my eyes like a wall, let his tongue part my lips, hands undo clothes. We made love as though the time were already ours.

As I dressed, I said, 'I have to tell Ryan.'

Alexis leaned on one elbow, hair clogged with sweat, the duvet rucked around his waist. His grandmother's blanket was gone, irreparable, a formulaic grey fleece in its place. 'When?' he said.

'After the conference,' I said. It sounded like I was making excuses. Maybe I was. 'It's important,' I said. 'I can't fuck that up for him too. He's away Sunday to Wednesday, and I'll tell him when he's back.'

Alexis nodded. I sat with my tights halfway up my legs, staring at the window. Would I live here next week with him? With Gracie, when she came? With my own kids, half the time? I tried to imagine it, to envisage Simon coming here, treading the slow stairs, pulling out his headphones, making small talk with Alexis.

I couldn't make it real, even in my head.

Alexis ran a finger down my spine, held it curved against my thigh. 'Are you sure?' he said.

I caught his hand, afraid it would slip from me. 'Yes,' I said. 'Yes.'

'Then we'll make it work,' he said.

I was twenty minutes late to get the kids. Evie grabbed my

legs and cried. Mhairi barely spoke to me. Back in my own house, I locked the door, and realised I had forgotten to look for shadows.

62

Laura

13 March 2019

I slept little last night, and when I did, I dreamed the children were being taken from me. Their faces were turned back, mouths stretched and soundless. At 3 a.m., sweat-smeared and frantic, I decided to work from home. An hour later, I determined to collect the kids myself. At 8, after pots of coffee, when I'd dressed and fed my babies and wheeled the buggy through drizzle to nursery, Yazzie was there. A Yazzie apparently reformed, disconcerting. She welcomed Evie with outstretched arms; she was even fairly cordial to me.

'I will see you later,' she said. 'Anja told me what to do.' To Evie, she crooned that she would bring her home that evening, give her tea. 'Won't that be nice?'

I hung up Evie's coat, not speaking. I wanted to say not to bother, that I'd made other plans. But in the face of her determined smile, the words failed me. I saw Ryan's scathing expression, recalled my own unbalanced tears.

'I'm working from home today,' I said, weakly. 'You won't need to stay so late. I'll be in the study if you need anything.'

I told myself that was enough. I got home and decided it wasn't, woke up the phone to call nursery, pressed it off again. I could still see Ryan's face. This way madness lay. This way to losing my children. *Unfit mother.*

Instead, I called Danielle and told her I couldn't come in.

'That's not convenient,' she said.

I said it was a family emergency. 'I'm sorry.'

'And *I'm* sorry to hear that.' Like hell she was. 'But if you knew how I've fought to keep your job for you, you might prioritise things differently.'

Well, that was a new angle on it.

She called back after lunch, less resigned, even less sympathetic. 'This is getting stupid. Bloody Kai is still off. And now you.'

I stared at the window, slashed with rain; asked what I had not, yesterday, thought to ask. 'What's wrong with Kai?'

'His ma's in hospital.'

'His mum?' I heard my own voice, flat as a computer. 'Don't you mean his aunt?'

'Aunt, mother, whatever. She had a stroke on Monday. He found her after work. That's why he was off yesterday. I need you to come in for the meeting with Design. You know what they're like.'

'I'm sorry,' I said, through a mist.

'I wouldn't ask if it weren't important.'

'I'm sorry,' I repeated. 'I'm working fr—'

'Yeah,' she said. 'I get it.'

'I could dial in.'

'If it's not too much bother,' Danielle said, and cut the call.

'Ryan's left me,' I said, to nothingness. Maybe that would have silenced her.

I decided not to call her back, drafted an email instead, then deleted it. I sat in a trance in front of the computer, opening messages, clicking on attachments without reading them. Useless.

I made toast, couldn't eat it. I fell asleep instead, forehead on the kitchen table, crumbs stamping my skin. When I woke, it was after three, I was freezing and I had five voicemails from Danielle. I hadn't dialled in to the meeting.

I deleted the voicemails, then checked my email. She'd sent me a second warning. No apologies this time. I closed my eyes, felt the downward spiral dragging at my limbs. Real as clutching hands.

I shut the email, counted to ten in my head, like I tell Benjy to do when he's having a meltdown. I put on another jumper, made another coffee and drank it in one gulp, shivering the caffeine into fingers and toes. Back at my desk, I tried to draft a letter to current account customers, but it was like writing in a language I'd never learned.

Danielle's words crawled back into my mind. *His ma. Monday.*

Then Kai's voice, Antipodean accent, an unthinking aside, cut off sharp. *Let us not become weary . . .* Another voice, deeper; another accent. A man I had never met. *Relatives, somewhere south.*

I typed what Kai had said, the half-phrase lying neat in my tired brain. Google completed it. *Let us not become weary in doing good.* I clicked on the drop-down menu, my fingers moving through a fog.

Galatians 6:9. So there we were. The Bible regurgitated as unthinkingly as most of us remember song lyrics or nursery rhymes. And something else struck me, with a sharpness that pulled the breath from my lungs. *South* needn't mean London or Kent or Surrey. On the globe, Australia was south.

I sat with my head in my hands, wondering if I had, at last, lost my mind. I sat there for I don't know how long. Then the doorbell rang.

I jumped to my feet, ran to the window. I looked down at narrow shoulders and streaked gold hair, too brash on the grey street. At an arm in a peacock sleeve, a hand still resting on the bell.

I felt no surprise. Only the sense that this had always been going to happen.

The bell rang again: long, imperious. My hand tightened on the shutter. His head tilted up. I dived back into the room, slamming my thigh on the desk corner, shouting with the pain. I reeled a moment, seeing speckled black, hearing nothing. I wondered where I had left my phone.

Then I realised that the bell had stopped ringing.

I crept back to the window and peered like a prurient widow round the frame, searching the street for that bright retreating head. I saw nothing. No blue-green back turning away; not even the thin figure still waiting. Fear crept, clinging, into my gut. I listened for something – for anything – but heard nothing. Until a stair creaked.

I ran swaying to the study door. I must have cried out, though I didn't know it, because the steps came faster, harder up the stairs, and as I reached the door, it opened towards me and he stood there, hands out.

Kai Fredericks. Isaac Mitchell.

63

Hope

1 April 1999

There's no car outside our house. My father is working late. I am late too, later still because I lingered on my way home. I push open the front door, and a creeping anxiety mires my elation. It is very quiet.

Isaac runs through the hall, up the stairs. I call to him, and he turns from halfway up to look at me. His face is striped, red and white like bacon. His eyes dart into corners, then settle unblinking on my face.

'What's happened?' I say, but he only stares at me, shrinking away into the dim landing. His bedroom door creaks shut.

The kitchen is dark but the door to the sitting room is open. I kick off my shoes and put my bag beside them in the hall. I take off my coat, watching the light, reach it onto the hook. The coat swings, thudding softly, the knife in the pocket hitting the wall. I put my hand inside and touch the hard metal, then leave it there. I stand by the sitting room door, hearing Her breathing.

I swallow bile. I go in.

She sits on an upright armchair, still and straight-backed. This room is always dull in the afternoon; now, with the curtains shut, the last of the dreary day is lost. I jerk my hand to the light switch, startling us both. The ceiling lamp sends orangey rays across the beige carpet. Behind Her, the striped wallpaper shakes into visibility. Before Her, tight in clenched hands, I see what my brother was afraid to tell me.

A foil-wrapped packet. Mine.

I stand there, watching her knuckles, waiting. When She moves, it is all in one go, like a pouncing beast. The packet falls to the floor. She is standing, She is in front of me. I can smell the bitterness of her breath. She hits me across the face, one way, then the other. I stumble against the door frame. I hear it all as from a distance: the clean, tight slap, the thump of arm and shoulder against wood. Then I feel it.

I wrench upright, step forward. She leans hissing into my face.

'*Slut*,' She says, so near, my skin mists with Her spit. The insult, so intensely inapt, almost makes me laugh.

'It's for my face,' I say, but I know it will do no good. She jabs a finger into my cheek, pulls at the skin. If She's looking for make-up, She won't find it.

'Vanity,' She says. I watch the lines deepen round Her eyes, thin lips stretching. Then, before I can recoil, She clutches my arm. 'Where have you been? Who is he?'

'I was at a revision class.' I cough acid. Her grip loosens; I pull away. 'I told Father. At least . . .' I cover myself, paint over the lie, 'I think I did.'

She watches me, stepping backwards, weighing my words in the balance. Her heel crushes stiff foil. She lifts her foot and the packet falls back, scattering white dust on the carpet. I am following Her eyes and I know that I am lost. She kicks the pack with the toe of Her slipper. She looks around the room, slowly. Perhaps She has forgotten the belt, ever ready in the hall. Perhaps it is not enough for Her tonight.

She moves fast. She goes to the fireplace, where the fire is almost never lit, and takes the poker from its hook. She weighs it in her hands.

'Shut the door,' She says.

I view the metal, heavy in Her curling fingers. I look at Her, and we are the same height. Something breaks. That same something that was set moving weeks ago, when last She beat me. Sooner, perhaps. The day I found out about Mark.

I kick the door shut.

'Turn round,' She says, but She has sensed it too, this new dynamic. I know it from Her voice. I stay where I am until She moves, and then I move too. I catch the poker as She swings it towards me. I yank it from Her, so She stumbles back. I hold it in both hands and I smash it against Her legs.

So many moments, but this is the one my life has been working towards. She's caught off guard. She roars. She falls against a chair, flailing, skirt rucking as it has never been allowed to rise in thirty years. I hit again, before I can think, before She can raise a hand to stop me. I strike an arm and She screams. I slam the poker down again and again, years of hitting. I beat legs, knees, arms, ribs. I hear bones crack. I listen as terror rises over rage then sinks into a whimpering silence. I drop the poker. There is a thud, then only stillness, and Her moans.

I stand over Her. I have not touched Her face. Her eyes narrow. She will not beg, even now.

'You made me,' I say. 'You made me this way.'

'God made you,' She whispers. 'He will punish you.'

I go out, shutting the door behind me.

64

Laura

13 March 2019

I stumbled, then straightened. I searched his face for the boy who had hidden in corners, barely seen, even when I was at his home. The eyes were the same: so blue it abashed you to look at them. But that had been a drab-haired child, bones fairy-thin; this was an adult, lightly beautiful, skin and hair bright as a sunlamp. And he looked younger, years younger, than he was.

I couldn't have known.

There was nothing of Hope in him. Perhaps there might have been if I had seen her grow into her new face.

'Hello, Isaac.'

His hands fell. 'So you worked it out?'

I nodded. 'How did you get in?'

'It wasn't locked.'

I stared at him. I saw myself returning from nursery, preoccupied by Yazzie, fighting the zip on my raincoat, pulling it half undone over my head. I heard Simon's voice.

You should be more careful. I tried to make my mind see my hand on the chain. But there was nothing to see.

I laughed, then choked. In all this fear, to omit the most basic precaution.

He said, 'My mother died two hours ago.'

I said, untruthfully, that I was sorry.

He smiled. 'I told the nurses I was relieved. They said it would hit me later.'

An unfortunate choice of verb.

I said, 'Why was she here? In Penicuik, I mean.'

He looked puzzled. 'Where else could they send her? She needed care, and I was here. She disapproves of big cities, so I agreed to live out of town.' He shifted, leaned against the door. 'I'd come back, you see. From Australia.'

'To look after her?'

He smiled again. 'Oh no. That was a not very welcome side effect. I came back for you, Laura.'

I swallowed, stared into those pellucid eyes. 'Well, you found me.' My voice surprised me, calm as ice. 'And you went *on* finding me. Quite some stalker you make.'

Just like your sister.

Outside, a car revved too loudly, then faded down the street. Kai said, as though I had said her name out loud, 'I used to think you were the only other person who loved her.'

Did he see me wince? Did it even matter?

He said, 'I saw how she looked at Alexis. I saw it destroy her, you and him being together.' The gaze seemed to go through me. 'I know that you know more about what happened to her,' he said. 'All these years, I've been thinking about it.'

I said nothing. He smiled: a brittle, boy's smile. He said, 'I suppose you think I should have come straight to you, not hidden under an assumed name.'

I cleared my throat. 'That's one of the things I'm wondering, yes.'

'When it came to it,' he said, 'I couldn't. *She* would never discuss Hope. She never said her name. Not even at the funeral. Maybe it was that. A kind of ... prohibition. Maybe it was not knowing whether I could trust you.'

I watched his face: the fading tan, the rings round the blue eyes. They said you were supposed to keep a killer talking. But this one wanted to listen.

'Tell me,' he said. 'Tell me about that night.'

My mouth was dry as ashes. He came closer, unblinking eyes on me. 'I know you were there,' he said.

65

Hope

1 April 1999

I go back to school. I expect distress, cancellation, disarray.
I see lights in the main corridor, but when I creep close,
I find it empty. I go round the long way, past grim houses
and up the covered steps to the bridge. From there, I can see
lights in the dressing room, hear music feeding through
open windows.

The school band, sounding almost like a proper orchestra.
Laura's voice, sharp as glass. Alexis's, contracting my chest.
Stacy's, soaring clear. I inch along the walkway, forming the
words along with them, feeling them in my stomach. None
of them, not even Stacy, can sing like I can.

In the dark, I press close to the door with its frosted pane.
The room is tidy, curtain in place, the torn petals of Laura's
dress swept away. I see it blurred through the glass, like a
TV with bad reception. Girl extras sit around, listening,
talking in whispers. Some are in jeans and vest tops, others
in their school skirts, rolled up, and shirts with undone

buttons. Mums in overalls tweak curls into place, daub lipstick on puckering mouths. Not Laura's this time. The girls take it easily, as though they are already stars.

The make-up wasn't there earlier. Or I would have destroyed that too.

I want to see what Laura and Stacy are wearing, but I dare not stay. I run back across the bridge and wait at the top of the steps, ready to dip out of sight, listening to the threads of sound to tell me when the show has ended. But before it does, the rain starts. I slip down the steps, finding shelter. Music fights the rain, and mostly the rain wins. At last I hear applause, shouting, faint through the downpour, chairs pushed back in one great sigh. I know it's over.

I wait. The cast will be changing (those who can), pulling on outdoor clothes, griping at the weather. I know there's a party at Rick's house. They'll come this way, giddy and self-loving, while the audience files along the main corridor. When they do, I leave my shelter and sneak into wet shadows between the houses. I watch them, my cast mates, scuttling under umbrellas, pulling up hoods.

Rick and Stacy are together, among the first. He has his leather jacket off and is holding it over their heads. She is laughing, triumphant. They stop near my refuge to kiss, until one of the Jets yells at them to get a move on.

No Laura, no Alexis. When the others have gone, footfalls in water, I climb back onto the bridge. I lean on the parapet, hair flattened, wet through my coat, and watch as a cyclist splashes through puddles, the light scribbling white on the glossy road. I hear the door to the dressing room open and I know it is Laura.

I turn. She calls something over her shoulder. I don't know what. The door shuts behind her. She is singing, zipping up her coat. Then she sees me.

'Hope,' she says. 'What are you doing here? Did you see the show?'

'I came to see you,' I say. 'It's been a while.'

'Oh,' she says. Light from the doorway hangs about her face like some kind of halo. 'That was nice of you.'

'Was it?' I say.

She blenches. 'Are you OK?'

I say nothing. The rain hammers the ground between us.

'It's very wet,' Laura says. 'Maybe we should . . .' She moves as though she'd pass me. My hand finds the knife in my pocket, fondles the metal. I wait until she is very close.

'Shame about your pretty dress, wasn't it?'

She jumps back. Silence hangs, shivers between us. She says, 'Was that you?'

'Ah well,' I say. 'Mummy can always make you another one.'

'I thought you liked my mum.'

I shrug, though I doubt she can see me. I wait, listening to the rain, watching her think. When she speaks, her voice is her mother's voice. 'Hope, I think you need help. I'm sorry, I hadn't realised, hadn't noticed.'

'No,' I say. 'You haven't noticed much.'

She holds out a hand. I see her hesitate, but she does it. Despite myself, something lifts in my chest.

'Maybe we could talk?' she says.

A car slides under the bridge, its headlights throwing everything into bright, brief relief – Laura, the parapet, the hanging rain. Then darkness wraps us again. It takes me an instant to realise it's deeper than before. The light in the room behind has gone off.

Laura realises too, and we both know what it means, even before we hear the door shut. She turns from me, hand falling. I see only the shadow curve of her body, yanked towards him, but it is enough. She corrects herself, swings back, reaches for me again. Too late.

'Hope?' she says.

I say, 'We're beyond talking.'

Alexis steps forward, two paces in an instant. He stands by her. 'What's going on?' he says.

I can hardly see him, but I know his voice like I know my own breath. I hear it all. Pity and revulsion and fear. I run a few shaking steps to the parapet. Then I haul myself up. The stone is wet and hard, scraping palm and knee, but I don't care. In Laura's in-drawn breath, I know my power.

She is watching me now, not him.

They step towards me like they are trying not to do anything fast. I hear Laura sobbing. 'Hope,' Alexis says. 'Don't do this.'

I laugh. I tilt my head up so the water drums into my eyes, slides into my open mouth.

They are close to me now, their heads level with my chest, their faces frightened blurs. Alexis reaches out, and I take his hand. I feel warm skin and strong fingers through the wet. Is it like I have imagined it, his skin against mine? I don't know now. I cannot think. Victory swims up, burning in my cold chest. My ribs incline as though I would fall towards him, let him close his arms around me.

Then he spoils it. His hand tightens on mine, he draws me forward, but his head turns from me and he speaks, instead, to her.

'It will be all right.' It is a whisper, but I hear it. 'It will be all right, love.'

I pull back upright. My hand finds the knife, slides the blade forward. I have a moment of exultation, living the anger. Then I bend again, striking down hard and fast. I feel the blade touch. Then I feel his arm, iron hard, and Laura's. Pushing me away.

The knife falls at their feet.

I sway.

I see Mark as I have imagined him, bike skidding from him, body curling through the air, crashing into the lorry. I hear Her bones cracking, Her voice, which has always destroyed me. I feel my shoulders pulling me sharp back, my feet wrenched up.

God will punish you.

I fall silent though the wet dark. It is Laura who screams, long and high. And in her terror, I find joy, though I know it is the last sound I will hear.

66

Laura

13 March 2019

I talked.

I told Kai, who is Isaac, about *West Side Story*. About crouching in the ruins of set and costume. About Stacy crying and Rick swearing and Mr Balmore, red-faced, unlikely statesman, assuring the audience that the show would go on. I told him how we stood on the stage afterwards, with our hands clasped. Stacy and me in school skirts and vest tops. Rick and Alexis in grey trousers and white cotton, ripped at the edges. Stacy's hair falling like sunshine as she tilted forward to bow. The audience cheering and calling to us.

I loved Stacy then. I loved all of them. I loved myself. I didn't know there would never be another moment like it.

I said all this and Kai sat still as a therapist and did not speak.

I told him how his sister had waited for us on the bridge, that she was angry, that she had a knife. We took the knife, afterwards, and threw it into the canal. But I didn't tell him that. I didn't tell him how Hope sliced at Alexis, and how the blood mixed with the rain, dark in the darker night.

I looked into his fragile face, hating myself. And I lied.

'She jumped,' I said. 'She got onto the wall and jumped. It was all so fast. We couldn't stop her.'

Kai watched me.

I remembered Hope's face as she fell from our frantic hands.

I thought of how Alexis came to me a week later, dull-eyed, when the lies were all told. After we had denied seeing her that night: to the police and to everyone. He told me he couldn't live with himself, or with me. He said he was going to his mother in Paris. He held me while I clung and sobbed and begged him to stay. He kissed me like it was a vow. And he went.

Kai took my wrist, not roughly, but as though he could read the truth from the blood in my veins. 'I don't believe you,' he said. 'Who are you trying to protect, Laura? Yourself, or him?'

'Neither,' I said. 'It's too late for that.'

Another lie.

'It's never too late,' he said. 'Not for redemption.'

Anger settled on me, hot and unexpected. 'God,' I said. 'You sound just like your mother.'

I wasn't afraid now, in this all-consuming rage. I wrenched my wrist away, spat the words in his face. 'Did you offer redemption to Alexis, too? Did you ask him for the truth before you stabbed him?'

Kai crumpled, more completely than if I had hit him. 'What are you talking about?'

'Or did you just kill him without giving him a chance?

He stared at me, eyes terrified. 'I didn't know,' he said. 'I didn't even know that he was dead.'

I watched his shaking hands and knew that he was telling the truth. His mother's victim, not her echo.

Outside, someone shouted across the street. I stood there, not touching Kai, until, at last, he moved. He walked past me, out of the room. I followed, watched from the top of the stairs as his pale head dropped past pictures of family holidays. Evie in a red swimming costume. Benjy and Simon rolling down dunes. Ryan holding me close with the Bridge of Sighs behind us.

I saw Kai's narrow hand on the front door. Suddenly he looked up. 'You shouldn't have lied,' he said.

'Please go,' I said. 'I'm sorry. But please go.'

He looked at me. His words were spiteful, but his expression wasn't – and that scared me more.

'If you're lying for Alexis,' he said, 'he wasn't worth it.'

My fingers tightened on the banister, sticky from children's hands. I said, 'You know nothing about him.'

'You weren't the only one he was seeing,' Kai said. 'I know that. There was someone else.'

67

Laura

3 March 2019

On Wednesday, Ryan will come back and I will tell him the truth. Tonight was the last night we will meet surreptitiously. But still, we should not have done it.

Alexis came here to me, to do what we could not do months ago: lie together in Ryan's house. It is as though we have sullied ourselves, broken something, started our new start off on the wrong foot.

It wasn't the plan. I was in mother mode, eating tea with the children, about to suggest a film to Simon. But Simon told me he was going out.

'With Bella?' I said, and he nodded.

I smiled, as though I wasn't about to hurl a bomb into this normality. 'When will I get to meet her?'

Simon said nothing. Benjy asked, 'Are you going to marry her?'

I got up to put the lasagne dish on the side. I told Simon, 'At least eat something first.' He hadn't touched his plate.

'I'm not hungry.'

'When will you be back?'

'I'm not sure. Why?'

'Darling, you're fourteen, not twenty-four. I'm allowed to ask. Besides, you've got school tomorrow.'

He sighed. 'I'll be back around eleven. We're going to the cinema,' he added, as though that made it legitimate.

I should have haggled. I should have asked the name of the film, at least. But I was already grabbing my phone, making an excuse, going into the hall. I stood with my back to our family pictures, messaging Alexis.

When he arrived – when Simon had gone and Evie was a caterpillar, dormant in her duvet chrysalis, and I had begged and bribed and snapped at Benjy until he too slept – I took Alexis to the study. We stripped with furtive tenderness, rolled together, made hasty, gasping love, stifled cries with kisses.

At last we lay together on the rug on the floor, cushions for pillows, under a blanket I curl under with my children, reading stories.

'Where will we be,' I said, 'at the end of the week?'

He kissed my shoulder. 'Together,' he said.

Together, yes, but where?

'We'll get somewhere new,' Alexis said, as though I had asked the question aloud. 'As soon as we can, with space for the kids.' He held my face, knew I was thinking of Simon. 'All of them,' he said.

Simon wouldn't come there. I knew it in my gut. Would he see me, even for café lunches and trips to the bowling alley? I held my mouth to Alexis's, blind comfort, for I had made my choice.

68

Laura

13 March 2019

I closed my eyes.

'I love you,' Alexis had said, the first time, in his grandmother's rose garden. And again, hours later, naked and gasping, his head on my neck, his body hot and salty and desperate. 'I love you. I love you.'

I opened my eyes. 'You're insane.'

'Not at school,' Kai said. Had he read my mind? 'Here, in Edinburgh.'

I'd heard Alexis, ten days ago, planning our future, felt him hold me. I walked down the stairs, feeling each step.

'It's not true,' I said.

'I saw them together.'

'When?'

'End of November.' He turned the door handle. 'Maybe early December. They were kissing, outside Innis & Gunn.'

While I was turning my life inside out to be with him. I swallowed twice, before I could speak.

'He wouldn't do that.'

If Kai heard, he made no sign. He said, 'That was the first I knew he was in Edinburgh. It was funny, I suppose, recognising him straight off after all those years. But I did.'

It wasn't true. It couldn't be true. But there had been those footsteps in the shadows, the torch beam on our weaving bodies. The watcher who had not been Kai. Ice shards, in my chest. I twisted my fingers, feeling where my wedding ring wasn't.

'I wondered if you knew he was here. Then you said something, that night in the Cumberland, and I knew you'd been sleeping with him too.'

Alexis loved me. *That* was not a lie. I sought reason through dazed anger. And if he loved me, he would have left this other woman, whoever she was. Would have made her hate him.

I said, 'Who was she?'

Kai was in the porch now, turning to leave. 'How could I know?'

I grabbed his shoulder. 'What did she look like?'

He closed his eyes, tightened up his face. The child again, playing a memory game. 'She had a ponytail like you used to. She was wearing a grey jacket.' A pause. I heard his breath, and mine. 'Her hair had purple streaks.'

My hands dropped. Kai opened the door, walked out into street light and drizzle and the darkening sky.

'I didn't kill Alexis,' he said. 'I couldn't kill anyone.'

'I know you didn't,' I gasped, to the empty house. 'I know who did.'

I found my phone on the kitchen table. I pressed buttons

wildly, stared at the time through my children's laughing faces.

5.40.

Oh God.

I forced limbs and hands to act, pulled trainers onto my bare feet, ran coatless into the wet dark.

Straight into a man's chest.

14 December 2018

From: Khaleesi8690

To: AlwaysHaveParis

Subject: The truth

You bastard. Months together, and you wouldn't even let me in. How the hell do you think that makes me feel?

Not a good time, Yazzie. Like hell it wasn't. Well, I've got news for you. Now is a very, very bad time for me.

You know what I'm thinking, right? You know what's going through my mind while I sit here reading all your old messages, still crying like I cried so I could barely see, all the way home? Going over every moment?

I'm thinking there's someone else. You'd better have the decency to tell me the truth, because believe me, I'll find out. And I won't forget being treated like this.

Y

69

Laura

13 March 2019

A boy's chest, not a man's. Simon's, in his school coat. But he's as tall as a man now.

'Thank God.' My voice was a squeak. I saw startled eyes, an exhausted face. There was no time to hug him. 'Come with me.'

I dialled nursery, already moving. I heard him slamming the door, following. The drizzle was rain now, quick and relentless. The phone rang on and on.

I ran. The street was wide and wet in the deepening dusk. Parked cars like rocks. And Simon, beside me now, shouting through the rain.

'What's ha—'

I held up my spare hand, cutting him off. *Answer. For God's sake, answer it.* I pictured them all out in rooms and corridors, pulling on coats, gathering up shoes. Evie's shoes. Pink and bright and too small for her.

I hadn't taken her to the shop, had forgotten to book a fitting. *I'm a terrible mother. I'm sorry. I'm sorry.*

I heard my own footsteps, hard and fast. I heard Simon's voice. 'Laura, *tell* me!'

I hushed him again, as though he *was* Evie. I tried Anja's mobile, but it went straight to voicemail. I dialled nursery again, lurching on with sliding feet.

Engaged.

I didn't scream. I hadn't the breath. I rang off and tried again, over and over and over, all the way along Hermitage Terrace and down Braid Avenue, slippery-steep.

Let me be on time.

I heard that bloody engaged sound, as though I would hear it for the rest of my life. Past tall windows and houses with stairs that curled up the side, past two girls jogging and an old woman who shouted when I dodged her. I heard Simon's breathless apology, the old bat's mollified sniff.

At last, almost at the traffic lights, the phone rang out again. I waited, staring at the red man, for the answer. And it came. Not Anja. Not Yazzie. Not the American manager, who thought me an unfit mother. What did it matter who?

I gasped down the line. 'I'm collecting Benjy and Evie myself. I'm on my way. Tell Yazzie I won't need her.'

The voice came back, polite over mild annoyance. 'Just let me check.'

I crossed the road, the phone hard against my ear, listening to the distant sounds of the children. I tried to pick out Benjy's laugh, Evie's shout over the pelting rain. But there was only an indistinguishable babble, and then the young woman's voice again.

'I'm so sorry. They already left.'

Across the road, I staggered a few metres, straight ahead, then slumped against a stone wall. I should have turned right for nursery, but it didn't matter now. Trees spat droplets onto my spinning head. I yelled into the phone, but she had long gone.

Simon caught me up, pulled me upright. 'What is it?' he said.

I sobbed, half screaming, into his jacket, 'She's got Benjy and Evie.'

'Who?' His voice rose. 'What are you talking about?'

'She killed Alexis.'

'*Who?*'

Cold water sliced down my neck. Images burst into my brain: flash cards I could not push away. Benjy's slight fingers, tugging at my sleeve. Evie's face, warm and smooth against my lips. My children, going trusting into the dark street.

'Yazzie.'

I tried to think, but it was like assembling pieces in the dark while terror tore at my chest. I counted breaths, three in, three out, until I had them straight. Capaldi. The red queen.

I'll tell you everything, you supercilious cow. I'll do anything if you'll get my children back.

'The police,' I said. My phone was still in my hand. I swiped at the screen, but it was too wet. 'I have to call the police.'

'No.'

The word cut through my panic. I looked up at my stepson, his face like a papier-mâché mask in the half-light. He snatched the phone from my slippery fingers, sent it skating across the ground.

'What the hell are you doing?' I tried to dive after it, but he pulled me back. 'Simon, for God's sake—'

'You're not calling them.'

I twisted in his grip. I wanted to scream, tried instead for calm. 'Simon,' I said. 'This isn't about you.'

Headlights lit his sallow skin, the damp wall, and the rain hanging in the air. Then vanished.

'But it is,' he said. 'It is about me.'

He let me go. I saw dots, silver on black, before my eyes. I put out my hands, to save myself from the rising ground.

30 January 2019

From: Khaleesi8690

To: AlwaysHaveParis

Subject:

Well hello to you too.

I don't know what the hell you mean. I haven't been near your flat since the night you turned me away like some kind of salesman. Why would I? Of course I was angry, being treated like that, but I'm not a psychopath.

I may as well tell you: I know who she is now. I heard about your little Meadows date. To be honest, I have nothing but contempt left for either of you.

Her husband is lovely. Did you know that? And using your kids as cover is stooping really fucking low.

So please, no insane accusations. Just leave me alone to get on with my job and my life. I'll do my best for your daughters, since neither of you gives a shit about them.

Y

70

Laura

13 March 2019

I twisted on the wet stone. I made my eyes open, pushed myself up with wrists that felt ready to snap.

'It was you,' I said.

I heard the words and felt them as impossible. But above me, in the sodden night, Simon's head moved. Up and down.

I tasted vomit, hot and sour. I said, 'I don't understand. How could you . . .?' I swallowed, speaking into silence, desperation sharpening my voice. 'You never even met Alexis.'

'I was following you.'

I retched, bile and toast, into the gutter. A cyclist spun past, gave me a disapproving look, and was gone. I crouched there, watching the rear light, a red dot weaving up the hill. I saw another figure on another bike. A knife, red-dipped, in a thin hand. Fingers on secateurs, cutting my mother's rose.

Simon began to talk, leaning over me, quick and confessional. 'You were acting weird,' he said. 'I went after you. I kept on following you.' He gulped, looked away. 'I went after you on New Year's Eve.'

I put my hands to my face, kneeling on the wet pavement. I said, stupidly, irrelevantly, 'But you were with Bella.'

'No,' he said. The word was almost a shout. Then his voice dropped again: a child's helpless admission. 'There is no Bella.'

'*What?*'

'You were so chuffed to think that I had a girlfriend. You and Dad both. You were desperate for me to fit in. I didn't want to let you down.'

I got up somehow, grabbing at certainty. 'Mhairi met her.'

'Mhairi met a girl from computer club. She just assumed, like you all did.' His face twisted. 'I wanted to stop. But then it was easier to keep on lying.'

He looked at me, then away into the darkness. 'I wanted to stop all of it. But I didn't know how.'

'Simon—'

'Please. Please, just listen. I broke into his flat. I slipped the lock. I didn't think it would work, but it did, and then I was so angry. I went crazy, I think. I got a minicab and said it was for a bet and followed you out of town. I thought if I scared you enough, you would stop seeing each other.' The words were sobs now. 'That was all I wanted.'

I thought of the shadows that had grown under his eyes, of how he had withdrawn from me, day by day.

I thought of Alexis, bleeding in the dirt.

I stumbled away, bent at the waist. He came after me, pulling at my jumper, pleading through tears.

'I didn't mean to.'

I stared at the ground.

'I heard you,' he said. 'That night, I watched the house. I saw him come. I heard you planning. You were going to break up our family. You were leaving, for him.'

This is my fault.

'I was so afraid. I knew I couldn't let it happen, but I didn't know what to do. And the knives were *there*, on the kitchen wall. I don't even remember taking one. I don't remember going after him. Only running, and how dark it was, and . . . the sound he made.'

Alexis. Alexis.

I made myself breathe. I forced another picture into my mind. The child who had watched me, waiting to give his trust. The young boy I had cuddled to sleep.

My child.

A car passed, then another. Little bright worlds. Simon stood with his head hanging, crying in gulps.

I wrapped my arms around him. 'It's OK. It will be OK.' I spoke into his ear, felt him yielding like an infant to the hug. 'I understand,' I said.

I thought of Capaldi, and my heart misgave me. I thought of Morse, who had sons of her own. I tried to see it with a jury's eyes.

'Everyone will understand.'

'*No.*' Simon snapped straight, pulling away from me. I gripped tighter. He said, 'They'll lock me up.' I felt the panic in his writhing arms, heard it in the tight, piercing voice.

'You're a child,' I said.

'I looked it up. I'm fourteen.'

'It wasn't your fault.'

But I felt his staring eyes, and knew mine were frightened too.

He thrust me from him, fast and sudden. My breast slammed against rigid stone. I closed my eyes with the pain. I heard shaking breath, felt him moving away.

I opened my eyes, reaching out, and saw what I had not seen before. The drop over the wall. Trees below us like black skeletons. Parallel lines of dark, rusty metal. I could barely see them in the near-night, but I knew they were there.

Not here. Oh Christ, not here.

Here. Another bridge. And Simon was climbing, fast as she had, onto the wet parapet.

I moved, quicker than I'd thought I could, but he was faster. He stood above me with the darkness behind him, and I stopped where I was, frozen, with my hands held out.

'Swear it,' he said. 'Swear you won't tell the police.'

If I didn't tell them, how long before they found out anyway? I saw Capaldi, determined as a hawk. Watching us, pecking on and on for months, until one of us cracked.

I said what Alexis had said. 'Don't do this.'

I moved my hands a fraction towards him. 'Don't do this to Dad.'

Simon shifted sharply, so his whole frame wobbled on the narrow wall. I lurched forward as though I would grab him. But he was steady again, and I stopped myself.

'You hypocrite,' he said.

'Simon—'

'You bitch. To talk of Dad . . .' He spat the words, so I felt his breath in the air above me. 'You *promised*. When you married him, you said we were a family. You said we would always be.'

'Oh God.' I said it aloud. Because he was right. I had.

The rain had stopped and there was only the still, wet emptiness, the cars indifferent on the main road. They might as well have been miles away.

'I saw his face,' he said. 'In the hospital, when Mum died. They made him go and identify her. He didn't know I knew that, but I did.'

I saw it all then. Naomi crushed to death in her own car. Naomi distracted for one fatal moment by her crying child. And that child, whom we had thought we had healed, still just a frightened boy. One who would do anything rather than let his father lose another wife.

'Simon,' I said. 'Dad loves you. You matter more to him than I ever could. He needs you. Benjy and Evie need you.'

He shook his head. He stretched his arms, up and outward like unfurling wings. I swallowed.

'I won't tell the police. I'll make it all right. Please get down.'

Seconds, but they felt like days. He stared into my eyes.

I said, 'I swear it.'

I waited, not breathing. Then he jumped, towards me.

71

Laura

14 March 2019

I sat with Simon until he slept, after midnight, holding my hand. Then I crawled downstairs and phoned Ryan. He came round at once, shattered-eyed, to argue for hours in the cold dark. When it was over, he fell asleep where he was, half upright on the sofa. I covered him with a blanket and sat with him until the dawn light flickered across his sleeping face. Simon's face. Benjy's. The face of a man who had never lied to me.

'*I'm sorry,*' I whispered.

I showered and dressed. My hands felt like someone else's. I woke Benjy and Evie with kisses that nearly broke me. I made pancakes for breakfast: a treat that made them squeal, then fight over who got the first one. They shrieked again when they saw Ryan.

'Daddy! You're home.'

Ryan hugged Benjy without replying, then Evie. He took the coffee I held out to him, spread butter and sugar on pancakes, responded to the children's chatter. He ate nothing himself.

Simon came in late, in his school uniform, so entirely as normal that I was suddenly discombobulated. Then he saw Ryan, glanced from him to me, and froze.

I took both his hands and pulled him to the table.

'It's all right,' I said. 'Have your pancake.' I poured lemon juice, applied sugar with an almost-steady hand. He ate in silence.

Afterwards, when Evie had refused to have her teeth brushed and Benjy had put on his own shoes and was tugging at Ryan's wrist, Simon still sat there, staring at his plate.

I put Evie into the buggy, zipped up Benjy's coat, pressed my face into his clean hair. He wriggled away, wanting Ryan.

Evie wailed, high and sharp. I knelt before her, smelled toothpaste and milk. Her arms went tight about my neck. Behind us, I heard Simon's chair scraping back. I stood up, freeing myself from my daughter's clinging fingers. I held my own out and she put hers against them, tip to tip, until Ryan turned the buggy.

I put Simon's coat and bag on him, as though he had been Benjy.

'You'll be OK,' I said.

I watched them go. Ryan put a hand on Simon's back, then on the top of Benjy's head. When they stopped to cross the road, he leaned forward and kissed his daughter. I called, 'I love you' after them.

I stood there a long time, by the open door. Then I moved. I walked.

I saw Edinburgh beautiful in the morning mist, like an image on a fading screen. I saw my babies' bright faces and bit my lip until it hurt. I saw Yazzie welcoming Evie with cuddles. Yazzie, whom I had barely noticed when Simon and I got back last night. She was reading stories, snuggled close with my children in a tidy sitting room. When she left, she looked at me, and her eyes were almost pitying.

Yazzie, whom I had thought a murderess.

Yazzie, who had lain, like me, in Alexis's arms.

Oh God. Alexis.

I zigzagged through the Grange, along streets I had walked with him, had run along *to* him. I saw him, a new boy in the school corridor. I tasted him, his mouth sweet and living on mine. I saw him kissing Yazzie outside a pub. I saw him spinning on the stage, falling with the gunshot, lying in Stacy's arms.

I would have given up everything for you.

Would I ever know now how much he had betrayed me? Only Yazzie could tell me, and I could never ask.

I was in Marchmont now, the tenements reminding me of Alexis's building. Students were emerging in clusters, crossing the Meadows, bleary-eyed, for nine o'clock lectures. My feet stung, blistered last night in my wet shoes.

It didn't matter.

I thought, *I still believe in him*. If I didn't, it would destroy me.

Then I thought of my husband, and how I deserved, after all, to *be* betrayed. I saw Ryan weeping over his dead wife.

I saw him grim-eyed on the evening he came back from Frankfurt. I saw him desperate and disbelieving, as he had been last night. I saw Simon, wavering on the parapet.

I followed the edge of the Meadows. Crocuses, white and purple and yellow. Trees, everywhere, coming into bud. Figures moving along the paths. The curve of Salisbury Crags, a shadow through the haze.

I love this city, like a living being.

The play park. Vibrant colours, children scrambling on frames. The mural on the toilet block. I saw Alexis, pushing his daughter on a swing, Evie and Gracie and Benjy playing among the woodchips.

I went on. My heels felt ripped and bleeding.

St Leonard's Street. Nearly there. The police station waiting, with its great, windowed eye. Revolving doors, hard against my pressing hand, and a constable indifferent at the desk.

In the interview room, I waited for the recorder. I heard Morse's prescribed words. I saw Capaldi before me: nails cream and smooth; face tired and impatient.

I saw Hope, falling through a wet screen. Perhaps I will stop seeing that now.

I spoke to the tape.

'I did it,' I said. 'I killed Alexis.'

Acknowledgements

Thank you to my wonderful agent Camilla Shestopal, to Hannah Wann (world's best editor!) and to Krystyna Green, for your faith in this book and in me. To the whole team at Constable for helping to shape the final product. To Jaime Marshall and Louisa Pritchard, for going well beyond your job descriptions to help me to get this dream off the ground.

So many people read *Obsessed* in various iterations, and all of them made it better: Sarah Jones and Vivien Cripps (here's to many more writing weekends!), Lisa Baylay, Tom Baird, Victoria Blunden, Ros Claase, and Gillian Mapstone. Thank you, Gill, for the Scots expertise, Helen King for insights into corporate marketing, and David Alexander for lending me the ideal writing retreat. Thank you, Emma Krousti and Sarah Jones (again!), for Prosecco and enthusiasm, and Helen Mabelis and Alan Saunders for being the perfect home from home in London.

I could never have done this without my lovely husband Tom (you in no way inspired me to write about having an affair!) and in-laws Kate and David. Thank you for making me the time to run away and write. Nor without my amazing parents, Viv and Harry, who gave me my love of crime fiction and have constantly encouraged me. Nor my daughters Alice and Lily, who make me prouder every day.

And thank you Edinburgh, my beautiful, evocative city. For being what you are. The perfect setting for love. Or murder.

If you enjoyed *Obsessed*, don't miss the next
addictive thriller from Liza North . . .

The Weekend
Guests

A weekend on the wild, beautiful Dorset coast.
Seven adults, six kids. A childminder,
the ultimate special treat.

It should be perfect: old friends, a stunning house,
champagne and wind-strung beaches. But it isn't.
Relationships won't stay still. Memories won't stay put.
Then the parents take a night out, and come back
to catastrophe.

Fourteen years earlier, five students in Edinburgh made
an irrevocable mistake.

One they thought no-one else knew about.
Until now.

Turn the page to read the opening chapters

Prologue

Dorset, 2019

The last caller had dropped his keys down the gutter. The one before had stubbed a toe. This was different. A bad line, dropping in and out of signal. A woman's voice gasping panic, gabbling sentences he couldn't decipher. Then something that might have been *he* or *she* or even *they*, and three words, suddenly clear, that gouged through a year's experience.

'. . . took the children.'

The call handler felt his mind empty immediataely, as if it had been shaken upside down. He stretched out fingertips and balanced them bloodless on the desk. Through the phone, he could hear the shriek of the wind, then the woman's voice again in incomprehensible snippets. From the next desk, his colleague turned to him, eyebrows raised. He shook his head, speaking into the handset. 'Can you tell me where you are?'

The woman yielded a phone number, an address. Her voice held ice-still, then disappeared into the crackling line. The words emerged isolated, distorted. 'A gun…' His mouth seemed to dry of itself. He held his breath, to catch every whisper. 'Please help us. Please.'

The handler keyed words into the computer, recalling his script with an effort. 'Help is on its way,' he said. Did she even hear him? *He* heard only the wind, a wild drumming like stones on metal, and a high keening that could have been a baby's cry. Then that serrated breath, close to the phone.

'The others…' The rest of her words were lost. The handler heard himself barking questions, sharply efficient. Around him, as if in a different world, he could see lines light up. More calls coming in.

'It's so dark,' the caller said. 'I can't see— I can't see anything.' Then the voice was clearer, as high and sharp as a scream. 'What if they're all dead?'

1

Brandon

Dorset, 2019

The weekend, which would flirt with farce and end in horror, began with a kiss.

Brandon stood by the panes of what his wife called their 'second home', congratulating himself that the setting, at least, was proof against modernisation. Above him, that Dorset countryside which was alternately Cornwall wild and Cotswolds tame. In front, the English Channel. Grey as tin on this late winter day; deep sapphire when he'd seen it first. Despite everything, he was bewitched by this piece of coast. He would go to his grave loving it.

Aline came to him with her lioness walk and stood before him like a figure in a poster: pale hair and long legs with floor to ceiling glass and that unreal view, behind her. Beyond the panes, the ground dropped, almost at once, into crag and scrub. Far below, unseen from here, it rose and fell and fell again, landing at last in the oatmeal curve of the bay.

'God,' she said. 'We were so right to do this.' She indicated to the glass, the opaque stretch of sea, with one hand. 'It's like you could run straight into it.'

'Fall into it,' he said. Fifty metres down, those tilting waters.

She slid her fingers down the back of his jeans, pressing long nails into his buttocks. He twisted his head and his lips touched the scented sheet of her hair. She turned him to admire her handiwork. Ripped out walls and an interior stripped and started again. Wood and glass, white space, and what their architect had called a 'statement staircase', rising from the shining floor. Blue-edged lilies in a vase the colour of the sea, on a table carved out of driftwood.

A designer's dream. Aline's dream.

'It's perfect,' she said.

'It should be,' he said. 'It cost enough.'

He yelped as she ripped her hand away, nails scouring skin, and swung off to the table. He thought how strange it was that the same pain, caused by the same movement by the same person, could be entirely erotic or entirely not. Upstairs, he heard his children fighting; behind him, the rain starting.

He watched her set a bottle of Bollinger on the table and arrange about it the crystal flutes that had been her grandmother's, getting the right angle for a photo. She showed him the picture gleaming on the screen, and the message she'd typed to go with it.

I have champagne. And surprises.

'OK?' she said.

'It looks great.'

'You could sound more enthusiastic.'

'You know what I think.'

She laughed, pressed send. 'It's too late to argue.'

'Aline . . .'

She turned back to him, so close that he could almost taste the cherry gloss on her lips. Nearly seventeen years together, and she was still the sexiest woman he had ever met – and the most frustrating. 'Anyone would think,' she said, 'that you didn't want to see our friends.'

'It's not that.'

'If you're worrying about how Rob will react...' She ran her lips down the line of his jaw. 'Then don't. He has his new girlfriend. Besides, you think I wouldn't have got over *you* in sixteen years?'

He let her mouth move onto his. 'Maybe,' he said, while he could still speak. 'But you never wanted to.'

**The Weekend Guests is available now to
pre-order**